The View from Here

THE VIEW FROM HERE

A Novel

LYNNE HINTON

NEWSOUTH BOOKS

Montgomery

NewSouth Books
105 S. Court Street
Montgomery, AL 36104

Library of Congress Cataloging-in-Publication Data

Names: Hinton, Lynne, author.
Title: The View from here : a novel / Lynne Hinton.
Description: First edition. | Montgomery, Alabama : NewSouth Books,
[2018]
Identifiers: LCCN 2017049318 (print) | LCCN 2017060212 (ebook) |
ISBN 9781588383488 | ISBN 9781588383471 (hardcover : alk. paper) |
ISBN 9781588383488 (ebook)
Subjects: LCSH: Wilderness--Fiction. | Tree houses--Fiction. | Wildlife
conservation--Fiction.
Classification: LCC PS3558.I457 (ebook) | LCC PS3558.I457 V54 2018
(print) |
DDC 813/.54--dc23
LC record available at https://lccn.loc.gov/2017049318

Design by Randall Williams

Printed in the United States of America by Sheridan

ACKNOWLEDGMENTS

There is so much goodness in the world, so much love and tenderness. Thank you to everyone who helps me *see*. Thank you to family, friends, all the beloved who love me and who support and encourage my storytelling.

For the sharing of this story, I am deeply grateful as always to Sally McMillan. I am also grateful to Suzanne La Rosa, Randall Williams, and the other beautiful people at NewSouth Books. Thank you for believing in this book, for all the kind words, great ideas, helpful suggestions, and the unwavering commitment to make it happen. It has been a lovely ride.

To Kristin Gerner Vaughn,

who sees the world in beauty and with grace.

Thanks for sharing the view.

Something opens our wings. Something makes boredom and hurt disappear. Someone fills the cup in front of us. We taste only sacredness.

— RUMI

One

Some people will claim it was the plight of the great loblolly pines nestled in the White Oak bottomland behind the Garver farm that drew my eyes skyward and pulled my feet from the earth. That it was the plans of Hatch and Brownfield Construction Company that made me climb and perch—their senior housing, nursing home village, and rehabilitation center a nightmare for the blackwater river basin but a Medicare bonanza for the developers. A few may make mention of the divorce as the cause, Dwayne finally packing up his model car collection and sweeping out the garage, tidying up his side of the room like he was getting it ready for my next husband.

But the truth is not one of those reasons really explains why I came up here.

It wasn't grief or boredom or political grandstanding. It wasn't even the red-cockaded woodpecker, critically endangered and not usually expected in a loblolly but rather in a longleaf pine forest, that was spotted first by Lilly Carol sitting high on my shoulders sixteen days ago on the outing to plant pine saplings back behind the dilapidated barn and deep into the tangle of old trees.

No, there was not any good reason that caused me to step from the forest floor to the fallen sweetgum, scramble up a few feet and then walk high along the trunk until I was standing on intertwined limbs from separate pine trees that leaned into each other and made a fort, a sturdy green-needled fort. And there was no real moment of decision making, no aha event, no glaring epiphany that pushed me up a tree. The truth is that I started climbing because I was curious about whether I could do it and then once I got here, well, I guess if there was a decision made, that's when it happened.

I had taken Lilly Carol back home, assuring Ray that his daughter and I had a fine and restful time at the park. I placed her back in her wheelchair and walked out, leaving her with the gesture of two fingers, the middle one crossed over the first, our sign that our newly discovered secret of the red-cockaded was to remain just that, a secret, and him with a nod, a way of thanking him for the afternoon with his Lilly. I left their house, went back to mine, packed a bag of fruit and cheese, two bottles of water, a sweater and jacket, gloves and hat, binoculars, my bird guide, a book of poetry by Rainer Maria Rilke I have been reading, and an extra pair of socks, and then I walked to where we had seen the bird.

I stood in the silent stand of tall and spindly sentries and suddenly noticed the large sweetgum that had fallen into the pair of pines. I saw a limb that I could grab and I reached and pulled, saw another and reached and pulled, walking up and up and up along the sweetgum trunk until I landed at this very place where I now reside. And I stood up as tall and straight as the pines around me and I could see everything I had not seen before.

It was just stupid luck or curiosity that got me up here, a simple childish act, a moment of careless skyward wandering; but I stayed for something even I hadn't expected. I stayed up here because of what the old Book Lady told me when I was thirteen and I had just spotted my first woodpecker, when I first fell headlong and for life in love with birds.

I can still hear her cackle while she spoke the words that had not meant a thing until I had lived almost three more decades, watched my husband come and go, found my mother living in Florida, finished six years of college, and then climbed up a loblolly pine. I never understood her meaning until I was standing in a tree.

Book Lady lived behind the library in a cardboard box and was cared for by most of the people in town. Some said she went crazy when her son died in the Iraq War, but others, who knew her when she was young, claimed she was always a little off. Still, she was as much a part of the town's landscape as the Baptist church and the Piggly Wiggly, and everybody called her the Book Lady because she always had a row of books cinched around her waist with a belt.

She worked a few hours every day at the library, shelving the returns, making enough money to buy bags of chips and keep a stash of cigarettes and red scarves that she liked to tie in her hair. At night, she slept in her box on a stack of blankets and quilts supplied by the women from the local churches. On several occasions she was given a room in a boarding house and her own furnished apartment; but she always came back to the box. She said she preferred living on the land even though she sometimes moved inside the library when it rained or when the winters were brutal. Miss Hansley, the librarian, had given her a key when she was newly hired.

I was standing near her box when I saw the bird, a male woodpecker, the red stripe vibrant on his cheek and forehead and she startled me when she crawled out of her bed and stood up beside me, a collection of Agatha Christie mysteries wrapped around her.

"That's a pileated woodpecker," she told me. "*Dryocopus pileatus*," she added.

I nodded. I had been reading up on the birds native to North Carolina, having just completed my science project on the woodpecker species found in the southeastern states.

"He lives back of Hardy's pond, has a wife and a couple of babies. Named him Charles," she said, like she thought I'd want to know.

I turned to her and for the first time got a close look at the town's most notorious homeless woman. She was wild-eyed and flicked her tongue in and out of her mouth. Her hair was white and uncombed, a thick crimson scarf tied in a bow on top of her head. She was missing most of her teeth.

"You like him?" she asked.

I nodded and watched as he pecked a few times on a downed pine tree.

"Yeah, he's a good one," she said, her tongue darting in and out. "But a wild one, he is, Charles Red." She looked back at me, squinting. "I know all the birds," she told me. "Raptors, sparrows, hummers, I know them all. You wanna know anything about em, you just ask me."

I nodded again. I wasn't afraid of the old woman. I had come with my mom on several occasions when I was small to bring her a plate of cookies or a coat we found on sale. But I still kept my distance, not wanting to give too much away.

"They can tell you things," she whispered. "Coming of storms, lunar eclipses, death. They always know about the deaths."

This was news to me. "What do they say?"

"Oh, they give me a sign, give me a name, drop a feather."

I stared at her.

"You don't believe me." And she leaned in close. "You think I'm crazy like everybody else?"

I shrugged. She did live in a box and she did talk to herself in the library while she returned the books to their rightful places, and then there was the lining of her belt with paperbacks. "Well, maybe I am," she said and then slid her hand across her belt of books. "Are you?"

I stepped back. Of course I was not. I shook my head.

Then she leaned in again and sniffed, like she was trying to smell whether I was or not.

"Well, if you do get crazy, get it right," she instructed. "Do it big. Crazy is better if it's big." And she winked at me and clicked her tongue a few times on the roof of her mouth, sounding very much like the pileated woodpecker's kent.

Charles flew away and I heard my mom calling for me and I turned to leave. When I glanced back, Book Lady was grinning at me, nodding, and waving for me to go.

I saw her a few more times after that. I brought her a sweater I found on a bench at the park and I gave her candy bars that I was supposed to sell for the science club and a stack of pocket size paperbacks that I thought might be lighter to wear; but she never talked to me again like she did when I was thirteen and saw the pileated woodpecker, when I met Charles. And then one day she was gone; and as far as anybody knows, she just left. No trace, no body, no reports of where she was going, no birdsong that anyone heard in the woods, no whistle of her name to claim a death, no path of feathers; she was just gone.

To this day, almost thirty years later, I still remember that conversation. And that's the real reason I'm doing what I'm doing, why it is I've climbed a pair of trees and moved in. I'm finally doing crazy, and heeding Book Lady's advice I'm doing it big.

Now that I'm up here, it just seems like the right way to go.

Two

"Wanda Kathleen Sinclair Davidson, you have the right to remain silent." Franklin Massey is standing under the tree. He's wearing his summer uniform even though it isn't yet April. It's tan and he looks like a brown thornbill even though this isn't the land down under.

I peek out from under the blanket. It's still early and the news truck from the night before is gone. "You arresting me again, Deputy?" I ask, yawning and scratching my head. There are a few twigs in my ponytail and I pull them out, placing them beside me.

I slept pretty good last night, the piece of plywood Ray brought me tucked nicely in the branches. In fact, unlike the other restless evenings, I only recall waking up once after dark and that was when I heard the pair of owls, the female roosting in a gray squirrel's old leaf nest that is in a pine not too far from my landing, and the male standing guard in the cherrybark oak just a few feet away.

They're great horned owls, *Bubo virginianus,* and I'm pretty sure they have eggs. The female doesn't make a lot of noise since it's nesting season but I've heard her at least once or twice responding to her mate. His call is deep and resonant whereas the female's pitch is higher. They speak to each other like an old married couple and I imagine them planning dinner, checking in with each other, or talking about their young.

A few nights ago I watched the male catch a mouse or a vole, some small unsuspecting rodent, his descent upon his prey quick and fatal, crashing upon it and carrying it away before I even knew what had happened. It was stunning and fierce and I can't decide if I felt terror or excitement bearing witness to such raw violence.

On a couple of occasions very late at night I thought I saw the female's yellow eyes staring at me from across the trees, both of us protecting our roosts. But then again I could just be making things up; it can get spooky out here at night, even though I've never been afraid of the dark and I've spent about as much time sleeping under the stars as I have in a bed indoors.

From as far back as I can recall, it was a weekly occurrence for my dad and brother and me to camp outside, spending the nights in our tents, the three of us together in the darkness. And then when I was old enough to carry my own equipment and Daddy worked the graveyard shift, it was just my brother and me. Even when Nathan was playing ball and had become the big shot on campus and I was four years younger and certainly not the cool kid in school, it was still the two of us spending our free time together. After he'd come home from a date, we'd throw our sleeping bags on our four wheelers and head back behind the pasture and be there all night.

During his first year in college he'd come home and we'd stay outside all weekend. We'd talk about his freshman classes, the stars, and the girl he was convinced was the one he would marry. He'd tell me about the new workouts he had been given to strengthen his throwing arm and then show me how to pitch a slider or knuckleball. I'd tell him about my bone collection and show him the birds I had taken pictures of and we'd fall asleep listening to the barn owls. When he died I headed out to the woods and wouldn't leave the tent. Daddy came out there and stayed in a sleeping bag close by, leaving me to my grief for days but finally having to pick me up and take me home when the weather turned and it snowed for hours, me kicking and screaming the whole way. I didn't want to leave. I was never going to leave. I kept thinking if I stayed out, if I didn't go inside, he'd show up. He'd come for me somehow, as a star or a bird, some way he'd come back and get me, somehow he'd show up from the night sky.

"Sheriff told me to come out here again after you made the six o'clock."

I lean my head over the limb. I can see the top of Franklin's head because he isn't wearing his hat. There's a bald spot starting and I am about to mention it but then think better of it. He's has been out here about four times already; I know I'm wearing his patience thin. He's a timid bird and doesn't like a show.

"How long have we known each other, Franklin?" I ask.

I hear him blow out a long, deliberate breath. He raises his hands to rest on whatever he has attached to his belt. I can't tell if he has a gun or a Taser or just the handcuffs. All I can see from up here is his elbows riding high. The first couple of times he would look up at me; now he just keeps his eyes straight ahead. I don't blame him for not looking up, though; after so many years tracking birds I know how stiff your neck can get staring at treetops and patches of sky.

He shakes his head. "I don't know, Sinclair, long enough to know you hate being called by your first name."

"Fifth grade," I say, and I watch him turn and glance up. "We were in fifth grade and I got moved to the desk behind you because you said Timothy McMillan kept putting things down the back of your shirt. Miss Wooten asked for a volunteer to change places and I raised my hand since I didn't like sitting next to Dixie Sulley because she was always trying to look at my answers on the tests." I sit up and rest my back against the cool trunk of the tree that isn't dead. I roll up the blanket and put it behind my head.

"It was sixth grade when we ran on a relay team together during PE. And it wasn't just *things* Timothy McMillan was putting down my shirt, it was bugs."

I can see him step out and grind his foot hard into the ground, probably killing an ant. "I hate bugs."

"And I could run faster than you," I reply.

"Maybe until high school."

There is a pause and I think of Franklin Massey as a boy, small and thin, jumpy and nervous. His mother wrote a note that got him out of biology when we dissected worms. I remember the other boys making fun of him.

"How is the sheriff?" I ask.

"You know how the sheriff is," Franklin answers. "He's not happy that you're living up in this tree."

"I'm not living in the tree," I reply; but then think that maybe I am. I've actually become quite comfortable up here with the piece of plywood and the camping gear I've been given. It's actually kind of roomy and you can't beat the view although there are still a few problems. For instance, the bathroom situation is a little tricky.

For the first few days I just hopped down and went behind the chestnut oak that stands a few feet away; but that was before all the media attention and the threats of being arrested, the big Hatch and Brownfield earthmover still parked at the edge of the woods. When I climbed up here I honestly did not realize it was only a couple of days before the groundbreaking and the forest deconstruction, but of course nobody believes that. When the word got out, more than likely from one of the heavy equipment operators for Hatch, the local papers reported my tree climbing as an act of civil disobedience, and the whole development project has since been put on hold.

On the sixth day LuAnn Hightower from the local Sierra Club, coastal chapter, came out here to support my protest. She noticed the bathroom situation and rigged me up a bucket with plastic bags inserted in it to serve as my toilet. It's not been easy straddling it while I'm standing up here but I think it would be much worse being at the bottom and having to empty the bags every day.

LuAnn said she read about the toilet bucket idea from that girl in California who lived in a redwood for over two years. That girl was evangelical about the trees and has become a kind of environmental celebrity. I've heard all about her since I got up here. She did this same thing twenty years ago, but the truth is I never knew about Julia Butterfly Hill until last week when Langston Williams from the *New Bern Sun Journal* told me about her.

He mentioned that he heard her speak once when he was in college and that she was beautiful and graceful, like some angel, he said, and then he glanced back up in my direction as if he was trying to make a connection between me and the Butterfly girl; but then he just drew lines across something he had been writing and didn't mention her again. I'm not sure if he realized I wasn't as heavenly as Butterfly or that he had written something he didn't like, but it was clear he was taking his story in a different direction.

"You know we can make you come down," Franklin says, pushing me from my thoughts. "We could cut down that old pine." He kicks

at the tree I'm sitting in. "We could shake it until you fall out." He
puts a hand on both sides of the tree like he's measuring it. "We could
shoot you." He looks up when he says that.

"You'd do that, Deputy?" I ask, peeking at him through the leaves
and needles.

He drops his hands at his sides and glances back down.

I know for a fact that Franklin Massey has never shot a person. I
also know he can't see well enough to shoot fifty feet ahead of him. I
read his file when I was at the county office. He's almost legally blind.

I can hear him sigh even with an airplane flying overhead and a
warbler singing three limbs up.

"Just come down, Sinclair. Winston Hatch is at the office every
day wanting us to do something. And the sheriff is driving me crazy."

I throw the twigs I had in my hair down at him. "I will sometime,"
I answer and I watch as he jumps when the tiny sticks fall on his neck.
He slaps at his collar and starts to walk away.

"He's not happy with you," he says in parting.

And I yell back. "Yeah, well tell him I'm not happy with him either."
But even as I say it I'm sure this will not mean a thing. My father has
known that for years.

Three

"What'd you do to make Franklin so mad?" It's Ray. He's brought
me breakfast.

"Oh, I don't know. The sheriff keeps making him come out here
to try and talk me down. Deputy Massey clearly doesn't have a career
in negotiating."

I see Ray putting a paper bag in the other bucket I use, the one for supplies, not the toilet. I'm hoping he doesn't notice that the other one hasn't been emptied.

I pull the rope and the bucket starts to move.

"It's a couple of biscuits," he tells me. "Cheese and egg."

I close my eyes and smile. I hadn't eaten since breakfast yesterday. I've run out of groceries and haven't seen anybody from the high school science club. Normally I would just ask Charlene from the Forest Service to pick me up some things since she comes by most afternoons, but the teenagers decided I was to be their spring project so I agreed to their help. They came, the bunch of them, took pictures, and made a list of my favorite foods, promising to deliver them every day.

Unfortunately, it appears that the president of the club just found out he's been wait-listed at his first college choice, Duke, and he's gone into some state of depression. The vice president told me this when she brought over some things a couple of days ago. She brought me stuff that I'm sure was from her kitchen cabinets at home since I know I didn't write spaghetti sauce and green beans on the list I sent down from the tree last week.

She means well, this young girl; but truthfully, I don't think her heart is in this project. Her name is Tiffany and it seems to me that she's mainly in the science club because she's in love with Stanley, the president. The last time I saw her she teared up when she told me about his college rejection and the depression medications she found in his bathroom cabinet. After that visit I have a pretty good idea that I won't see Tiffany again unless Stanley gets it together and returns to the science club; feeling this hungry makes me think that maybe I should ask Ray to call Charlene to come out before lunch.

"You got water?" he asks.

I pull the rope until the bucket of breakfast makes it to me. "No, I drank it all."

"I'll get you a case this afternoon. Here . . ." He pulls a bottle of water from the pocket of his jacket and I can tell that he's going to throw it to me.

I ready myself and he pitches it perfectly, right through the branches, above the ply board landing, and into my open hands. I surprise myself, catching it so easily, and for a second I think of Nathan, how he and Ray threw the baseball to each other in the front yard every day before school. I always watched from the kitchen window waiting for Daddy to fix me breakfast.

Ray was as torn up about my brother's death as I was. They were best friends.

"How's our girl?" I ask, as I place the bottle of water beside me, open the bag, and unwrap the biscuit. I take a bite; it's still warm. I lean against the trunk.

"She's begging me to bring her to see you, says I can park at the barn and carry her on my shoulders. It almost sounds like she's been out here."

He squats in his catcher's position; I guess old habits are hard to break. He tosses a pebble like he's throwing back the pitch. "She's making a scrapbook with all the newspaper articles about you. She says she knows which tree you're in."

I can tell he's fishing for just how far I brought his daughter into the woods and I fill my mouth with the biscuit so that I can't answer.

Since Lilly had the accident, Ray is such a worrywart that I don't say much about our activities. He'd probably kill me if he knew all that the two of us do during our outings. For instance he has no idea that I took her swimming in Hardy's pond last summer or that I let her sit in my lap and drive the Jeep, or that I carry her on my shoulders into the woods at least once a week.

He thinks we go to the city park and feed the ducks or go shopping at the mall, when we're really out here checking the saplings we plant and listening for wrens and bluebirds. Sometimes I sit her by a tree and leave her while I clear the brush that's become a fire hazard or make my measurements of the creek. She's been stung by a bee and gotten too close to poison ivy; I even tripped once while I was carrying her and we both almost landed on our faces. Anyway, he'd be really upset if he knew how we spend our time together.

"I've shown her pictures," I lie, finishing one of the biscuits and wiping my mouth on my sleeve. When I do that I get a whiff of myself. I'm going to need some more of those campsite bathing cloths and another set of clothes.

"Right," he replies.

He doesn't say anything else and I drink the entire bottle of water and then stretch my legs out in front of me. We are both quiet and there is birdsong close by.

"That a catbird?" he asks.

I shake my head and keep listening. I know catbirds are rarely in the woods, especially these woods with all the pines. They nest in thickets and briar bushes. "Brown thrasher," I answer. "Hear how it repeats the call twice."

We listen together.

"Catbirds repeat the phrases only one time; thrashers sing it twice."

The bird calls as if on cue, two song phrases, melodic, male.

"They're breeding," I tell Ray.

"It's a little early, isn't it?"

I glance around the still-barren forest. Spring has not quite sprung but we're close. "February and March is actually their usual time," I say.

I look between the branches and watch Ray nod. He's wearing a baseball hat and I can't really see it but I'm fairly sure that it's the one Lilly bought him last year for Father's Day. It's the one he wears most of the time. We picked it out from a website. It has NYFD on it. She said they were known as heroes ever since the "big explosion," which is what she calls 9/11. She wasn't even born in 2001, but she read about it in her history class last year and she spent a lot of time contemplating the horrible acts that were done, trying to understand why someone would fly a plane into buildings. Neither Ray nor I had good answers when she raised her innocent questions.

"Why did they do it?"

"They just hated us," I said.

"But why did they hate us?" she wanted to know.

"Because we represented everything they despised," I replied.

"But how does a person know how to hate that big?"

I had glanced over at Ray when she asked that question and he wouldn't look at me.

"I don't know, Lilly. It just happens sometimes."

"Well, I hope it never happens again," she said, her innocent child brain trying to wrap itself around the problem of evil.

"Did you know the brown thrasher has the largest song repertoire of any North American bird?"

I can't see his face but I know he's rolling his eyes. Between me and Lilly, Ray hears a lot about birds.

"There's over a thousand. And they mimic other calls like mockingbirds." I stop and we listen. "In fact, I think this guy is trying to sound like a cardinal."

We hear the whistle.

"Well, he probably knows they're better-looking, which means he'll have better luck finding himself a girl thrasher."

I laugh. "That's funny," I say. "Girl-thrasher."

Ray stands up. "You need anything else besides water?" He brushes off the back of his pants, though I doubt he ever sat on the ground or leaned against the trunk. Ray has a strong back and even stronger legs. He works at the lumber store, dragging around two-by-fours and tools.

"I need everything," I answer.

He looks up at me.

"I'm afraid the high schoolers have forgotten me."

"You got a list?"

"Just get me stuff you'd eat."

I see him take off his hat, scratch the back of his neck and shake his head. "All right, I'll come back after my shift."

He starts to walk away.

"Ray—" I stand up so I can see him even though I doubt he can see me. I feel powerful standing so straight against the pine. It's sort of like the "tall-thin" position horned owls take when they hold themselves as slim as possible, resting on a limb in the daytime, camouflaging themselves from the other owls, trying to appear bigger than they are. "Thanks for not calling me crazy or trying to make me come down."

He glances up and I see his face. Even from this far I can tell he's just shaven because his cheeks are pink. He shrugs. "What have I got to say about crazy?" he asks and slaps his cap against his leg and puts it back on.

I nod without responding because he's got me there.

Four

There is a swish, swish, swishing in the ground cover beneath me. I stop and glance up from my book. Something is approaching.

"Yewww-hewww."

I hear the call and I sit very still, trying not to bring attention to myself.

"Yewww-hewwww." Swish ... swish ... swish.

Maybe I won't be seen. Maybe that petite creature with its tiny head, the deliberate, bulging eyes, the sensitive ears, maybe with all that flapping and swishing through the leaves and needles it won't know I'm here.

"Yewww-hewww, Katie Sinclair." Swish . . . swish . . . swish. "Well, there you are."

Too late. I've been spotted. I clear my throat and ready myself for this unwanted forest encounter. I put a marker between the pages of the book.

It had been so peaceful until this moment as I had been enjoying a wonderful morning of quiet reading. I was trying to memorize a poem by Rilke. It helps pass the time and I like to pretend it will prevent me from losing my memory when I'm old.

"The laboring through what is still undone . . ."

I close the book and set it behind me next to the rolled-up blanket. I throw my legs over the side of the board and look down.

"You are really up that tree!"

From my perch I see her standing about ten feet away from the tree. She has on a pair of khakis, perfectly starched and ironed, a button-down dress shirt, soft pink, her signature color, a handsome white vest that she probably ordered from REI or Land's End with next-day delivery just for this visit, new hiking boots, and a hat that looks a little like the one Indiana Jones wore in all those movies. I'm sure she's been shopping for days planning her trek out here. I can only hope she's not going to stay or make a habit of hiking in the woods.

She's staring at me, her hands on her hips and bright pink lipstick, her painted-on, made-up smile, turned in my direction. There's a backpack next to her that she has just laid down, and she has walking sticks leaning against her. It's not more than a mile from the road, but she needed walking sticks.

"Will you look at what you have done. I heard you were out here but I just couldn't believe it; but bless my soul, there you are." She makes that "tsking" noise with her tongue like she does when she disapproves of something, which happens a lot when she's around me.

I don't respond, which is how we usually communicate.

"Kathleen Sinclair Davidson, as I live and breathe." She pushes her hat off from the front, letting it drop behind her head. There's a string tied around her neck that keeps it from falling. She waits there, just looking up at me. It's actually a nice angle for the two of us, me perched up here, her standing beneath me .

"Hey, Marge," I finally say. "You lost?"

"When I heard you had come out here to impede the progress of Riverview I did not believe it. I said I have to go out there and see this bit of shenanigans with my own eyes."

There's a long pause and I'm not sure what's she's waiting for. Usually Marjorie Williams doesn't take a breath in her conversations.

"Rivervew?"

"Winston Hatch and Thomas Brownfield's development," she tells me.

"That's what they're calling it?"

"Yes, that's what they're calling it. How could you not know that?"

Well, there are certainly lots of reasons I would not know or have guessed the name of Winston Hatch's latest construction project including the fact that there is certainly no view of the river from here; but I decide not to answer what I assume is a rhetorical question. There's that "tsk . . . tsk . . . tsk"-ing again.

Marjorie Lewis Williams is the sister I never asked for. Her mother, the widow of Starling Lewis, married my father about fifteen years ago, manufacturing all kinds of relationships I did not want and do not need. That's just one of several reasons he and I don't see each other anymore.

It isn't my new stepmother, however, that keeps me from my old house; I can take Millie just fine; she's kind to me and has for the fifteen years of their marriage stayed out of my business. She doesn't try to make unnecessary conversation with me or get to know me by taking on some maternal role; and she has a certain respect for the

Sinclair history, the grief of losing Nathan and the disappearing act of my mother.

She never comments to me about the burdens of the shared and tattered past of my father and me or about how we remember and order our life together. She doesn't try to get me to open up or share secrets. She knows she has no part of the original Joseph Sinclair family and I doubt she troubles the sheriff with any well-meaning ideas of reconciliation with his only child or tries to remedy what has been broken. Millie is quiet and good-natured; I'm sincerely glad she and Daddy found each other.

But her daughter Marjorie—Marge—is intrusive and meddlesome. She has an opinion about everything and she works incessantly to make sure everybody knows it. She chatters on and on about politics and religion, fashion trends, and the evils handed down by the school board. She cannot seem to keep herself from getting in the middle of other peoples' private affairs.

I know for a fact that she's been the cause of at least three preachers leaving the Methodist Church where she claims to work "behind the scenes serving Jesus." I know this because the pastor at the Lutheran church, Jim Stallings, is my best friend, and he tells me everything he knows about the inside workings of the local congregations. That's why I don't go to church anymore—way too much information about the good Christians of Jones County.

Marge may say that she works behind the scenes at Clydes' Memorial Methodist Church; but it doesn't sound to me like she is serving Jesus unless the Lord has somehow become deeply concerned that the altar cloths match the window treatments and that Marge gets to serve as the chair of every committee. I would say that she's more a handmaiden of the devil; but then Marge and I have not seen eye-to-eye since we were in the same Brownie troop and I beat her up, ending my career as a Girl Scout before it began.

She's a mockingbird, a noisy, possessive nuisance for everybody.

She repeats everything she hears, embellishing just enough to make the things she says about other people sound dirty. She hoards money, praise, and damaging information that she especially likes to use against the unlucky folks she targets and those who won't agree with her. She's bossy and pretentious and I can't get her out of my business with insults or rumors, a super soaker water gun or a black eye when she was only nine years old. She's an intruder and I cannot believe she is now right here, standing under my trees. If the toilet bucket was up here I'd tip it over on her new clothes.

"How's Wilford?"

She rolls her eyes and turns to look up in another tree, one near the owls but I know she'll never see them. She crosses her arms across her and I can see I'm getting to her. She hates it when I call her husband Wilford more than she hates me calling her Marge. Everybody else in Maysville and Pollocksville calls him J. W. or Will or Doctor Williams; but since I know it bugs her so much I call him Wilford. One has to celebrate the small victories.

"J. W. is in Atlanta at a convention. He is fine."

"He take Gloria?"

She snaps her head back in my direction at the mention of the nurse she made him fire last summer. It was rumored J. W. was having an affair with the young assistant but I don't really think that was the case. J. W. is a little creepy, tipping the scales at three fifty; and he's a podiatrist. That's hardly sexy to a college girl. It didn't matter to Marge however whether it was true or not, she made him get rid of her as soon as she got wind of the gossip.

"Oh no, wait. She moved to Florida." I let that linger just for a beat. "Well, that's not so far from Georgia, is it?"

She swats at something flying around her. "I don't know why I even bothered coming to see you," she says.

"Well, I don't know either, Marge. Why did you lather up in insect repellent and buy a new vest and hike out here?"

"I came to bring you this," she answers, picking up the backpack and holding it in front of her.

I glance down at the pack she's holding and for a second I don't feel so disgusted with Marge. I have a tiny hope that maybe Marge is doing something kind. I entertain the thought that maybe Millie has sent brownies or a pie. Maybe I'll get some chocolate cookies. Everybody in Jones County knows that Millie can cook just fine, but she bakes like a professional.

"It's from the Women's Circle."

The disappointment descends quickly. I doubt that means there's pie; Millie goes to the Baptist church.

"It's a Bible and a prayer shawl," she informs me, unzipping the pack.

"Don't you give those to sick people?" I ask.

"We crochet the shawls for those in need." She pulls out the bulky outerwear and lays it across her arm while she yanks out the Bible. "It was not my idea to bring it out here but it's my month to deliver. I've got to go to the nursing home and then to New Bern to the hospital. Mr. Finney fell and broke his hip."

"Well, why don't you give my prayer shawl to Mrs. Finney? She can probably use it more than I can, sitting in the waiting room."

"Because the Circle voted to give you one since Nancy Peterson thinks you're having a spell of nerves and in dire need of Christian charity; and once the vote is taken, the shawls must be delivered."

"Look, Marge, I don't want the prayer shawl. Just give it to someone else at the hospital."

"I'm going to leave it down here with the Bible. You can climb down and get it when you want. Maybe you could read some and it would help you be a little nicer."

She puts down her sticks and walks to the base of the sweetgum. I watch as she puts the shawl down first and then places the Bible on top.

"Yeah, I wouldn't hold my breath," I say, moving away from the edge of the landing and leaning back against the trunk.

"Well, whatever," she says and puts her arms through the backpack and picks up her walking sticks and starts to turn away.

"Tell Wilford I said hey," I respond. "Unless he finally figures out what's best for him and decides to stay in Georgia."

She stops, twists her head around and looks up. I can feel the indignation from thirty-five feet above. "You know you are a disgrace to my family," she says, her voice all tight and high-pitched.

"I could care less about your family," I say without apology.

She steps back to the tree, almost tripping over her sticks. "I know you don't care about J. W. and me but you could think just for a second about what you're doing to your father and to my mother, what you did to Dwayne and your own marriage. You're an embarrassment to everything the sheriff stands for and even though he won't say it, you're a complete disappointment to him. You sitting up there in a dead tree like somebody who's lost their mind. I'm glad Dwayne finally came to his senses and left you but why your father and my mother won't cut you out of their lives for good, I will never know. Why he keeps looking for some reconciliation, wanting for some word of relief from you I will never know." Her face is bright red. I've certainly succeeded at my job in getting a rise.

"Okay, thanks for stopping by, Marge, and oh yeah, thanks for that Bible, I can sure see how it's helped you."

I watch her spin around in a huff and stomp away and I thought getting her goose like I did would make me feel good. Surprisingly it didn't at all.

Five

I started my career in the Forest Service as a forestry research technician, specifically to study the southern pine beetle, a pesky insect that kills its host to reproduce and wreaks havoc en masse. I worked in Asheville first, up in the Smoky Mountains, traveled around doing other research, and then I moved back home to study the beetles again. The infestations were out of control in forests near the Atlantic Ocean, including all of the Coastal Plain ecosystems like longleaf pine savannahs and pond pine forests, as well as some wetlands like the elevated swamps in Jones County known as pocosins.

When I moved back to the coast a few years out of college I was originally assigned to the station in the Croatan National Forest, near the southern rim of Catfish Lake. I rented a house on the water, a cabin that was a real fixer-upper. My job was to measure plant coverage, tree age, height and diameter, and specifically to check the levels of pine resin and formations of pitch tubes that kill the beetles, ultimately saving the trees.

I set up the equipment for performing the field tests and studies to learn more about the beetle, and as a consequence to my insect work I began to uncover the effects of infestation including forest fragmentation which led to a population growth of the cowbirds. It was an exciting study in which I learned a lot about this species and became quite an expert on brood parasitism.

For about three years I was outside all the time and mostly alone except for the birds and beetles. Then Charlene joined the forestry office, an accomplished researcher of the exotic earthworm in the west; and we became good friends. A year or so later on a trip to her parents' home at Myrtle Beach I met and later married her brother,

Dwayne. Of the two relationships, it's the friendship with Charlene that has persevered and is the one I have always cherished the most.

Still, Dwayne is a good man. From the very beginning he displayed genuine interest in my work in the forests. He'd find journal articles that spoke to the research I was doing, copy the pages, punch three holes, and place them in plastic folders for me. He brought home flowers for every major holiday and sometimes just on a Tuesday when he would take the long way home from work and drive past the florist on Main Street. He kept me in bird books and he sent me cards in the mail because he knew I always got home before he did and that I liked to find good mail in the box even though I never addressed a card to him or wrote a letter to anybody else.

He calls his mother every Sunday at five, sends her chocolates at Valentine's and Easter. He would listen to me complain endlessly about aspects of my job I despised, the harassment from the other agents, the long hours tromping through the woods, the paperwork required, and then quietly suggest that maybe I might like to go back to school and finish my doctorate. He'd go on to explain that with some budget-tightening at home and his yearly cost-of-living raise from the bank where he worked we could manage it and even brought home catalogues and brochures about PhD programs in biology in schools all across North Carolina.

He never told me what to do about my father, never griped about all the time I spend with Lilly Carol and Ray, the long hospital stay when she was alone, the late-night calls to go over and help with her care, and never stood in the way or sulked when I wanted to go out to the lake and camp by myself.

Dwayne was a good husband by everybody's standards, and before he left, trying to salvage the doomed marriage, he even asked what he might have done differently as a spouse. Just as it been throughout all eight years of matrimony, I had nothing to tell him, nothing to say, nowhere to point and explain here's where you failed me, here's where you really missed the mark. I could only reply that it's just me, it's my fault, or that we've just gotten in a rut, or maybe deep down I didn't want to be married. He listened to all my responses, stared at me like he wanted to be criticized or given a task or a step-by-step guide on how to be a better husband. But in the end there was no real cause for the demise of the relationship that I could pinpoint for him. He probably would have stayed with me even though we were both completely unhappy, but a new teller named Debbie came to work at the bank and suddenly his eyes were opened to how "real love" can feel.

The night Dwayne cleaned and packed, the day he left, Charlene called and came over. I told her that if she needed to be with her brother, be his ally, stand *by* him which I assumed to mean *against* me that she should do it, that I would understand. She waited for just a second, shook her head and then balled up her fist and hit me hard in the arm. I thought she did it because she was mad at me for messing things up for Dwayne, that I was completely to blame for the break-up. But when I said I was sorry that I caused her family so much pain, she hit me again in exactly the same place, making a huge red mark, and then just walked in the kitchen over to the refrigerator and took out a beer and said, "I didn't do that because of what you think you did to Dwayne. I did it because of what you're doing to yourself."

I remember following her to the table where she sat down. But I remained standing, rubbing my hand up and down my arm because she swung pretty hard and twice. I waited for the explanation, the accusation, conviction, and sentence that I had anticipated when she asked to come over a few hours after Dwayne left.

"I did it because you're acting crazy, like a killdeer running around pretending it has a broken wing."

She's talking about a distraction display used by killdeer to distract predators from their nests. The bird walks away from the nesting area holding its wing in a position that simulates an injury and then flops around on the ground emitting a distress call. The predators follow because they think they've spotted an easy prey and are distracted away from the nest.

I was more than a little confused.

"You are not a cowbird egg."

I sat down at the table still rubbing my arm. First a killdeer and now a cowbird. She will need to explain.

"You aren't a brood parasite."

I shook my head; I still was not following.

"Your mother didn't drop you off in the perfect Davidson box. You didn't get born in the bluebird nest. You didn't take anything from Dwayne or from me. You belonged with us; you still belong with us, with me."

It was clear she could see the big question mark situated over my head.

"Katie, you're not a bad person. You didn't steal Dwayne's innocence. You didn't steal anything."

I knew a lot more about cowbirds that Charlene did. I was the one who got her interested in the species in the first place. I had even shown her the brown speckled egg situated next to the three blue ones in a bluebird nest box, the hole large enough for the cowbird female to sneak in and make her deposit. Even though I have always been intrigued by the cowbird I never imagined myself as one.

"You think, you've always thought, that you weren't good enough for my brother, and where you got that from I don't know. I never see you act like that with anybody else at the office or in the field but you do with Dwayne. And you need to stop."

"I don't think I'm a cowbird," I reply.

"You don't think that Dwayne is somehow better than you and that you poisoned your marriage? You don't think that you're the reason it's over?"

I shrugged.

"He's the one who fell in love with somebody else."

"Yeah, but . . ." And I was going to list the reasons I made a mess of things, causing him to fall for Debbie, but she interrupted me.

"You want me to hit you again?"

I grabbed my arm protecting it.

"It just didn't work out. You didn't usurp from him or spoil anything for anybody. You got that?"

I nodded but without conviction and she put her bottle on the table and acted like she was getting up to come over.

"Okay, okay, I got it."

She sat back down.

But I see now that I really didn't get it at the time. Of course, Charlene was right on the money and even with a bruise on my arm that lasted more than a week and even with her scientific reasoning about our breakup I still felt responsible.

I did love Dwayne; I even enjoyed being married to him for a while. But from the very beginning of our relationship I felt as if I was always trying to be a better person when I was with him. Even thinking about that now, being able to name it for myself, I realize that wanting that in itself is not a terrible thing.

I could do with being a better person. Even Jim, my friend the Lutheran minister with whom we met a few times before he married us, said that a good marriage should make you want to be better, help you be better. I thought it was a fine quality in any marriage and have always conceded that I need that kind of inspiration.

It's just that I started feeling like I needed to be better all the time. I would look at myself in the mirror day after day thinking I *can* do more with my life. I can eat a healthier diet and read more on meaningful and interesting subjects. I can get a good haircut so that I don't always end up pulling my long stringy locks back in a ponytail. I can wear more make-up, learn more words, and broaden my vocabulary. I can take classes and learn Spanish and quit asking Jorge to translate everything for me when I need to talk to the

THE VIEW FROM HERE

researchers in South America about the mosquitos in Brazil.

I would look at myself and realize that I could forgive and let go, stop sneaking cigarettes after I had too much to drink. I could quit having too much to drink. One habit and then another, one failure and then another, one goal missed and then another, and suddenly somewhere along the way, all that inspiration started making me do worse than better.

For the entire time we dated and for the eight years we were married, I genuinely wanted to push myself to be better, always looked at Dwayne and thought he deserved more, caught my reflection in the mirror and always fell short. Dwayne never put that pressure on me but it was always there and eventually it wore a thin place in my heart.

Thinking about it now, alone in a tree, maybe I do see myself as a cowbird egg, taking up space and food from the truly authentic children, the ones who really deserve the care and attention. And maybe that's why Marjorie's words still sting even though she swished out of the woods over an hour ago.

Maybe, just like she thinks, I also believe that I am a disappointment to everyone, a source of shame and endless frustration and regret.

Maybe I also think that I will never really deserve or find my own nest.

Six

"Shreep . . . . shreep . . . . shreep."

I recognize the call. It's the song sparrow, the elusive small bird, brown and plentiful, noted as a bird of "least concern" to the International Union for Conservation of Nature and Natural Resources because the species is so common. Various classes of sparrows can be found in practically every area of the country and most are usually flitting along the ground, near bushes and at the edges of backyards.

"Shreep .... shreep .... shreep."

I smile and put down my Rilke poems. This call, however, isn't coming from the song sparrow. This call comes from Jim, my friend the clergyman, my confidant and birding companion for more than a decade. We met when I moved into town and started leading bird counts in the area for the Forest Service. Jim was the first volunteer. He had only just moved here as well, a fairly new pastor from South Carolina.

Today, I am happy to hear his whistle since I have not seen him in over a week. He left just before I made my tree climb. He was traveling back to his home state to visit his mother. Mama Stallings is frail and elderly, and has been for years in need of her only son's care.

"Well, I see now that I can't let you out of my sight for a minute." He is standing near the sweetgum. Hanging on his arms are several plastic bags filled with supplies, I imagine. He has something on his back, looks like one of those folding camping chairs in a canvas bag with straps. He's wearing his short-sleeved black shirt, his clergy collar, black dress pants. He's tied on a straw hat.

"Why are you dressed like that? You on a religious pilgrimage?" I ask, sitting on the edge of my landing. "You planning to save me?"

He glances around, puts his bags down, and his eyes appear to stop at the prayer shawl and bible left at the base of the tree.

"Looks like somebody else already tried."

"Marge was here."

"Oh, how nice for you." He peers up at me with a big grin on his face. "Good ole Marge and the Methodist Women's Circle, bringing the love of Jesus into the woods. That probably counts as this year's foreign mission project."

I roll my eyes.

"How's Mama?"

"Resting," he answers.

"How do you know that?" I ask.

Because I just left her.

Charleston is at least a six-hour drive. I'm not following.

"She's at the parsonage in a hospital bed. We're calling in hospice tomorrow. I think this is probably it."

"Wait. What? You brought her here?"

"I did indeed."

In all our conversations about this visit, Jim never mentioned that he was going to fetch his mother, only that he was going to his childhood home to set things straight. "Wow, so Mama Stallings is living with you now, here, in Maysville?"

"It happened somewhat abruptly and in truth, I am not properly prepared for this life change; but the answer to your question is yes."

"And hospice has been called?"

"Heart Hospice of Jones County is going to be the primary health-care provider. Jane Wyatt is her nurse."

"Hasn't this been about the fourth hospice your mother has used?" I know of at last that many trips he's taken to line up care.

"Third, but lucky for us, hospice agencies can discharge a patient and then sign them back up again. Apparently, a person can come near death and back away more than once."

"Yeah, I would imagine that's true." Jim's mother has done that more than a few times.

He lets the straps fall from the bag on his back and I can see now that it is the camping chair he uses when we go birdwatching. He pulls it out of the canvas pack, unfolds it, and sets it up where he's standing. From there we have a good view of each other through the branches. We smile at each other and nod; it is good to see my friend.

"You see Bernard?"

He settles in his chair. "Many times," he answers.

We stop for a second because we hear a couple of crows nearby. Jim and I never talk when a bird is calling. A calling bird is holy.

"Have you read the study that shows that the fish crow is somewhat more resistant to the West Nile virus than the American crow? Survival rates of up to 45 percent have been reported for fish crows, compared with almost zero for the American."

"I did know that," I reply. Originally I was assigned by the Forest Service to research the species as a bioindicator.

"Of course, you knew that."

There's another pause as the crows fly toward the other end of the forest. The government officials gave the study to researchers in Florida instead.

"So . . . ?"

I have waited as long as I could and finally say the word for him to begin as the place around us has become momentarily quiet.

"So . . . Bernard got a promotion at the university library and he doesn't want to leave Charleston."

This was not what I was fishing for.

"That's yesterday's news. I thought you were going to South Carolina to tell your mother once and for all that you and Bernard are lovers, have been for ten years and that you were quitting the church here to look for a job there."

He doesn't reply.

"You were going to tell her the truth. We stayed up all night talking about this before you left. You were going to tell her that the two of you were moving in with her and would take care of her until she died at which time you and Bernard were going to paint the entire exterior of the house *soft buttercup* and the interior of the house a slightly more intense yellow—*spring sundress*, I believe, was the name; and you were going to use an eggshell finish, open up the front room using French doors with classic clear glass and move the master bedroom upstairs. I thought you had plans for a B and B."

"We changed our minds to satin because we prefer more of a gloss to the interior paint and we'll need to completely redo the upstairs bathroom if we're taking that space. The French doors are still a go and so is the bed and breakfast idea; although that was never in the works to tell Mama Stallings that part."

He hesitates.

"My plans to tell her changed on the fourth day of my visit when I finally got up my nerve and she suddenly took a turn."

"What? In her wheelchair?"

"No, not in her wheelchair, in her health, with her health. She started coughing, wheezing, saying she had chest pain, her arm was going numb; so I took her to the emergency room and they kept her for three days."

I shake my head and blow out a long breath.

"I don't want to hear it," he tells me, knowing exactly what is running through my mind. I just couldn't do it, not now."

"Not now?" I reply. "How about not ever?"

"It is what it is, Kate. I just couldn't do it."

If I were beside him, I'd squeeze his leg or grab his hand. We've been over this territory so many times. He gets his nerve up to do what his heart has been telling him to do for years and then can't see it through.

"What did Bernard say?"

Jim doesn't answer right away.

"He said that the albatross life is better than nothing and that he understands."

"That Bernard is quite a guy," is all I say.

When I first learned of his long-distance relationship with a friend from college and his fears that it couldn't last I told Jim about the albatross and how the seabirds mate for life but rarely spend much time with their partners. The birds don't nest together every year because the process of raising a chick is a long one and so when they're not nesting, the albatrosses travel thousands of miles and usually alone.

They live much of their lives as solitary animals. It seemed like a good analogy years ago when the long-distance arrangement seemed necessary; now it just feels like a rationalization for not putting forth the necessary effort in a relationship needed to take it to the next level.

A light breeze stirs the needles and dry leaves in the trees and along the ground. The pair of crows return, call to each other, and Jim and I are quiet, listening once more to the sacred sounds we have come to honor in the woods.

Seven

"Okay, now it's your turn." Jim lifts his chin up at me. I see his kind eyes. "Why did you leave your home and move into a loblolly? And why didn't you call and tell me?"

I lean my head back and take a long look at the sky. It's going to rain, I'm sure of it and I wonder how I'll manage. For the past nine days I've only encountered easy spring weather. I have a tarp and a jacket with a hood, compliments of Charlene and the Forest Service; but I still dread sitting in a tree getting soaked.

"Like yours, I suppose it was a kind of a spur of the moment thing," I finally reply.

He nods like he understands.

I'm curious. "So, what do you hear about me? What are the Lutherans saying?"

"The Lutherans aren't saying much. It's Lent, they're clamping down on wine and chocolate and, I'm happy to report, loose chatter."

"What a good pastor you are."

"No, I doubt I had anything to do with the cessation of gossip for the last few weeks; I've always believed Lent was a waste of time. If there's something you need to let go of or cut back on you should really try to do that more than just forty days out of the year."

"Well, if it wasn't the Lutherans, then who told you I was out here?" I ask.

"Dwayne called me."

"Dwayne?" I guess Charlene must have told her brother.

"Yes, your ex-husband left a message at the church, asking me to contact him when I returned from my trip. I called him this morning and he told me of your whereabouts. I guess you might say he was worried."

"Well, that's sweet, but it's hardly his business to worry about me. He should know that I'm fine."

"Are you fine?"

"Don't I seem fine?"

"You're a bit high up for a reliable mental state assessment; but yes, I suppose you seem like the Kate I know and love, just sitting in a tree."

We're both quiet, both trying to put some order to the decisions we have made and trying to understand how it is that we made our choices, our life-altering choices, without the input of the other. Betrayal comes in many forms.

A question dawns on me. "Why did Dwayne contact you?"

"Because I imagine like so many others in this county he still thinks you and I are an item."

Well, that's possible, I suppose. He did at one time question me about my relationship with Jim, why we spent so much time together. I explained about our mutual interest in the birds but I'm not really sure he believed it. I'm not really sure I believe it.

"Why didn't you ever tell your husband that I'm gay?" he asks, surprising me with the question. We hadn't talked about this in a long time.

"That's not for me to tell," I explain falling back on the same reasoning I did when he asked me before. "And as you know, I shouldn't have to defend my friendship with you to Dwayne or anybody else. It shouldn't matter if you're gay or not that you're my best friend. Either he trusted me or he didn't."

"And did he really trust you?"

The question gives me pause. I think he did; I never really saw him act jealous but then again I'm not really sure I was paying very close attention. Maybe this was one more reason for choosing Debbie.

"Well, it doesn't really matter now anyway, does it?" I watch as the clouds gather overhead.

Jim doesn't answer and we are silent again.

"So, do tell, who have you seen out here since abandoning the human race and joining the frail forest ecosystem?"

I think about the red-cockaded. Jim will be so excited; but I just can't bring myself to share that sighting. In the same way I have never spoken of my friend's sexual orientation even with people I know would keep it secret I feel bound to a certain degree of confidentiality not to *out* the spotted bird.

"There's a pair of great horned owls," I say, knowing this will be fairly pleasing to Jim; he loves the owls.

He lifts up the pair of binoculars and holds them to his eyes.

"Look at the pine that would be at about two o'clock if I'm standing at noon." I watch him move his vision slightly to his right. "Now, go down about two inches." He follows my instructions.

"The dead pine? The snag about twenty yards from where I sit?"

"Yes." I wait as he adjusts his view.

"Is it a squirrel nest?"

"Yeah, is she in there?" I hadn't heard her all day.

"She's sitting on the nest, and I think she's watching us."

"I named her Delores." I stand up and look in the opposite direction. "Her beau, Mr. Delores, is in the cherrybark oak to your left. Maybe ten feet from us."

He turns in the direction I have instructed.

"He's asleep."

"Typical," I respond and sit back down on the landing. "There's a nest of whip-poor-wills somewhere behind us."

"I haven't heard one of those in years," he replies, sounding almost dreamy.

"I know. It's spooky hearing them."

"Death omen," he notes.

I don't respond but it is what I think about when I hear them, death; and Hank Williams, of course, hearing the whip-poor-wills, feeling so lonesome that he could cry.

"What else?"

"I think I saw a chimney swift even though it's still a little early for them to be back and there's a pair of chickadees using an old woodpecker's nest in a tree by the creek; I can see them from here. A family of brown-headed nuthatches lives in the flat downstairs."

We both glance to the limbs below me.

I go on. "The mornings are filled with the Wilson's warblers and house finches. By the afternoon it's crickets and cicadas. Late day it's robins and thrushes, geese flying home, blackbirds and doves. And once it's dark Mr. and Mrs. Delores have long conversations for most of the night.

He puts down his binoculars. "I almost envy you up there," he tells me softly. "You and your honorable birds."

This brings a smile. Jim once read a Dorothy Sayers story about a group of Japanese men discussing the doctrine of Trinity within Christian theology. One of the men said, "Honorable Father, very good. Honorable Son, very good. Honorable Bird, I do not understand at all." This has become a sort of inside joke for us, Holy Spirit, Honorable Bird.

"Your buddy Ray was at the store when I went by there and he gave me the stuff he was buying for you, said to tell you he'd be out here

tomorrow at lunch. I brought you some peanut butter and a couple
of apples. There's a box of protein bars and three of bottles of wine.
He begins rifling through the bags at his feet.

"Do you want me to open the bottles for you since they aren't
screw top?" He reaches in the front pocket of his pants and pulls out
a knife with all the fancy gadgets attached. He holds up the corkscrew.
"This is what it looks like."

He makes me laugh and I watch as he opens the bottles and then
sticks the corks back in. "Now, how is it that I get them up to you?"
He sees the buckets.

"You'll figure it out," I tell him, watching as he takes the top off
the toilet bucket, recoils, and puts it back on.

"Mother Mary and Joseph," he says, shaking his head. He begins
putting his bags of groceries in the other bucket and I start to pull.

"If you're keeping your mama at home, you're going to need to
learn how to empty one of those."

"Good God, I have done a most dreadful thing, haven't I?"

The bucket gets to me and I reach in for the goodies. "You need
me to come down and help?" I am serious with the offer; I don't really
think he knows what he's taken on.

He shakes his head, folds up his chair, and leaves it at the base of
the tree.

"No, we each have our own paths to take. Mine is with my dying
mother and yours is with an owl named Delores and a nest of nuthatches." He pauses now. "I'll be back soon. You are okay, aren't you?"

"About as okay as you," I answer.

"Well then, may God have mercy on us both."

"Amen," I respond and cross myself for good measure.

A meadowlark sings out and Jim nods his approval and walks away.

Eight

"I'd like to do a story about you," she says, standing so far away that I can hardly hear her. I never saw her approach. It was as if she suddenly appeared out of nowhere—surprise tactics of a bird of prey.

"Why?" I ask, leaning down to see who it is.

"Because you're interesting, I guess."

"To whom?"

She finally moves into the clearing so that I can get a good look at her. She's tall, blonde hair, small head. Her neck looks thick because she's wearing a dull yellow scarf that bunches under her chin. She's wearing glasses, black-framed glasses on her face. If she had a black beard, she would look like a lammergeier, a bearded vulture, translated from German as *lamb vulture*.

She shrugs. "People."

I step back so that she can't see me through the branches but still giving me a bird's eye view of her. She's young but that's no matter; she's dangerous. I can tell this already, the way she stares up at me, the way she stands, laser-focused, eager to pounce. I watch her closely, recalling that the lammergeier has a shrill whistle and favors the soft marrow inside bones. The long-winged bird is known for waiting until the other vultures are done and then carrying the bones high in the air and dropping them to shatter below. Lammergeiers are thought to be the largest Old World vulture still around.

This bird is not familiar to me, not native to these parts, and I don't think I've seen her face on any local television broadcast, her picture in the local papers.

She's wearing a light-colored pair of slacks, a black overcoat, and has a small reporter's notebook in her hands. It appears as if she's alone and she's glancing all around the sweetgum, writing down notes.

"Was that a priest?"

She must have seen Jim when he left. He's been gone for an hour and she only just showed up. This makes me wonder how long she was standing close by and exactly what she might have heard.

"He's a friend," I answer cautiously.

She nods, writes something down.

"Who told you I was up here?"

"I read about you in the paper last week. You're a Forest Service agent, right? And you're disputing the Hatch and Brownfield development."

"Not really disputing anything, no."

"You're in a tree that they intend to remove for the construction project and since you're up there the project has been put on hold." She pauses, waiting for a reply, I assume, but I don't have one to give. "That's a dispute, I'd say. Actually, it's more than just that, you're breaking the law, you know?"

I don't respond.

"Is it the tree?"

"Is what the tree?"

"Is it the tree you're trying to save?"

She walks closer and I watch her place her hand on the trunk of the sweetgum, then she moves over to the loblollies and she runs her fingers along the spine of one. I bristle at her touch. "The other one, the fallen one is dead, right?"

"The sweetgum?" I ask and then shrug. I don't want to talk about any of the three trees that are holding me.

"Is it this particular tree that you're trying to save?"

"Who are you working for?" I suddenly remember that she has not identified herself or the media outlet she represents.

"Tonya Lassiter," she answers. "I do mostly freelance work."

"So, you're not a television reporter or write for the *Sun Journal*?"

She shakes her head and then angles herself so that she can get a better view of me. I slip back just a bit.

"It's Wanda Davidson, isn't it?"

"Kate," I answer. "I go by Kate and the Davidson part is wrong, too."

She flips back to another page in her little notebook. "Oh, that's right. You're recently divorced." She reads over the page in her hand. "You're taking back your maiden name?"

"Eventually," I say, cautiously.

I watch her jot something down.

"Is this act of civil disobedience because of religion?"

She's back to Jim's visit again.

"No."

"So the priest who was here and brought you gifts wasn't offering you some spiritual guidance or religious support for your actions? Did he put you up to this?"

I don't respond; I certainly don't want Jim mentioned in any story about me being up this tree.

"If it's not religious, it's ecological, environmental then? The trees, the land?" She pauses. "The bird?"

It seems odd to me that she said that in the singular tense, not *birds* but *bird* and I immediately wonder if she somehow knows about the red-cockaded.

She corrects herself before I answer. "Birds, I mean," she says.

"Maybe," I respond and then take my seat on the board, lean back against the cool wood. The sky is darker now. I can hear thunder in the distance. There's a sharp wind. None of the afternoon birds are singing but I feel them close by. I wonder if this is how it is for them, if this is how they feel waiting on a storm, watching for predators, careful with every call or move.

"You have help." She is walking around the base of the tree. She is noticing the buckets, the chair, the shawl and Bible. "The Sierra Club? The Audubon Society?"

"Jones County High School Science Club," I reply, choosing not to list the names and organizations of my friends. I even shield Marge's women's circle.

She nods, makes another note.

"And your father, has he visited, does he approve of this action?"

Who is this woman?

She taps the pen on her notebook. "Never mind, I can get a statement from the sheriff later."

"Do I know you, Tonya?"

She shakes her head, realizing that I can see her. "I don't think we've ever met," she answers and then meets my stare. "Nathan's death, your brother's accident, even though it was a long time ago was a painful experience for you, wasn't it?"

I stand back up and think about leaving but I don't really have anywhere to go. As high as I am, as free as I have felt since moving up here, I realize now that I'm trapped. I look out towards the path that leads to the road, hoping Charlene is on her way or that Jim might come back; but I don't see anyone else around.

"Look, Tonya, I'm not sure what kind of angle you're trying to take on this. I don't know who you're writing for or what you're hoping to get out of this interview; but I don't want to talk to you anymore. I'd like it if you would leave."

"Well, you can't really make me though, can you? It is, after all, a free country and you've chosen to climb a tree that's on private property and so that doesn't really give you much authority to run me off, does it?"

I stand and move up a limb, feeling a little shaky.

"I mean, if you were trying to get away for solitude, have some private time, you kind of chose the wrong place to go, wrong thing to do, wouldn't you say?"

I watch her closely.

"Should the people of this county be worried?"

I glance at my watch, willing Ray to finish work and get back.

"Is this a political statement about the government, your employer?"

She stands where she is, gazes in my direction, waiting for a response but as before, I don't make one.

"Do you have a gun?"

I reach for the next limb.

"I have a quote from your boss," she says, her voice sly and provocative. She pauses, flips through her notebook.

I stay where I am, turn back towards Tonya and think about Don, his red face and sweaty palms, his beady eyes and nervous tic. Don and I have never had any real problems between us; my annual performance evaluations are always good. I think my work at the Forest Service is exemplary. Still, I'm quite sure he's unhappy I've done what I have. He may not have any complaints about my work but he's probably getting lots of distracting calls about his field researcher moving up a tree. And Don Rich doesn't like distractions.

"Don't you want to know what he's saying about you?"

"Don Rich is a good man and has a pristine reputation with the Forest Service. I have nothing to say about him and I don't really care to hear what he's saying about my recent actions. My work and this climb are in no way related."

She glanced down at her notepad. "Wanda Kate Davidson is no longer employed with the Forest Service. She has not shown up for her assigned workdays in more than a week without just cause thereby giving her employer ample reason to release her from her duties. She was an outstanding employee until this recent irrational behavior and we have no further comment at this time."

Well, it's not as bad as it could be, that's for sure. This bone didn't shatter.

"Would you care to make a response?"

"Tonya . . ." I hesitate.

"Lassiter," she fills in the blank. "Tonya Lassiter."

"I don't know who you are or what kind of story you're hoping to write. I've got nothing to say to you. And since it's getting ready to rain, it would be my suggestion that you head back to your vehicle before you get stuck out here."

She looks above me up at the sky, the tops of the trees beginning to sway.

"It's spring, you know, so that means the cottonmouths are starting to perk up. Maybe you didn't know this, but they like to spend their winters near dead pines and old stumps, woodsy areas sort of like right where you're standing."

I watch her jerk just enough to let me know she doesn't know anything about this habitat, giving me a little authority of my own. I do have an upper hand, after all.

"Studies show that they're most active this time of year and I'm sure being such a smart reporter as you appear to be, so familiar with your subjects and their personal landscapes that you've heard about snakes and spring storms."

I can tell I've got her attention.

There's a loud crack, right on cue. "The thunder seems to draw them out, wakes them up, makes them cranky."

Tonya folds up her notebook, sticks the pen in her pocket. She looks carefully around her feet as she steps away from the sweetgum and pines.

"I'll be back, Kate, and I imagine when I do I'll have lots of other quotes from people in your life to share with you."

I watch her peer up at me one last time, smile, and then walk towards the path. I hear a flapping sound and glance up in the swamp blackgum that stands near my perch. Close to the top, on a large limb just starting to bud, I see a Cooper's hawk with a small bird, probably one of the chickadees, in his long flesh-tearing beak, eyeing me.

When I look back to see how far the lammergeier has gotten on the path, she's already gone.

Nine

"I thought I should come out here before it rains."

I'm busy trying to tie the tarp above my stand. I have to keep waiting for breaks in the wind. I barely make out the voice of someone else who has ventured out this evening. I lean over the limb to get a better look.

"I brought you food," the person says, stepping closer and holding out a bag.

It's Tiffany from the science club. She's by herself and she's wearing a rain poncho and rubber boots.

"Oh, okay," I answer, thinking I am well supplied for now. Jim and Ray made sure of that. "Thanks." I look around for the bucket I had already stowed. I take the rope and lower it near where Tiffany is standing.

She walks closer and puts the plastic bag inside and I pull it up.

"I wasn't sure you'd still be up there," she says, stepping back.

"Yeah? And I wasn't sure I'd see you again," I confess, taking out the bag. "How's Stanley?"

She doesn't answer and I stop what I'm doing and peer down in her direction.

She shrugs. "He got into Wake Forest," she tells me, which I assume means he's no longer in deep depression.

"Go Deacs," I say, trying to sound enthusiastic.

"Right," she replies softly.

There's another rush of wind and the unsecured end of the tarp flies up.

"There's an umbrella in there," she tells me.

"Oh, okay," I reply, not sure how that will help.

"Plastic garbage bags if you need to put stuff away."

"Thank you, that's very thoughtful." I open the bag. There's some granola bars, Gatorade, toilet paper, three black bags. I glance around my stand; I'm running out of room for stuff.

"So, what about you?" I ask, making conversation because Tiffany is still standing beneath the tree and it seems like she wants to talk.

"What?"

"Where do you want to go to school?"

She shrugs. "I've got some time before I make up my mind."

"Well, you've had time to think about it, right? You've visited a few campuses?"

She shakes her head. "I'll probably just stay close by."

"East Carolina then?" I ask her. That's the favorite of most students in eastern North Carolina.

"Lenoir Community College," she notes.

"Well, that's a good school, too," I reply, feeling slightly embarrassed that I made the assumption that she would go to a four-year school.

"It's just for the associate degree. We can't really afford anything else right now. I have a sister at State."

"What do you hope to study?" I ask, wondering how long she's going to stay, wondering about the coming storm. I can smell the rain.

"Biology," she answers. "Maybe specialize in entomology. I'm interested in wildlife work too, maybe with the Forest Service like you."

"So, bugs then? And you really do like science?" I ask, realizing that I may have been completely wrong about Tiffany.

She nods. "I'm in the advanced class this year."

I put the food in the bag I had already stowed in a hole in one of the pines. I stick the toilet paper in the toilet bucket along with the garbage bags and put the cover on it, and then I tie it with the other bucket onto a limb.

"Are you scared?"

The question surprises me. "About what?"

"The storm? Being out here by yourself?"

I move back to where Tiffany can see me and shake my head. "No, I've been outside during storms before." But then I realize I was never up a tree in one.

"Isn't it dangerous to be standing up there during lightning?"

I look around me at the other trees, the nests I've discovered, the places other animals are hiding. I shrug. "I guess we'll see," I say.

"You could come down and hide down here, nobody would know. And then, you could just climb back up there when the storm is over."

I can't say that I haven't thought of this. It would be less scary, that's for sure. "But that sort of defeats the purpose, doesn't it?"

There's another rush of wind and I hang onto a branch. The sky is getting darker.

"If you don't mind me asking, Ms. Davidson, what is the purpose?" she asks. "I mean, I support you for trying to save the trees, trying to keep one more fragile ecosystem from being bulldozed, but don't you think that will happen regardless? Don't you think they're just going to wait until you come down and then do it anyway?"

Tiffany does have a point. I don't really plan to spend the rest of my life up here. Basically all I'm really doing is probably just delaying the inevitable; but then again, I'm not just up here because of the trees.

"Have you ever done something without really thinking it through, Tiffany?"

She pauses and I can see she's having trouble with the question.

"My mom says I do that a lot, especially when it comes to the boys I like."

"Like Stanley?"

She nods and pulls the poncho tighter around her. "He's with Courtney Hutchens now. She's a cheerleader." She drops her head. "He put me in charge of the spring project so that he can spend more time with her."

Poor Tiffany, stuck with taking care of the crazy lady in the tree.

"And you spent all that time trying to nurse him back to good mental health?"

"I did his homework in three classes, baked him way too many cookies, typed his U.S. History paper. Yeah, basically I wasted a lot of time. I don't know what I was thinking."

"You weren't thinking," I say to her. "You were just doing; you were just being nice, helping out a friend."

"Yeah, right, a friend." She pulls the hood over her head.

"Hey, don't beat yourself up for liking a guy. We've all done that before. And you know, if you don't want to bring me stuff anymore, if you've got too much to do in your classes, I can sign something for you, verify what you've done already. You don't have to keep coming out here."

Tiffany shrugs. "Nah, that's all right, I like coming out here. It's nice to be outside, away from school. I don't mind. Last time I came, I found an oil beetle."

"You didn't touch it, did you?" I know that the American oil beetle emits a chemical that can blister human skin.

"I just took a picture of it; didn't have my collection kit."

The wind fills the trees now and a few drops of rain fall. I look up at the sky; the storm is very close. "You should probably go now, Tiffany. I don't want you to get caught out here when it starts to come down."

She nods. "Yeah, okay. Be careful. And I'll see you later, maybe in a couple of days."

"Great, thanks."

She hesitates. "You want my poncho?"

The young girl's generosity is touching. I shake my head. "I've got a tarp and now I have an umbrella."

"Right."

And just as the first rumble of thunder fills the sky, Tiffany holds up her hand and leaves.

Ten

It is a long, drawn-out storm. At first, the sky threatened and cleared, threatened and cleared, until finally the rain clouds were thick and heavy enough to break. As darkness settled only a light breeze danced through the leaves and needles, but now it has grown and the howling has become deafening. The loblolly limbs begin to dip and sway and the forest is filled with wind. It sounds like a train coming through.

Rain batters the tarp that I placed above me, having just gotten it fastened to the branches after Tiffany left, right before the storm began. I've stuffed my books and binoculars into my jacket and tied together the sleeves and hung it on a limb. I did what I could to secure my other belongings, food, a thermos, my toothbrush, lantern, and toiletries into a hole near my perch. I've put the flashlight in my pants pocket and wrapped the blanket around my shoulders.

I've found my hat and gloves and put them on but still it's cold and water comes down from the sky in sheets and I'm hanging on for dear life to the top of the trunk of one of the pines. I have tethered myself with a rope even as the earth beneath me seems to pitch and roll; I suddenly feel as if I'm in a ship on the stormy sea, standing in the crow's nest above the masthead, the swollen waves lifting me and then slamming me back down.

I think about slipping, falling, buried under all my belongings. I think about being thrown from the tree stand, hurled by the sweet-gum, crashing to the ground. I think about being struck by lightning or the pines being ripped apart, me tumbling between them. But mostly I'm just thinking about holding on and not letting go, driving my fingernails through my gloves into the pine bark, shoving my shoes far into the crevices between limbs on both sides of the trunk even as three trees bend and sway under and around me.

I press my face against the bark, the wood wet and fleshy, and when I open my eyes between the pitching, I catch a glimpse of Delores, her brown wings flapping around the nest in the dead tree near me. I think about the eggs that have been beneath her for so many nights, wonder if they might fall and break, wonder if she will grieve like I would if I realized all that work, all that maternal care had been spent for nothing. She flaps and in the flash of a bolt of lightning I see her long talons reaching for and grasping the branch under the nest. She hangs on just like I am doing.

The wind barrels through again, the thunder rolls, and there is another crack of lightning, closer now, and suddenly I feel like I'm in a dream, a nightmare. The rain turns to hail, pelting me even with the tarp overhead; no matter how hard I try to shake myself loose from what I know is only my imagination, what is not real and is instead the shadows dancing in the forest, the dark recesses of my mind are now open.

I stand in a shaking tree while images flash before me but not the images I long for; these are not my moments of sweetness rising from stored memories to comfort me in this dark hour. I do not see my mother, young and unburdened, showing me how to roll out dough for a pie shell, her easy smile, the dust of white flour in her hair. There are not images of my father lifting me high on his shoulders, above everyone else, above the top of the fence, to watch my brother play ball.

There was not a picture of the songbirds I followed as a child, the early ones I noticed outside my window, the robin and bluebird, the first nest I found. No treasured holidays, no graduations. There are not moments I know I have kept somewhere, moments of loveliness, sweetness. There were none of the memories that would otherwise ease me, filling my thoughts. None of those images arrive in this wretched night.

Instead, in the thunder it is the muffled words I hear of the police officer at the front door whispering to my father after I have been ordered to my room, the push and pull of my own hard breath as I try to make out their closed and hushed conversation. Instead of the lightning giving me vision into this span of forest I know and love it is the sight of Nathan's pickup truck smashed and burning in a ditch not more than a mile from our home.

Another flash and I am seeing my dead brother's body shoved into a wooden box, his eyes closed, his lips pulled into a tight line, his arms down at his sides, his face flat and bruised, my father slamming his fists against the weeping willow. I see only that horrible night waiting for my brother to arrive and sing the birthday song, opening wide the door looking for him only to find uniformed officers at the door instead.

The only visions that come from this violent spring storm are of those terrible days that followed, days of death and silence and nothing I even yet can understand; and just like I felt so many years ago, there is a growing part of me that just wants to let go and fly into the brutal wind and let my body be cast about until it finally crashes and breaks into pieces, just like my heart had already done. I even hear the laughter of someone tempting me to loose myself from the bindings of this world, this forest, this tree, tempting me to surrender.

But I don't.

And whether it is a basic primal instinct that keeps me holding on, fundamental survival skills that disallow me from giving over to the storm, or someone from the other side, something keeps me clinging to life, holding and holding, something within will not let me let go. And I pitch and sway, refusing to fall, refusing to be thrown from my stand, refusing to give in or give up or let go. It becomes a battle of wills and I am determined not to let the storm win even though I clearly remember the times when I have desperately wanted to die. Still, I fight, knowing that I will not die tonight.

When the last rumbles of thunder disappear and the lightning has passed, when the tree is upright and still, and the final drops of rain have fallen, I feel my ragged breath. I am weary and spent. My body is exhausted. My fingers cramp, the muscles in my neck and back shake in spasms, and I am soaked to the bone. Even then, I don't let go for the longest time. I don't stop clinging even as there remains nothing around me but night and silence. I am still unwilling to drop my arms and step away.

And finally there is a sound.

I hear Delores's voice. She is okay, too. She has survived and she is calling her mate, checking on him, asking for him; I'm not sure. But she calls and she waits. She calls and she waits, until finally from the edge of the woods more than a hundred feet from his usual roost he answers, and she doesn't call again.

I let go of the trunk and stand still for a few minutes trying to get my bearings in the dark. I reach down and feel the board beneath me; it survived. But the limb of the sweetgum where the ropes to the buckets were tied has broken and fallen or been thrown somewhere else. I reach in my pocket for my flashlight, pull it out and try to turn it on but it doesn't work, the batteries dead or wet. I put it back in my pocket and grab at air, feeling around my feet like a blind person because there is only a sliver of moon, the stars still covered in clouds.

I can't tell for sure but it seems most of my belongings I had thought were secure on the landing or that I tried to stow in the holes and crevices have also fallen. I feel nothing near where I am standing except the jacket tethered to the branch—my books and binoculars still in place—the tarp, now torn, sagging overhead and the blanket tied around me.

There is nothing to do now but lie down, slide my knees up, pull the blanket tight around me, and try to get some sleep. My watch reads two o'clock in the morning. No one will be visiting for hours. I cannot see well enough to climb down and try and gather everything that has fallen. I can only be still and try to get warm. I will not be able to assess the storm's damage until daylight breaks.

I hear rustling nearby, close, and I sit up to see a pair of yellow eyes on the branch right above me. Mr. Delores has flown over from his perch in the storm and apparently has seen about his mate and eggs, checked on the safety of his family, and now it appears he is checking on me.

Eleven

"You coming down then?"

Charlene is the first to arrive the morning after the storm. She's seen everything littering the ground beneath my stand and now she's just looking up at me like she thinks this is it.

My throat is sore and my clothes and blanket are still wet from last night. My feet are numb; I'm cold and my shoulders and arms are stiff. My back is against the pine tree trunk, the one I was clinging to during the storm. I hear the nuthatches below me. It appears their nest survived as well but I wonder if they aren't just as spent.

Charlene can see me from where she is standing. I shake my head.

"No. Okay."

I can't tell if she's mad or disappointed or just tired of me.

She starts picking up the things that fell from the tree. She holds up my toothbrush. "I don't think you want to be using this again." And she throws in the plastic bag she has to collect the trash. "You lose all your food?"

I nod.

She puts down the plastic bag and reaches in the pocket of her vest. She's dressed for work and I know she can't stay long. She has to report to the ranger's station this morning to start on the invasive non-native plant maintenance project. We were assigned to the same field area a month ago and we had been looking forward to working together. When we got the job notice we had celebrated with Mexican food for lunch. Now, she'll be stuck partnered up with Tim Weston or Phil Nobles, our least favorite colleagues at the Forest Service. Tim can't stop talking long enough to catch his breath and Phil, we both agree, is a little sketchy; he stares at you a lot and touches his mustache more than he should. I know she's no longer looking forward to the project.

She fishes out a protein bar and pitches to me. I don't catch it but it lands on the board near my feet.

I watch her pick everything up, putting the salvageable items in a small pile. I watch her as she finds the two buckets. Both are empty. She holds up the rope that had been used to get them to me. "How did the girl from Emerald Isle throw this up to you?"

She's talking about LuAnn Hightower from the Sierra Club.

"She tied it to a brick."

Charlene glances around, eyes the brick, and heads over in that direction. "You want me to try and get it up there to you?"

I stand up. "Okay," I answer.

She ties the rope through the brick and secures a knot. "Stand back," she tells me.

I shimmy around the pine tree trunk and wait. It takes three tries but she finally gets the brick and rope to the board. I step back around.

"Which one is the toilet?" she asks, holding up both buckets.

"The blue one. I had garbage bags up here that went in it. It has a top."

I hear her sigh and she starts looking around for the top and the bags. I can't see her for a few minutes until she returns. She puts the box of garbage bags in the bucket, places the top on, pulls the rope under the handle and ties it. She looks up at me and I grab the rope and pull it up.

As I untie it and throw the rope back down for the other bucket, she gathers everything in the pile and places it all inside. When the end of the rope is back down, she ties the second bucket and I pull it up. There's the thermos, lotion, bug spray, some protein bars, bottles of water, socks—everything soaked and dirty.

"I need something else to wear," I tell her.

"I know. I went to your place yesterday and got some more clothes." She goes over to the backpack she had put down when she started cleaning the mess from the storm. "Do you need other shoes? I didn't bring any other shoes."

I shake my head. "No, I'll hang these up; they'll dry in the sun." I throw down the bucket still tied to one end of the rope.

She places the clothes inside. "There's something else." She stuffs everything in the bucket. "You'll see."

I can tell that the bucket is full and I pull my end of the rope slowly until it arrives.

"Okay, I guess I need to get over to the station." She straps the backpack on her back, shields her eyes with her hand and looks up at me.

"I got fired," I tell her. "I found out from a reporter who was here yesterday."

Charlene nods.

"You heard?"

"Yeah. Don told me."

"I guess I shouldn't be surprised, right?"

She shrugs.

"You mad?" I ask, feeling slightly nervous.

"Nah," she answers and then hesitates, dropping her face.

"What is it?"

She waits before answering. "Eugene was at the gym last night."

I sit down on the landing.

"He ran into Winston. They played basketball together."

Eugene Watson is the guy Charlene has been dating for years. She saying that she's going to break up with him because he claims he's not getting married; but she can't seem to leave the guy.

Eugene was a jock in high school, works as a fireman now, and likes to play pick-up games at the YMCA. He's been doing that for years. Sometimes I go with Charlene to watch him play. He's pretty good.

"He asked him a lot of questions because he knows you and I are friends and that Eugene and I are dating."

I can only imagine the conversation.

"Eugene said he didn't say very much to him, claimed that he didn't really know what was going on."

I don't say anything because I know there is more she has to say. I brace myself. Her whole manner this morning, the way she's talking, I realize now that it isn't that she's mad about me not being on assignment with her; it's something else completely and seeing her now, I don't think this is going to be good news.

"Winston told him about the hospitalization. You know, because of . . ." Her voice trails off.

I feel my face flush a little. Charlene didn't know that I spent some time on a psych unit. I hadn't told anyone about that, never really saw the point. It was years after Nathan died but I was having a bad time and Daddy didn't really know what to do with me. Finally, we both agreed that maybe it might help to go somewhere and he promised he would take me to a place out of town and nobody would find out. I was there over a summer break after my sophomore year and it did help a little. But I never told Charlene or Dwayne and I thought that Daddy had kept it secret, too. Now, I'm not so sure.

"So, what does Winston Hatch think he's going to do with that information? That doesn't mean anything now."

Charlene won't look back up at me. She's sliding her feet around, kicking at pebbles or sticks.

"What Charlene? What did Eugene tell you?"

"Winston's going to a judge, trying to say you're mentally unstable."

"And what? Get a dragnet, shoot me down from here with a

tranquilizer gun? Wrap me up in a straitjacket and take me to Cherry Hospital?" I feel hot, the wet clothes I'm wearing starting to feel thick and scratchy.

Charlene shakes her head. "I don't know what will happen," she answers. "I just thought I should tell you."

I take in a breath. "Okay, thanks."

"You need me to stay with you?"

"No, you need to get to work. You don't want to lose your job for being late and cavorting with a crazy person."

"Hey."

I won't look at her.

"Hey," she says again.

I find her through the branches. She's staring right at me. "You're not crazy and Winston can't do anything about you being here."

But of course I know he can. I'm trespassing. I blow out a breath and close my eyes. "Thanks, Charlene," I say, and then for reassurance I make sure she can see my face. "I'm okay."

She watches me for a minute. "I'll see you tomorrow."

"Okay. Thank you for everything."

She nods at me and walks away.

Twelve

Inside the bag Charlene left, there is a small book, a journal with the pages without lines, blank, meant for drawing, and a box of colored crayons. She remembered that I used to love to sketch when I went on field trips. I told her that a long time ago, but I haven't actually drawn anything in years. Truthfully, I have missed the sketching, but it just got to be too much trouble trying to pack a sketchpad and paints in my equipment. Mostly, like the other agents doing research, I just took a lot of photographs; I have some beautiful shots of the birds. Besides, I never seemed to have the time for sketching anymore. Well, until now. I change into the fresh set of clothes and throw my wet ones over the branches near me. I stand for a bit, do a few stretches, raise my arms above my head and then bend and touch my toes, balancing on the plywood. I do this a few times and then sit back down. I work out some of the kinks in my spine and shoulders, twisting and turning from one side to the other, and then I am done.

Now I listen. It's active in the forest this morning. A male cardinal, bright red, flies right into my little perch. He sits on a limb close enough for me to touch; but of course, I don't. I just watch him as he watches me, trying to understand what species of animal this is, tall and looming, sitting in a tree. He tilts his head from side to side satisfied that I bear no harm and then flies off.

I hear the songs of the pine warblers, the forest filled with nesting pairs. The small yellowish birds sing with a steady musical trill, often mistaken by birders for the chipping sparrow or the dark-eyed junco. This species is found in most pine trees, hence the name, and their sweet songs are common in these parts. I close my eyes and listen, think about the storm, the images in the flashes of lightning, the way I wouldn't let go.

I think about Tiffany, how she reminds me a little of myself, timid, a science nerd in love with the popular boy. She seems bright but apparently not smart enough to get a full ride for a four-year education. I figure she'll do okay at the community college; a lot of people do. But I can't help wishing that she could know how it feels to be recruited, to apply to the universities and fill out all those essays, hopeful and confident, how it is to dream about what she might learn, who she might meet.

I was glad to leave home and go to school. I felt like I was finally getting away from all of this, finally forging my own path, out of these blackwater bottoms, beyond the White Oak River and the pine savannahs, the deep swamp of grief. I thought it would be unlike what it seemed that I have known forever, that it would be new and exciting; I would finally be someone other than Nathan's little sister or the daughter of the sheriff. And yet I got to college and still felt the same way I felt before I left, exactly the same way, small and different, unpopular, broken and loosely held together.

I met a few girls I liked, worked in the labs with the other science geeks, made good grades, and except for that long second year when I couldn't seem to get my footing, the academic setting of the university was good for me. I did okay for myself. Not like it was for Nathan, of course, big man on campus that he was, but I still managed to carve out a little place all my own, unlike what I was never able to do in high school. At least in college I could focus on my studies, taking as many courses as I could, learning as much as the professors would teach, as much as my brain could hold.

I loved books, loved the experiments we conducted in labs, loved the research, the classes and the lectures. I did well in my work and in my Bachelor of Science major of Biology; but even then, even after finishing third in my graduating class at a pretty reputable college, I knew I would only be saved by what I found outdoors. I would never feel at home anywhere but places without walls.

It was the birds and the trees, the earthy soil, the reptiles and beetles, this was the only way I would get through my life. It had been that way since I was a little girl and my mother walked out on us all, me finding solace in the willow grass and lofty pine trees; and it has remained, even as I ought to have forged new roads for myself by now, developed different patterns, even as I should know better. Still, I don't and I am saved by something other than my relationships; I am saved by the calls of birds and the thick woodsy arms of inseparable pines.

I pull out a granola bar that Tiffany brought and snack on it for a while, drink some of the Gatorade. I have to admit I miss coffee and a mattress, washing my hair in the shower, eating hot food, and having clean fingernails; but that's really all. I know people think I should want to come down now, that it's been more than two weeks without all the things others imagine we have to have to survive, but I'm really pretty content. In fact, I feel a measure of peace that I haven't felt in a long time.

I liked owning a house, driving a car, having shelves to place my skulls and bones, my framed photographs. I was perfectly fine with being married, enjoying the Nature Channel and playing board games, eating dinner on a plate; but I also really like it where I am, having nothing but what I can fit in pockets and hang on branches. It is oddly satisfying resting on a piece of plywood, eating granola bars, wearing the same clothes day after day, being close to the nests and the forest sounds, living in a tree.

I close my eyes and lean back against the loblolly and I hear him before I see him fly by. It's the same one Lilly Carol and I spotted, the same one I haven't seen in ten days. He's about six inches long, mostly gray and white with the well-distinguished red bar behind the eye. He's probably trying to find a nesting site, and for a second I wonder if I have taken away the place he was hoping to build.

I am in a loblolly and it suddenly dawns on me that it could be argued by conservationists that I am breaking the law not only by trespassing but also by modifying or degrading suitable habitat for the red-cockaded. By living in these trees, sturdy old pines that are favored by the endangered woodpecker, I may be harming him; I may be impairing his ability to feed or breed. I may, in fact, be blocking a cavity already drilled by this species. And yet I don't recall seeing one since finding my perch. There were a few holes, a couple of nesting places, but none that bears the marks of a cockaded.

There were no woodpecker cavities near the lowest branches, no entrance tunnels or resin wells that I could see, just one or two niches carved out between limbs, empty of nests and bearing no marks of recent habitation. I know that the red-cockaded woodpeckers live in clans and that the clans typically consists of a breeding pair and some male offspring called helpers who assist the breeding pair in maintaining cavities and feeding the young. The females leave but a few males always hang around the nest.

It has been reported that clans occupy clusters consisting of one to several cavity trees that provide roosting and nesting sites. I don't know why I haven't seen more than this one lone bird. I don't know where the clan is or where his old nest is situated. I just know he could be in a cluster that includes the trees I'm in.

My eyes are open as he is flying past and he doesn't even seem to notice that I'm here. He's on his way somewhere, doing something, and I'm confident that if there is one red-cockaded woodpecker, there is a family, a nesting pair, and probably eggs.

I feel myself getting a little excited just knowing I am so close to them. And I am getting out my binoculars hoping I can track his whereabouts when I hear the voice calling out beneath me.

Thirteen

"I wasn't sure you'd still be up there."

It's Ray and he's not alone.

"You think I flew off in the storm?" I stand up and lean over.

"Hey, Kate," comes the little voice.

"Hey, Chickadee," my term of endearment for Lilly Carol.

Ray has his daughter on his back; he has somehow managed to tie her on, like a pack, her paralyzed legs wrapped around his thick waist.

I look closer and see that he has rigged up an apparatus that lets her sit on an inflated tube he has around him and she's wearing pants that keep her legs attached and together in front. There's a strap around them both. From where I'm standing they look like one person with two heads, and the sight of this makes me laugh.

"That's quite a contraption you got there, Mr. Marcus."

He unbuckles the strap connecting them, reaches around and pulls the girl from the back to the front so that now it looks like she's hugging him and then gently places her on the ground. Using the strength in her arms she manages to slide around so I can see her face. She has the biggest smile and it almost makes me want to come down there and scoop her up in my arms. But I refrain.

We both glance over at Ray who is standing there with the inflated inner tube still around his waist, looking very much like a large beginning swimmer. He puts both hands on his waist above the tube and appears to be catching his breath. It's a haul out here with a twelve-year-old on your back; I know because I've done it.

"We tried yesterday to push the chair out here but it was just too sandy. We kept getting stuck."

I know this is her code for *I haven't told him how you brought me out here on your shoulders,* and I don't respond right away, thinking of something to say to let her know I am following.

"Well, it certainly appears as if you figured out a fantastic way to get you in the woods." I sit on the landing and watch as Ray slides out of the inner tube, reaches in the backpack that Lilly Carol is wearing and pulls out a blanket; he spreads it out and then picks up his daughter and places her on it. He also takes out a bottle of water, hands it to her, and then stretches out beside her.

"You want a protein bar?" I ask.

They both shake their heads. I watch as Lilly Carol drinks from the bottle and then hands it to her dad.

"I saw you on TV," the little girl announces.

"Yeah, how did I look?"

Ray takes a long drink and then wipes his mouth with the back of his hand.

"Small," she answers. "I think the camera guy was having a hard time getting a good shot of you up there. There's a lot of branches."

I remember the television crew that arrived under the trees on my fifth day here. There was one reporter, a young boy, the newest one on staff, I'm sure, sent out to all the remote locations with the weird stories, and there was one cameraman, not at all happy about having to lug his equipment this far out in the woods. They didn't stay long; I wasn't even sure it would actually make the news.

"And what was the story exactly?" I ask since Lilly Carol is the first one to tell me about my media coverage.

She turns to her dad at this point without answering and suddenly I'm feeling a little nervous.

"It wasn't really a story," he answers.

"Yeah, what was it then?"

Neither of them responds.

I wait.

"The kid reporter just said that a trespasser had been seen in the forest area that was set for development and the starting date for the retirement village had been put on hold." He pauses. "And then there was a shot of you up there." He shakes his head. "Not really a story."

Lilly Carol won't look at me and I know there's more; but I decide it must not be good if neither of them will tell me.

"So, how's school?" I ask. I let the television news report go.

"It's good. I made a 96 on my math test and I'm the spelling champion for my class."

This makes me smile. Lilly Carol is so smart and I'm so proud of her; I know how hard she studies, how hard it was for her to catch up after the accident.

"Spell Bachman's warbler," I tell her.

"B-A-C-H-M-A-N." She grins up at me. "Warbler is too easy."

"So it is."

"You have a tarp?" Ray asks. He must be looking at the rig above my head.

"Well, *had* is more like it. It's ripped; I've just put it across the branches right now; won't be much use next time."

"Pretty bad out here?" he asks.

I nod. "It was an ordeal. But me and Delores managed to hang on."

I turn towards the old tree where the owl's nest is. I haven't seen her all day but I'm pretty sure she's still there.

"Delores?" It's Lilly Carol and I forget that she doesn't know about everybody I've met since moving out here.

"The great horned mama in the old squirrel nest not too far from where I am. I don't think you can see her today, but she's there with a nest of eggs."

I watch her lean forward, trying to find the owls. I wish she could see the big bird, hear its call. But owls aren't known for daylight activity, especially after a night like we just came through.

"Thanks for the food and water," I tell Ray.

"Yeah, I saw the preacher at the grocery store; he said he was coming over so I just gave the stuff to him. I had to pick Lilly up at school early." Ray peers up at me like he's got more that he wants to say but then seems to think better of it.

"Yeah, he came by before the storm."

He nods.

Lilly Carol pipes up. "The spring dance is coming up."

"Yeah? You going?"

She shrugs.

"Well, when is it?"

"April," she answers. "Next month. Ms. Lennox said she'd help me shop for a dress."

I glance over at Ray but he's not looking at me.

Ms. Lennox is the school librarian and has had a crush on Ray for as long as he's been single. His head is down and I can't see his face.

"Well, Ms. Lennox has excellent taste; I'm sure she'll pick you out something beautiful." I don't know why but as I say this I feel a kind of knot in my gut. I suppose that if I was normal and out of this tree I would be the one helping her shop for a dress for the school dance. I'd probably even be the one taking her.

"I guess," Lilly Carol replies, and I can't tell if this is her way to ask if I'll be down in a month.

"So, spelling champion," I change the subject. "What does that mean? Do you go against the other class champions?"

She nods. "There's a school spelling bee in a couple of weeks and then the winner goes to a regional contest and then there's the state championship in Raleigh sometime in May."

I realize how much I am missing.

"But Daddy's going to tape it so we can show you if you're still out here," she tells me.

I catch Ray's eye at this. He clears his throat and starts to stand.

"I brought you some more stuff; it's in the car so I'll go and get it. She can stay here, right? You two will be okay, yeah?"

I nod.

He glances down at his daughter. "You comfortable? You need to reposition or anything?"

She shakes her head and he peers at me again. "I'll be back in just a few minutes," he says and we both watch as he walks away.

When he's out of listening range she whispers, "Have you seen him?"

And I know she's talking about the red-cockaded.

Fourteen

"Just before you showed up; it was almost like he knew you were coming and wanted to tell me," I answer.

She glances around. "Is he still around? Is he close?"

I shake my head. "I don't know," I tell her. "I hadn't seen him since that first day when you and I came out here and then it was not more than an hour ago right out of the blue he just appeared." I sigh. "And then just like that, he was gone again."

She twists and turns, peering into the tops of trees.

"You're my good luck charm," I say.

The nuthatches start to sing and we both listen.

She nods and lies back, puts her arms behind her head and closes her eyes, a perfect smile across her face.

I realize, looking down on her, seeing her this way, that she seems absolutely whole. From this angle, high above with this bird's eye view, Lilly Carol is like any other kid and a person would never know of her severed spine, her unusable legs. The way she rests, so easy, so relaxed on the forest ground, you would never suspect how close she came to death or how close Ray stepped to the edge. You wouldn't think a thing except here is a perfectly healthy girl who happened to be most at home, like me, in the woods.

"I haven't told anyone," she explains, opening her eyes, staring right at me. "I wanted to tell Dad, but I know it's a secret." She pauses, sits up on her elbows. "I read on the computer that he's endangered," she adds. "They call it the spotted owl of the east."

"I know."

"Did you also know that they used to control the beetles, they ate them?"

"Yep, I knew that too."

"That was one of your studies from college."

"It was. *The Red-Cockaded Woodpecker and the Natural Maintenance of the Southern Pine Beetle.*" It was the primary work from my junior year, won a prize from the science community, an honorable mention from the school's biology department.

Lilly Carol knows more than anyone about the research I have done. She heard all my reports and papers, my field studies, when she was in the coma. At the time, I didn't really think she could hear me and I only did it because the ICU nurse claimed that reading to coma patients helps in their recoveries, helps them wake up.

She saw me sitting in the room day after day, my helplessness taking over, and she inadvertently made the suggestion; read to her, she told me, tell her your stories. So, with Ray out of commission and me the only one staying with her, I lugged all my cartons, all my boxes of files to the hospital and read what I had, my stories, what I knew, what I loved.

And then, when she woke up, having taught me everything there is to know about desperation and Ray everything he knows about miracles, she remembered all of it, every paper, every hypothesis. She sat up in the hospital bed, paralyzed, the lower part of her body useless, the top in perfect working order, and started spouting off scientific facts about Southeastern ecosystems and natural habitats for songbirds, controlled forest burns and invasive insects. It shocked us all.

It was as if she had captured every word I spoke, and when the ICU nurse overheard Lilly Carol asking me about the studies, citing details from the work, she confessed she only told families to talk to the patients or read to them just to give them hope, that she thought it helped a little but that she hadn't ever really believed in a patient's retention of the information. She hadn't really thought it was possible that a comatose person could recount what had been said at the bedside and that she hadn't really believed such a thing herself until she heard all that the little girl recalled, all that Lilly Carol knew.

As she went through rehabilitation, she started asking me all kinds of questions about my field work, wanted to know why I didn't finish my master's thesis, why I quit studying the Neotropical migratory birds and became interested in the forest devastation caused by the pine beetle. She wanted to know how I learned to conduct routing forage production studies and how I learned air-dry weights of range vegetation. She had even heard my confession, late on a feverish night, one of her worst, and wanted to know why I thought I could find my brother in the trees.

When she got home, when Ray got better, she pestered him until he came over to the house and made copies of everything I had, the cartons and files emptied once more, and then read them all to her again, her bedtime stories, my papers on the prothonotary warbler, the bald cypress, water tupelo, and bottomland hardwoods.

Other little girls want to know about mermaids and fairy princesses; Lilly Carol wanted to hear about longleaf pines and Eastern bluebirds. She still does, still likes to hear the scientific journals read to her before she falls asleep, wants to know the funded projects of the Forest Service, the studies the government assigns, the latest information about migration patterns and waterfowl habitats. And this passion for science is only part of the reason I love this child like she was my own.

"You could tell somebody about him," she says, jolting me from my thoughts, and I don't respond for a second.

"The woodpecker," she reminds me, sensing that I have drifted. "You could tell somebody at your job, Charlene maybe, or your boss. You could tell them and they could make this whole area off limits to the bulldozers. The woods wouldn't be destroyed and you could come down. They couldn't develop it if they knew."

How this child knows so much is beyond me.

"Yeah, you're right, I could tell someone. And I will; I really will." I pause, wondering if I sound like I'm telling the truth. I glance through the branches and try to see her eyes to see if she believes me. "But I need proof first."

She turns away.

"We have to be sure it's a cockaded or they'll just think I'm making it up," I say, trying to convince us both. "They'll just think I came up with some other reason to stop the construction."

"But we didn't make it up," she replies, now sounding more like a child than a scientist and this makes me want to hold her. "I saw him. I know that's what I saw. And then, you saw him again today. Isn't that what you said? Didn't you see him today?"

"I did, yes, but I still didn't get a photograph and I'm not sure I can make anybody believe me without proof."

She tries sitting up a little more. "He's real. I know it."

"Yes," I say, stepping down to a lower branch. "You're right." And I step down one more and sit down, giving her a clearer picture of me, letting her see me the way she always has. "He is real . . ."

But before I can finish what I want to say I am interrupted.

Fifteen

"Who's real?"

"Well, perfect timing," I say, climbing back up to my perch.

"Yeah?" Jim squats down on the blanket next to Lilly Carol so he's eye to eye. He has two cloth bags hanging from his arms. "Hey there."

"Hey, Pastor Jim," she responds and then turns her focus back to me. It's clear she doesn't know where to take the conversation.

He's still in that squatting position and he crooks his neck so that he gets the same view as the girl sitting under the tree. We smile at each other, a slight raise of his chin.

Jim is in his priestly attire again; I guess he's working steady now, making up for the time off he took when he went to South Carolina. "How's our favorite forest resident?" he asks, and then back to Lilly Carol. "Might I join you here?"

She nods, puts her hands by her sides and tries to slide a bit, giving him more room. He makes a kind of huffing noise as he sits down on the ground. Jim prefers a chair. "So, do tell, who are you trying to convince yourselves is real and why is my arrival made with perfect timing?"

"Jesus," I answer, since I've now had time to think of something other than the red-cockaded and it's a perfect response for Jim to wrestle with anyway.

"Okay," he says, giving me a strange look.

I shrug, my way of giving him the stage. This is his bread and butter, after all.

"So, you're asking Kate if Jesus is real?" He puts the question to Lilly.

Even from up here I see her face turning red. She stares at me for help. At her young and vulnerable age, she is not at all prepared to lie to a minister.

"Not Jesus himself," I answer, taking her off the hook, well aware that I passed that age of vulnerability a long time ago.

"Oh, okay," Jim responds.

"We both accept the historical accounts of Jesus of Nazareth." I am actually enjoying this. "There is ample verification of his existence."

He glances at Lilly who still has the same red face and stunned appearance. "Good," he responds.

"Rather it's God she's most curious about." I pause. "Like the rest of us, I suppose." I swing my legs over the side of my stand, lean the top part of my body down a little. "How is it that you are so confident of the presence of God?"

And now he is stumped, which almost makes me laugh. I imagine he didn't hike out here to the woods this morning expecting to deliver apologetics to a twelve-year-old sitting under the thirty-five foot high perch of a woman in a tree.

He waits before answering, eyeing me very carefully.

"Why is it that I think Lilly Carol isn't questioning this at all but rather it is you, my heathen friend, who is just trying to start trouble?"

"Start?!" Lilly finally chimes in, making us both smile.

"So true, Lilly Carol, so true."

And the bright light that had been shining on the focal point of our conversation, the questions about the woodpecker, has lessened.

"How was last night?" Jim asks, quicker than I was to change the subject.

"Rough," I reply. "I felt like one of the disciples in the storm. I was hanging on for dear life."

"And was there a miracle upon these woodsy waters—stilled wind and a calming of the waves?"

I shake my head. "Not until everything I had was thrown out of my stand and I was drenched and exhausted."

"You didn't hear your name called and decide to step out of the boat like Simon Peter?"

"No, that's where the analogy ends, I guess."

He nods.

"Mama Stallings happy in her new lodgings?"

"She appears a little stronger today," he answers. "I've hired someone to stay with her while I'm working."

"Who's Mama Stallings?" Lilly Carol asks, joining the conversation.

"My mother," he replies. "I just brought her here to live with me."

"Oh," she answers. "That must be nice."

Jim doesn't respond and I suppose this could be for a couple of reasons. One, it's clear this isn't at all that nice, and two, we both are well aware of the absence of Lilly Carol's mother. We sneak a peek at each other, feeling the awkwardness, although we shouldn't be feeling that at all.

Unlike me when I was her age, Lilly Carol hasn't acted at all as if she minded her mother's disappearing act. She has always seemed perfectly well adjusted to a single-parent home. When my mother left home, sneaking away in the middle of the night, leaving her two children and her husband wordless and clumsy in her wake, I kept thinking it was somehow my fault.

For years I tried to change, tried to find ways to be better, act better, in hope that wherever she was that she would hear about her daughter's newfound ability to cook dinner and pack lunches, that she would find out that I had learned how to vacuum and mop with a real cotton string mop, the kind she preferred, that I could clean rust from the bathtub faucet, set a perfect table, and iron my father's shirts, and that she'd come home. She'd hear the reports of her spotless house and near-perfect girl child and come right back home.

I even knew what she'd say when she walked through the front door, carrying her suitcase, the orange one with the separate matching makeup case, wearing the same dress I knew she was wearing when she left, the blue one, navy with tiny pearl buttons. She'd open the door and hold out her arms for me to run right back into like I used to do when she was home and happy and ours and she'd say, "Well, my sweet Katydid, you have captured clean to a perfect shine."

Unlike me, Lilly Carol came home from school to find her mother's empty closet, the hangers swinging when she pulled open the door, her cleaned-out dresser drawers, the folded pages of magazine perfume ads still pushed in the corners, and just accepted exactly what Ray told her when he found her lying on her mother's side of the bed, which unlike the story I was given, happened to be exactly the truth.

Lonnie loved her daughter but knew she was sick and that her sickness was so bad that she was sure that it would hurt Lilly Carol, so she went away but she would never forget the two she left behind and she would always love her daughter more than anything or anybody. Ray told her that every night and every day for five years and now she says she doesn't need to hear it anymore.

"Hey Jim," Ray is back.

"Ray," Jim responds, standing and holding out his hand. "I must have missed you when I was coming in."

"We parked on the back side," Ray replies. He glances down at Jim's cloth sacks and then looks at the plastic bags he has. "You brought some stuff too?"

Jim nods. "A couple of books, long-lens camera," he answers. "Champagne crackers, sourdough bread, and some smoked salmon I found last evening in Jacksonville, at the Fish Market."

Ray seems to hide his bags behind him while he nods.

"Well, it's clear you are set with the finest company this morning," Jim says, which I understand is his way of leaving. "I'll stop by when I get finished with my sermon for Sunday and my hospital rounds."

"Okay," I say. "I'll send down the bucket for the goodies." And I go to the stash bucket, tie the rope on the end, and drop it down. "Thanks for the camera, that's perfect," I tell him. I can tell that Ray and Lilly Carol are talking but their voices sound distant and low.

Sixteen

"So, what are you doing the rest of the day?" I don't expect Ray and Lilly to stay with me all morning and afternoon. Nobody has done that.

"Daddy has a meeting and I'm going to Lindsay's for a play date." She picks at a pine needle she's holding. "It's a teacher's work day."

I knew this but had forgotten. It was supposed to be a day in which I took care of her. I get all the school vacation days with her. I wrote them down in the beginning of the year, marked them on my calendar and requisitioned time off from my job so that Ray could work and I could be with Lilly. I'm sure today is a hardship for him and a disappointment for her. Lindsay is a brat.

"I'm sorry," I say softly. And then I have a thought.

"You could stay here," I tell them both, but I'm talking about Lilly.

Ray is the one who answers. "We thought about it but I don't think it's the best idea. It's a little high for her up there and I don't think there's room enough for two of you."

I glance around at my perch. He's right. There's hardly enough room for me and all the accumulated stuff I now have.

"And I'm not sure how I'd get her up there."

Definitely a challenge I had not thought through but I don't see why she can't just stay where she is.

"It's okay," Lilly chimes in before I can make that suggestion. "I won't be at Lindsay's for long and then Daddy and I are going out for strawberry sundaes."

"Man, I am really missing out, aren't I?" I see Ray glance at his watch. "What time's the meeting?"

"Ten," he answered.

It's already nine. They need to leave, I know.

Ray goes to AA meetings, usually at lunchtime and just once or twice a week. He told me he goes more during those times he feels stressed and I guess this is one of those times since his number one babysitter climbed up a tree. I hadn't really thought of the hardship I'm causing for the two of them.

Ray's been in recovery for three years, ever since he got out of jail after the accident. He's been clean and sober long enough to make us all believe it will stick this time; but it's like he said, I guess, "No matter how many days has passed since my last drink, it's still a day-by-day life I'm living."

Everybody knew the wreck wasn't his fault. He was careful when it came to Lilly and to driving when he knew had too much to drink. But his blood level was above the limit even if just barely, and he was behind the wheel so it didn't matter to the law or to him that the other driver fell asleep and drifted into his lane, forcing Ray to run off the road and hit the guardrail. It didn't show up on the police report or change the protocol for the arresting officer that he was alert enough to keep his truck from sailing off into the river and that he was able to save his daughter's life, pulling her from the burning wreckage. He had been drinking and Lilly Carol is paralyzed from the waist down for the rest of her life. He served some time in jail and lost his driving license for a while. He blamed himself when it happened and I guess he still does.

"Well, thanks for bringing Lilly Carol to see me," I say to Ray. "You made my day," I add to her.

"I'll bring her back," he tells me. "Maybe the weekend."

"That would be really nice."

"You can take pictures now," Lilly Carol pipes up. "Pastor Jim brought you that camera. You can take lots of pictures from up there."

Of course she's talking about the woodpecker; she wants me to get a shot, and I'm sure wants me to come down. We enjoy our days together.

"She made you sandwiches," Ray tells me, holding up one of the bags.

"Peanut butter and honey," she chimes in, "the way you like."

"That is the best."

"And I copied some of the articles I found online about forest stuff," she adds. "I thought you might like something else to read."

"I do indeed," I answer, fetching the bucket again. I take out what Jim placed inside and lower it to Ray.

He walks over, stuffs the two plastic bags inside, glances up at me. "And you're okay, have everything you need?"

I nod, getting a good look at him from up here. He's broken in a way I can never understand, hurt that his wife left him, angry at himself for Lilly's condition, alone and flying solo, making it one day at a time, as he says.

From this view, he's so much smaller than he is when I'm standing right in front of him, having to raise my head to see his eyes. From up here he's little and straddled by his demons, pushing through life like it is a river flowing in the opposite direction from which he swims. I know things are hard for him, they have been for a long time; but ever since Nathan died, we've never been able to talk about the sorrow. He started drinking. I went to college. When I came back we were still in the same place, only older, with our hearts wrapped even tighter in layers of something I don't even understand, anger maybe, but I don't know. Grief can do a whole lot to a person; some of it you can't even name.

So after all these years, I'm sitting in a tree by myself, seeing things in a way I never saw them before but still alone, still defended, and Ray is a single dad employed at a lumber store and working a twelve-step program, both of us bound by the common loss of Nathan and by the shared commitment to his daughter. We quit a long time ago trying to define who we are to each other.

"You doing okay?" I ask him.

I glance over to see that Lilly Carol has dropped back and is lying down. She has her eyes closed.

"I'm good," he answers.

"I'm sorry about today," I tell him. "I know I would be with her if I hadn't climbed up here."

He shrugs. "We're all right. I have a bunch of vacation days I hadn't used so it's not a big deal."

"Still," I say softly.

"Don't worry," he tells me and pats the bucket as if to tell me it's ready to come up. He steps back.

"Today's made me think that it might be nice if we go somewhere together."

I feel somewhat confused.

"Maybe during her spring break, we might go to the beach or up to Asheville to see my parents," he adds.

And I suddenly understand that I'm not included in those plans. He's moving forward with his life which I've told him that he needs to do for years, only now that I hear he's doing it, well, I can't really say how it feels but it's certainly not great.

"Oh," is what comes out of my mouth as a response and I begin pulling up the bucket.

"I'll let you know if we do," he adds. "I'll decide something in a couple of weeks."

I nod and keep pulling.

"Okay, Miss Lilly Carol, let's get you hitched up so we can get out of here."

She sits up and I watch as he wiggles into the inner tube, hooks up the strap to himself, sits down in front of his daughter and waits while she scoots close. He reaches behind himself and grabs her legs and wraps them around him, attaching her pant legs together with what I can now see are strips of Velcro lining the inseam. She holds on as he slowly stands, the two of them one solid working unit.

"I'll just leave the blanket. Maybe Jim or somebody might want to use it later." And he smiles, waves, and turns toward the path.

Lilly glances back. "I'll see you again!"

"Okay," I answer, feeling the hole inside me open just a little more.

Seventeen

I hear them before they approach. They are a flock of tropical birds, colorful, lively. I feel like I just landed in a rainforest somewhere in the Amazon and the parrots and Moluccan cockatoos are dancing beneath the trees. There are at least four of them, maybe five, this bright band of creatures.

They're singing and calling and I scoot near the edge of my perch to get a closer look. I assume all the other forest inhabitants are doing the same thing, nuthatches, chickadees, the hawks and the squirrels. This is new for all of us, I'm sure. We don't see a lot of these birds in these parts.

"Hello . . ." one of them calls out, the one all in green with yellow hair. It's a parakeet. He's small, waving to all the trees—seems high or good-natured, I'm not sure which.

"Kind woman . . ." a blue and gold macaw calls. She has long blue hair, a gold dress, gray boots. She swishes through the dead leaves at her feet, pushes aside the branches of trees with her blue feathers, a navy cape that flows around her. "We come seeking your wisdom," she adds, trying to find me in the sky above her.

"We wish to honor your stand." This one looks like an antthrush. He has an orange mohawk, black head, dressed in brown. He finds me in the loblollies, stops and stares in my direction, pointing me out to the others.

"Okay," I answer, sensing that the flock is not native to Jones County, but they seem harmless.

They're hippies, probably from the mountains, kids really, part of the rainbow family, I presume. I met a few of them when I worked in the western part of the state. They know more about the outdoors than most of the forest reps, always pointed me in the right direction for fire hazards, insect nests. "Hi."

"Look! There she is!" another says. And this one, male I think but it's hard to tell, is as colorful as a bee-eater. He's dressed in blue and yellow and green, tie-dyed from head to toe.

They flock close together and when they find me up here, see me looking down on them, they pull out tambourines and drums and make even more noise, celebrating, I suppose, this sighting. I see the nuthatches moving to the edge of their nest, the robins and warblers watching from the limbs. I don't even want to see Delores's reaction. How do I explain this particular family of my species?

"We come with a blessing," the macaw tells me, and I silently wish it came without the drums.

She sings, chants really, not sure what words she's saying, and she spins around while the bee-eater beats his congas. The other birds clap, their feathers flapping about.

I wait until they are finished.

"Thank you," I say, without a lot of conviction.

"We honor your vow to save the trees from the evildoers and city planners," the parakeet says. "We think it's way cool," he adds. "We found out about you from a guy traveling from the beach last week. He read the article in the paper and we wanted to come here and show our appreciation."

"Okay," I answer, feeling a little nervous.

"We brought you some gifts," another boy tells me. He has on tan pants, a tan and white shirt, a red bandana around his neck. He looks like a cut-throat finch except he's taller than the parakeet, so too big for that species.

I watch as he takes off his backpack and unzips it. I can't see what he's holding up so I learn out over the stand.

"It's nuts and berries," he tells me. "We picked them from around our place this morning."

"And where's that?" I ask.

"Asheville," the macaw answers. "Near Mount Mitchell."

Bingo, I think. All the hippies end up in the mountains of North Carolina. I think they know they'll get shot at if they camp out anywhere else around here. Mountain people have always been more tolerant of the non-native species.

"How do I get them to you?" the finch asks, glancing around.

"I have a bucket," I explain. "You can just put them inside and then I pull it back up with a rope."

"Cool," the antthrush responds.

"We also have daisy chains that we made for you to wear around your neck, some lavender to help you sleep, and a picture of Lord Krishna."

"Awesome," I reply, not sure why.

"It's the portrayal of him as an infant eating butter," she continues. "You don't have that one, do you?"

"You know what, I don't."

She smiles.

"I'll send the bucket down." And I do. And then I watch as the macaw places the gifts inside.

"I got this bear claw, too," the finch tells me. "It has protective energy." I watch him remove a leather cord from around his neck and place it in with the other things.

"That is really nice of you," I tell him, thinking it must not have been so protective for the bear since he lost it but deciding I should just receive his unique and thoughtful gift without being cynical.

The macaw taps the side of the bucket and glances up at me expectantly. She has a sweet face. "Okay, I think that's all."

I start to pull. "So, how did you get here from Asheville?" I ask, wondering if they hitchhiked or took the bus.

"The van," the antthrush answers.

Or a van—what was I thinking?

"Of course, we're out of gas now so I'm not sure how we'll get back home."

"Oh," I reply, suddenly worried that the rainforest birds may not leave. I get the bucket to the stand and walk to the side where I can see them. "You know, the Lutheran pastor in town is a friend of mine. He'll give you cash for gas, I'm sure."

I'll deal with Jim later; I just really don't want to spend the night with the rainbow family.

"That is so cool," the finch responds for the group.

"Let's do our community dance of goodwill before we leave," the macaw suggests to the others.

And I watch as the bright birds take hands, and together they chant and dance around the tree. It lasts about twenty minutes and I wish somebody else was here to see it. I will never be able to tell this right.

I glance over to the cherrybark oak where Mr. Delores usually sits and he's watching with one eye opened. I shrug in his direction and I swear he shakes his head, closing his eye.

Eighteen

The day stretches long.

No visitors. No more hippies, reporters, deputies, high school students or well-meaning colleagues. No birds. It's just me and the loblollies. Even Delores seems to be hiding out in her nest, resting I suppose from the tough stormy night behind us and the loud guests who entertained us earlier.

I had hoped for just a peek to make sure she and the eggs are okay; but after her few calls to her beau once the rain ended, I haven't seen or heard from her all day. Maybe she's simply waiting for dark.

I've been sitting and reading most of the afternoon, a few poems from my book and the articles Lilly brought. There's one from the Area Extension Service about the woodpecker, its habitat and the loss of the longleaf pine stands, and another about the rescue efforts for savannas in Georgia. The girl really has done her research, and it makes me a little proud that she shares my same interests. I only wish she were here so we could talk about the articles, find out what she thinks, tell her what I've seen.

I confess I'm starting to feel lonesome even though I know this is what I thought I wanted, even expected. It's just that two weeks into a thing, a vacation, a trip, a move, sitting in a tree, a person starts to realize all there is in her life. A girl starts to recognize what she has and doesn't have.

And I have to say, it might have been better just to keep living the distracted life that I'd made for myself. It might be less depressing if I hadn't decided to forego the work and the daily grind of the Forest Service job. I might not feel as lonesome if there was just a little drama to keep me engaged, just enough office gossip to tend.

I don't know what I thought I'd find up this tree but having only myself to think of and sit with is not all that exciting. It turns out that I don't make such great company, and the birds don't seem to be all that interested in talking to me.

And yet, I'm still here. I guess, in the words of the rockers U-2, "I still haven't found what I was looking for."

I put aside the reading material and pull out Jim's digital camera and decide to take some pictures. I know how to use the one he's loaned me because it's exactly like mine. We bought them together, in fact, on a holiday shopping spree one day last December. It's the Canon Rebel T5 DSLR with the telephoto lens, costing us each more than five hundred dollars but making us feel smart and important and confident that we would take excellent photographs of all the birds we had come to love. It was our Christmas gift to ourselves.

It turns out neither of us has used our camera very much. I got saddled with a seedling project and divorce, and he had to deal with the church seasons of Christmas, Epiphany, and now Lent, in addition to another long dying of his mother. It's been almost four months and even though we promised this would not happen to us and we would get our money's worth, that we wouldn't be like all the people who buy expensive toys and never take them out of the box, neither of us has had the opportunity to set out and take pictures of birds.

Until today.

The stickers were still on the camera. I take them off, check the batteries, turn on the power, attach the long lens, focus, and take a look at all that I can see. It's a lot.

Zoomed in, I can tell that spring is starting to show all around in the forest. I see the conelet buds, the female strobili already here when I arrived, having emerged sometime during the first two months of the year; but now I register new growth. Looking about the stand I can see that the pine has arrived to its peak pollen shed and I recall that the conelet receptivity period usually ranges from late in February until late in March or maybe even into April.

I see the growth on the branches and assume that the flowering dates are right on time, even though in past years I've seen the seasons in pine tree growths like this one vary. Based upon my observations, these pines are somewhere in the middle of their spring activities; and as I realize this, I put down the camera and wonder if I also have hit a median mark for my own germination.

Maybe I only have a few days left and I will be ready to move on to something else, another season. I don't know what actually brought me up here so I certainly don't know what will eventually take me down; but maybe like the pines, there's a limit to how long I have to sow my seeds. Maybe I'm budding and don't even know it.

I put the camera to my eye again and focus on other trees around me. I can see that the white oaks are flowering, as are the cherrybarks. There are small green buds on a dogflower tree as well, a species not native to ecosystems like this one; it probably grew from seeds transported by the wind from the farm just north of here. Also present and close by are black willows and bald cypress. There are red maples and river birch trees, all starting their new year, their new foliage, all stretching out in response to the longer days of sun and the warmer temperatures in the soil.

Zoomed in, I see the animals in and near the trees and I watch the activities around me, feel a gentle afternoon breeze, and slide down on my board to rest. I watch the sky through the long camera lens, feeling so much closer to it than I have on the ground, the clouds light and scattered, the blue deep and hypnotic. After a few minutes, I place the camera beside me and let myself drift, falling asleep; I don't wake up until the afternoon has passed and the sun has lowered, changing the blue of the sky to pink and orange.

I sit up, check my watch and see that it's after six, and this causes me to wonder why Jim didn't show, wonder if something has happened to his mother or if the day just got past him like it does for everyone, disallowing him the extra hour to make a promised pastoral visit to a loblolly pine stand. I guess it will be tomorrow then.

I stretch and rise, think about dinner and remember the smoked salmon. The thought of a little fish and bread and wine suddenly makes my stomach churn and I rifle through my bags of supplies until I find what I'm searching for. Without much effort, simply tearing open the plastic packaging of the salmon, uncorking the already-opened bottle, and pulling the bread from its wrapper, I make myself a meal that is one of the finest I've had since living in a tree and maybe one the best I've fixed for myself since living alone.

Even though I did a lot of the cooking when I was married, even enjoyed trying new recipes, once Dwayne moved out and I was suddenly once again alone, I found myself less and less interested in cooking for one. Smoked salmon and a loaf of fresh bread is a treat compared to the bowl of Cheerios to which I had become accustomed. Once I start my meal, I see Delores peeking out of her nest. We stare at each other a few minutes, a forest neighbor's greeting, and she steps out a bit so that I can see her eggs, I think. I pick up Jim's camera to get a better look and I can see that she has three small ones, fairly uncommon for the great horned owl which I know typically have only one or two. I figure now that she is bragging and when I put down the camera, I raise my bottle of wine to her, my toast to her maternal skills and the three eggs.

I can still see her with my naked eye from my stand and I watch as she flaps her wings a bit and then turns back around to sit on her nest.

I pick up the camera again and with the long lens glance into and around the trees near me, notice the nest of nuthatches below me, and then over to the usual roost of the owl's mate but see that he's not yet arrived for the night. I am just about to put the camera down and pick back up my meal when I catch a glimpse of a man standing near the large black willow tree, the one that has started to bud, his binoculars turned right on me, a red glare coming off the lenses. We look at each other briefly and suddenly Mr. Delores arrives, sailing across my view, making one loud call, and diverting my attention to him.

When I focus back to where I had seen the man only moments ago, he is gone.

I put down the camera, step back on my stand into the branches, and sit down. I take another drink of the wine and pull my blanket tight around me.

Nineteen

"You sure it was Winston?" Charlene is back. She got here about an hour ago, brought me biscuits and the newspaper article about the retirement village plans. I told her about the man standing near the black willow, the one who was watching me with his binoculars just before dusk.

I shake my head and pull up the stash bucket. She's disposed of the bag from the toilet and put another one in. That's still on the ground beneath me.

"I don't know who it was," I answer. "I said I thought it was him." I grab the bucket and reach inside for my breakfast. She's brought me a thermos of coffee, too. I take it out and hold it to my heart. "Thank you," I say to her and to the Great Creator above who was kind enough to give rise to the coffee plants and those perfect cherry beans.

"Well, who else do you think it could be?"

I don't answer because I'm taking a drink of coffee, the first I've had since I've been up here—that's sixteen days without my usual morning fix. Ray brings me biscuits quite often but he spilled a cup of coffee in the bucket the first time he brought me breakfast and he hasn't tried since. I haven't said anything, haven't asked for a cup, because, well, who am I to ask for anything?

I pause because I have a little bit of heaven in my throat.

Charlene is looking through the branches trying to get a better view of what I'm doing. She sees and waits; she remembers how much I love coffee.

"I got the medium roast because they were out of the industrial strength."

I close my eyes, taking note of every nuance, every tiny bit of roasted flavor.

"I guess medium must be okay." And she cleans her hands with sanitizer and then plops down on the blanket Ray and Lilly Carol left and starts to eat her breakfast.

"Did you know that coffee was said to have been discovered by a goatherd in Ethiopia named Kaldi? The story goes that he noticed several goats from his flock nibbling on bright red berries of a bush and that they then suddenly jumped about. Curious, Kaldi tasted the berries as well and he later felt so exhilarated himself that he shared them with an Islamic monk in a nearby monastery. The monk, thinking they were some kind of evil drug, threw the berries in a fire, immediately drawing forth this wonderful and enticing aroma. The holy man, so enraptured with the smell, pulled out the roasted beans from the embers, ground them up, and dissolved them in hot water, thereby brewing the first cup of coffee." I take another sip, hold it in my mouth and swallow.

"And all this time I thought it was three college kids from San Francisco who moved to Seattle and named their stores after a character in *Moby Dick*." Her mouth is full and her words are mumbled but I think this is what she says.

"The guys at Starbucks didn't even come up with their own roasting techniques," I tell her. "They learned them from a man in Berkeley."

I see Charlene shaking her head, and I know I've done it again. She calls me a walking encyclopedia and says I carry around more useless information than anybody she knows.

"Alfred Peet," I add, "of Peet's Coffee." I take another sip and close my eyes, smiling. How lovely is today, I think.

"So, back to the creepy guy staring at you," Charlene says as she finishes her biscuit. "Who do you think it was?"

I blow out a breath. Now I wish I hadn't told her; she's going to be worried about me for the rest of the day. "I don't know. Maybe he was just a local guy checking me out." I throw down the rope so that she can tie it to the handle of the other bucket.

She shakes her head. "I don't like it, Kate. There's too many weirdos out there and now one of them knows you're out here by yourself. No cell phone, no means of protection. No mace, no rape whistle."

"I have a whistle," I say, trying to lighten things up. "It's custom made from some guy in Kansas, carved just for me, out of wood, hanging on a lanyard." I lean over the stand to get a look at my colleague.

"I gave you that whistle," she says, taking the bait. "And it's not meant to be used for safety purposes; it's for calling ducks. I'm serious, Kate."

I throw down my biscuit wrapper and we both watch it float towards her. "I know you are." I watch as she picks up the piece of trash, rolls it up in a tight ball, and stuffs it in her pocket. "But I'm okay, I promise. Nothing bad is going to happen."

"You don't know that. You don't know who this guy is." She stands up, brushes off the debris from her pants, front and back. "You don't know how mad Winston is."

"How mad is Winston?" I ask.

She shakes her head and I'm not sure what this means.

"Really, Char, how mad is he?"

She looks up and I can see her face. She knows something.

"What is it?"

"He's just saying stuff around town."

"What? Like how he's going to spread stories about my psychiatric history? That he's going to have me committed?"

I stand up and yank the rope that she's attached to the toilet bucket, pulling it up. "He's harmless. His brother is running for mayor and he's not going to do something that will jeopardize that political race and his opportunity to have another public official in his pocket."

The bucket arrives and I place it behind me. "Hey," I say, trying to get her to look back up at me again. "Hey."

She meets my eye.

"It's going to be okay, really. Winston Hatch is just a boy with a toy. He has a bulldozer and he wants to strip out every living tree in Jones County. He'll get tired of waiting me out and he'll go bulldoze some other piece of property that his daddy bought him."

She doesn't reply.

"Char... Charlene, do you hear me? It's going to be okay. I'm fine. He's not going to do anything. He's a coward. I've known him since he was in diapers. I beat him up in elementary school, for heaven's sake. He's not going to hurt me."

"I got to go," is all she'll say. "I got to finish pulling up knotweed and spraying browntop with Phil."

"Now see, that's who you need to be worried about. You and Phil out there alone in the clumps of stiltgrass; you're the one in real danger. What happens if some of those seeds fly into his mustache?"

I see the smile, ever so slight but it's there.

"Yeah, you're the one who needs the rape whistle, sister. You want the duck call?" And I reach inside my shirt and pull out the lanyard I always wear. I put the small piece of wood to my lips and give it a gentle whisper and the sound echoes around us.

"Just be careful, okay?" And she takes a long look up at me.

"You, too."

And she starts to walk away.

"Charlene..."

She turns back.

"Thanks for the coffee."

She nods at me and leaves.

Twenty

I know that I should probably tell them that I'm up here; but I don't know how to do that now. The conversation was well underway before they showed up beneath the loblollies.

"You said you were leaving her!" She pulls away from him and I get an even better view. She's young, in her twenties, I'd say, pretty; dark hair with an iridescent green bow, shapely; she's wearing a brown sundress, tan and white spots. He's pudgy, medium height, slightly red-faced. He's wearing khaki shorts and a pink golf shirt, a big bald spot on the top of his head. He's carrying a blanket under his arm; she has a picnic basket.

"It's just not the best time, Amy. I told you I'm working on it."

"Working on it? You sent her flowers."

I glance around at the birds. We're all just watching this from our perches. The nuthatch gives me a nod.

"It's her birthday; it doesn't mean anything."

Oh yeah it does, I want to say, but don't. What it means is that he's staying with his wife. *Girl, I can identify that song and dance from way up here. That little number is as old as, well, it's even older than he is. And with what I can see from up here, that's old.*

"It's her birthday, so you have to send flowers. It's her parents' fiftieth wedding anniversary so you have to go to Georgia for the weekend. It's your son's graduation." Her voice is high, screechy. "Do you not see this pattern?"

Of course, he sees it, I think. *He's working it from both ends; he just didn't think you'd see it.*

"It's not a pattern, Baby."

Oh, now he's going with the "Baby" talk. I raise my eyebrows at the nest of warblers in the next tree. The female flutters her wings. She gets it; I can tell.

"Amy, I told you when we started seeing each other that it wasn't going to be easy. I need to get some things straightened out. My lawyer said that I need to get us money set aside before I ask for a divorce, otherwise she'll take half of everything. And we'll have nothing. Baby, we need to have some money. Don't you want to be able to go to nice places, do nice things together?"

Yeah, cause it sure looks like he's spending a lot of money on you right now, bringing you out to the middle of nowhere for your shady afternoon getaway.

I still have a little coffee left so I'm just sipping on my java and watching the show. I can't believe they walked this far out to deal with their business. I notice Amy is starting to glance around and I slide back behind the limbs a little.

She looks back at him. "You told me it wasn't going to be easy but you didn't say you would keep giving her gifts and going to her family functions. You didn't tell me you were going to send her flowers for her birthday!"

He sighs.

I don't know how he thought this was going to work; but he obviously didn't count on the fact that Amy had a little more in mind than just a romp in the woods.

"Let me get through Stanley's graduation," he says, and my ears perk up. *Stanley,* I think and then, *no, it can't be that Stanley.* "He's going through a rough time right now. Did I tell you that he didn't get into Duke?"

It is that Stanley!

"I don't care where your son is going to college!" Amy is angry now and I can't believe I'm hearing the father of the Jones County Science Club President having a fight with his lover right beneath my stand. I'm embarrassed and terribly nosy all at the same time. Truth be told, I don't really know Stanley, didn't like him after what I heard from Tiffany, using her the way he has, but I have to say, I sort of feel sorry for him right now. With this guy as a dad, what shot does he have of turning out well?

"It's a difficult time for my family and I just can't deal with your demands. I told you when we first met that I needed some time to work through some things with my wife and children. And I still do."

"When Stanley graduates, then you'll tell her?"

Oh, Amy, I want to yell down. *Don't do it!*

"He's the last bird in the nest. Karen left two years ago and Sylvia has been out of college a year; so yes, it's almost over; and I just don't want to ruin this time for him right now." He reaches up and touches her on the cheek and all of a sudden I make a noise.

"What was that?" Amy asks, drawing away.

It wasn't loud; but it was kind of a gag reflex. I couldn't help it; I do it when I don't believe what I'm hearing.

"What was what?"

He's pulling her back into his arms.

"That noise."

"I didn't hear anything, Baby. Nobody's out here."

Uh, I'm out here, I think. *Delores is here. Whip-poor-will families, there's actually quite a lot of us.*

She moves away from him. "I don't like it here," she says. "It's creepy."

Creepy? I look over at the warblers, then at the nuthatch. *You going to let her get away with that?* The nuthatch calls out. It's a high-pitched whistle and it's right on cue. He looks over at me and I give him a thumbs up.

"It's the woods, Baby. Come on, you told me you like the outdoors. I thought you'd want to have a picnic, a little afternoon delight."

I can't help myself. I do it again.

"There it is. You don't hear that? I think there's somebody else out here."

Stanley's father takes his hand away from Amy's face and steps back. He walks around the area where they are both standing. He looks right and left but thankfully, he doesn't look up.

"There's nobody out here, Honey. It's just the squirrels and the birds and the bees," he says, all smarmy, walking next to her. He spreads out the blanket.

He is a determined fellow, I give him that.

"Isn't there some woman living out here?" She's still standing, glancing around her.

"I don't know," he answers, patting the ground beside him. "But I doubt anybody would be living in the middle of the forest."

"No, I'm sure I heard about it or read it somewhere. She's a forest ranger or works for the government, something like that."

I freeze where I am as Amy takes her first gander up into the trees.

"She climbed up a few weeks ago, protesting some development, I remember now." And she's staring right at me. "She's crazy, I heard." But she doesn't see me.

"Amy, are we going to do this or not?"

And that gets her attention. "Do this? *Do this?* You make it sound like some business deal, like you're selling a car or something."

"No, I'm pretty sure it's not a business deal because if I was selling a car, somebody's for sure getting screwed."

Uh-oh, I think. *You've blown it now, Daddy Stanley.*

"Well, then, maybe you should just go to the dealership and see if you get lucky there because there's nothing happening out here except you sitting by yourself in the woods. I'm leaving."

And she swings around, her black hair a swirl, the green bow flying, and her brown sundress whirling about. She looks like a mallard frightened from a riverbank, all flying dust and feathers. In a split second, she's gone.

I lean over a bit just to see the look on Daddy Stanley's face and he was peering right in my direction.

"Crazy lady in a tree . . ." He makes a huffing noise. "Maybe I'd have a better shot with her."

And I'm about to tell him what I think of that when he picks up the blanket and hurries off.

Twenty–One

It is a high-pitched whistle that I hear, squeaky, almost sounding like one of those rubber ducks I used to keep in the bathtub when I was a kid. It's a familiar call in these parts, but this time it isn't the nuthatch calling from a few limbs below.

"Is she dead?" I put down the binoculars and scoot close to the edge of the board, let my legs hang over.

He walks from around the nearby tree. "How did you know?"

"Well, let's see. I taught you all the calls, first off, and second I can see you coming from like a mile away. I've got a pretty great view, remember? And third, you're the only penguin in the forest." I say this because he's in his work clothes.

Jim walks over to where he had stashed his chair, picks it up, opens it, and sits down beneath me. "She isn't dead," he reports. "The hospice people say she's doing better today."

He glances up at me and I hold my hands up, part shrug, part gesture of fake praise.

"Stop it," he says, reading my every thought, interpreting my every move.

"I'm just saying . . ."

He lets out a long sigh. "You're right, I know you're right. She's never going to die."

"Not as long as she knows it keeps you from telling the truth."

"What is truth anyway?" he asks, like he often does.

"Ye shall know the truth . . . ." I wait.

"And the truth shall make you mad, I know. Alex Huxley said it better than our Lord." He smiles. "So what's with you and the hippies?"

And I suddenly recall that I had sent the rainforest birds to him.

"Sorry," I say. "They seemed like nice kids."

"Yeah, well you owe me sixty dollars."

"Sixty?" I thought they just needed gas money.

"For a van to drive to Asheville," he reminds me. "Have you been up there so long that you've forgotten how much gas costs?"

I shrug. I guess so.

He runs his hand through his sandy brown hair, interlaces his fingers behind his head, and then stretches out his legs in front of him and finally crosses them at his ankles.

Even from way up here I can tell he's tired.

"You know it's only been like two days that your mom has been living with you." I state the obvious since I know I'm the only one who will speak to him this way. Well, maybe Bernard, sometimes.

He shakes his head. "What's a son to do?"

"Tell his mother that he's gay and has a gorgeous boyfriend who has put up with his skirting the important issues for too long. Tell his parishioners that he's sorry but their pastor is not celibate like they think, and then tell that handsome lover that he has been a fool and wants to get married as soon as he can."

We wait.

"All that coming from a woman who lives less than a mile from her father and hasn't spoken to him in twenty years? A woman not unlike the famed short tax collector from the gospel of Luke, Zacchaeus, who has climbed up a tree and distanced herself from the world. All that from you?"

"A mile and a half," is all I say in response.

"A mile and a half?"

"It's a mile and a half from my father's house. And it's been more like twenty-five years, but who's counting?"

We grin at each other.

"Hey," I say to my best friend.

"Hey."

"You want some wine? It's good. Except it's not cold."

"It's red, it's not supposed to be cold."

"Right."

"What's going on today in the world of crazy ladies besides entertaining the rainbow family?"

"Well, let's see. I bore witness to a couple having a spat; he's married and not to her."

"What?"

"Yep, the view from up here has certain advantages."

"I'm sure. You want to give the scoop?"

"Nah, not that interesting, really."

"Okay, take the high road then."

I smile. "Delores has three eggs and she's working her man hard every night, making him bring two dinners home to the nest."

"Hormones," he responds.

"Another chickadee is missing. The Cooper's hawk again, I'm guessing."

He nods.

"I think there's a fox that shows up at night even though I thought they killed them all in Jones County last hunting season."

"Ah, what is a good Christmas holiday without a red fox to hang on the mantle with the holly and the white candles?"

"Hunters," I say, without any flair.

"Now, now, death is integral to nature and hunting is a constitutional right of all good citizens."

"And magpies had to learn how to conduct funerals because people shoot birds for no reason."

"I thought they only did that for birds that were killed on highways."

He's citing a study from a researcher from the University of Colorado in 2009 in which four magpies were reported standing beside the body of a fifth bird. The scientist concluded that these actions were similar to what is experienced at a human funeral. It was even noted that during the gathering two of the birds flew away and then returned to drop blades of grass next to the dead magpie. I copied the report and faxed it to him.

"You know, maybe that's where the colors of your clerical garb actually originated," I say. "Maybe it wasn't the penguins, maybe it was the magpies holding a memorial service."

He gives me a fake smile.

"Black is the color of mourning, symbolizing dying to oneself so to rise and serve the Lord."

"Well, I'm sure Mama Stallings loves you in your cassock."

"Stop," he says.

I drop a protein bar at his feet.

"Anyway . . ." He picks it up and tears open the top and takes a bite. "I can't stay; just wanted to come out here and make sure you've got what you need. And oh yeah, I have a question."

I wait as he chews a little.

Then he says, "What do you know about a reporter named Tonya Lassiter?"

I hear the woman's name, make a shrill whistle like the lammergeier; and I realize she's like a robin in winter, still digging for worms.

Twenty-Two

I didn't really get the chance to talk to Jim about the reporter. I don't know if she's been to the church or followed him on the street or to a nursing home or if she only called and left a message. I don't know what she's actually said to him or what he's told her because Tiffany came up just as he asked the question. He left before I could find out more and all I could tell him as Tiffany waited, listening in, was to be careful, hoping he heard the edge in my voice that he knows means that he should take me seriously. I still don't understand who Tonya Lassiter is or what she's hoping to find out, but I'm certain she's bad news.

Before she left, Tiffany asked if I would tutor her in her advanced biology class. I agreed. Mostly I'll just quiz her for the exam since the semester is almost over. She says that she's making an A but she has to do well on the final to keep the high grade. She brought me her research paper that she had just gotten back, a good solid A, written and circled with a red Sharpie.

She wrote about the orb-weaving spiders, those three-clawed engineers that use sticky silk to build spiral wheel-shaped webs, the spiders that are quite common in fields and forests and in gardens. She was looking primarily at sexual cannibalism and the advantages for the male in constructing and then vibrating a mating thread over trying to sneak into the center of the web and mount the female. It seems that the male, much smaller than the female, is less likely to be eaten if they mate while she's hanging on his deftly engineered thread.

And who says romance is dead?

"Smart," I told her. "You did your own study." I flipped through the pages, intrigued by her research. After reading her conclusions, I stopped and glanced down to catch a big, goofy smile plastered on her face, apparently happy to have my approval.

Just hearing her excitement about her research and reading her spider paper lets me know that we have a lot in common, and not just doing homework for the popular kids; she really does love the outdoors as much as I. Of course, she's more into the insects and bugs whereas I am still drawn to the birds, but she reminds me of myself when she talks about the moths and the beetles, the araneids and the walking sticks, the six- and eight-legged creatures. It seems to be for her the same way I feel when I talk about anything with feathers.

She brought along her bug collection to show me today, hoisted it up to me in the bucket, and I have to say I am quite impressed. She has specimens of species that I didn't know were around anymore. She found an *Augochlora pura* sweat bee, an eastern velvet ant, also known as a cow killer, and a southern devil scorpion, one of the North Carolina insects I had heard about but never actually seen.

She says she's been collecting bugs since she was eleven and found that being outside was much more interesting than sitting in her house watching her mother sleep. From the little bit she's told me I take it that her mother suffers from depression since the woman seems to be in bed quite a lot. Tiffany has an older sister, "the pretty one," as she calls her, and younger twin brothers, which may be the reason she's outside so much. It sounds like she is the primary caregiver for the two youngsters. Hearing what is required of her in their care makes me think of my early years, with just me and my brother and on the receiving end of a fair amount of respectable parenting from both a mother and a father at least until I was eight, and this makes me count myself as pretty lucky. I can't imagine trying to look after two little boys when I was just learning how to take care of myself.

I want to ask her questions about her mother, about her father, whom she never mentions and I'm not really sure is around, but we're just starting to get to know each other and I sense I need to move slowly in trying to be a friend to Tiffany, more like a beetle than a bee. I could see that letting me look at her bug collection was a giant step for this awkward teenager. She doesn't trust easily.

She stayed over an hour, which I think was longer than she should have. Since it's a teacher workday and her brothers are out of school, I assume she was supposed to be spending the day with them. I get the feeling that she snuck out in the few minutes her mother actually made a move to the kitchen around lunchtime. I could tell she felt a little guilty since she kept glancing at her watch and she pulled out her phone, which I explained was useless out here since there's no service.

Charlene tried again today to leave me a phone, snuck one of those disposable ones in the stash bucket when she sent up my breakfast. I found it after she was gone, beneath the biscuits and coffee and the sweatshirt she had placed on top. I turned it on before Jim arrived, but just like the one I was issued at work and my personal phone that I have taken with me and tried on numerous outings, there is no service fifty feet beyond the barn on Coda Garver's property.

Tiffany wanted to know about working with the Forest Service, what it was like and whether I was happy, and I found myself talking about how much I really enjoy the job. You get plenty of alone time, I told her, not ever really stuck in an office; and there are lots of different projects and positions that can take you many other places in the country if you want to travel. She seemed most interested in this part.

I told her about a summer job in Washington State researching the marine wildlife on the Pacific coast and about another stint I did in Big Creek, Kentucky, maintaining natural habitats for the big mountain cats that are losing ground in the area. I explained that I could work in any office in the state if I wanted to study regionally specific birds or plants, and how much I like the eastern side of the Carolinas.

I talked about my research, my love for the pines, the never-ending fights with landowners and developers who keep destroying more and more of the fragile ecosystems, creating higher rates of animal extinctions and pushing the limits on what nature can handle. I told her about the politics, about working for the government, and about how I felt at the end of most days, physically tired, maybe even a little discouraged, but still committed to the work and the agency and still convinced that what I do matters—maybe not to a lot of people, but to the animals, the wildlife, the trees, I think it matters.

"And that," I told the young high school student, "is more important to me than climbing some corporate ladder or making a lot of money."

"I don't care about money," Tiffany responded, sounding just like me at her age. "I just want to be able to get out of here, go somewhere else, study the bugs in some other place."

It sounds like she's over Stanley, which after "meeting" his father, I think is for the best.

She told me I could keep her collection for a while if I wanted, that it was nice to be able to share her work with a real biologist; and now that I'm left alone up here, I'm glad she brought it along and let me keep it. Even though I've never been a huge fan of pinning dead bugs to a piece of cardboard and putting them under glass, I can tell the amount of care Tiffany has gone to in making a professional display and in her work of classification and scientifically correct labeling. She will be a fine entomologist and I must make sure to tell her that the next time she visits.

I've read her term paper, studied her display, and now that it's dark and I can no longer see, I am carefully wrapping the glass panel, planning to store it in the crook of one of the loblollies. I have just stepped up a branch to put it in a safe place when I hear chatter, a rustle nearby, and realize whatever is making noise is quickly moving in this direction.

Twenty-Three

The sun has set, dusk has fallen, but there's still just enough light for me to see that a small gaggle has gathered beneath me near the cherrybark tree. I think it might be the Sierra Club, LuAnn Hightower scheduling a meeting near my stand. She told me on her first and only visit that she'd be back, that she wanted to make sure I had everything I needed and that the club would support me in whatever way I desired. I haven't seen her since then, but maybe she's returned this evening and on this occasion, coming with the others, she hopes for an introduction and seeks to bring me a kind of endorsement.

I don't really need any introductions since I know most of the members of the coastal chapter. They're birders like me, and we often run into each other at the volunteer bird count every year or following up on a lead we've gotten about a siting of a piping plover or wood stork. Everybody I know in the Sierra Club loves to catch a glimpse of an endangered species, loves to celebrate our small victories and the wherewithal of our feathered friends. When I get closer to the edge of my stand, however, and glance down, I don't recognize a single person in this group. And now that I can see them more clearly, they don't look like birders or Sierra Club members, they don't seem like any nature-loving group.

They look like a handful of young people up to no good, boys, all of them. They've flown in tonight for trouble.

"Well, well, well . . ." says one, the tallest, the most dominant. He's wearing a ball cap and has a pistol attached to his belt.

They're all wearing hoodies, gray ones or black. He kicks the bottom of the tree and struts a little. "She really does exist, the crazy lady in a tree. And all this time I thought they were making you up."

I don't speak but I can feel my heart beating a little faster.

"Hey, lady bird," another calls out. "Whatcha doing up there?

I am up a tree, trapped.

"I think we made it just at the right time, too," the third one hoots.

They wait.

"I think it's lady bird season."

They laugh.

"Is it just bow and arrow or are shotguns fine?"

More laughter.

"I think it's whatever brings her down," the leader answers. "But I don't know, now that I got her in my sights, what do you think, dudes? What is she? Would you say that's a bird or a lady?" He stares in my direction, pulls one hand behind the other, like he's pulling back the string on the bow. He lets his hand go and makes a whistle, like he's just shot the arrow up in the loblolly.

"Maybe it's a wild turkey," one of the other ones says, craning his neck to get a better look. "Maybe it's a female laying her eggs up there."

And they all cackle like crows.

"You got some turkey eggs in your nest, lady bird?" One of the smaller ones, one who hadn't yet spoken, calls out from behind the aggressive males.

Of course, wild turkeys make their nests and lay eggs on the ground, and I consider setting the record straight; but I don't think this is a group that's really interested in ornithology trivia.

I watch closely, feeling the nerves taking over. *I don't get scared. I am not afraid of you. I will not get scared.* That's what I keep telling myself. *I don't get scared.* And I stand next to the loblolly trying to convince myself of the words I am saying.

It was Nathan who gave me this mantra. I was only eleven at the time and we were camping in the backyard. In the wee hours of the morning, I confessed to my older brother that some of the boys in fifth grade were bullying me. They picked me as their target, circled me, taunting and pushing me after school and in the playground when the teachers weren't watching. They were mad because I told the principal that they were stealing the other kids' lunch money. Before that, unlike the other members of my class, I was never worried about them because they usually left me alone. They knew about Nathan, and up to that point, I was not the easiest prey.

Once they found out that I ratted on them, however, it was open season; they had been after me all week. I had not told anyone else and I didn't want to tell my brother. But that Saturday night, sitting together under the stars, finally having run out of all the stuff kids talk about, I told him. And I told him that I was afraid of these boys.

"Katie," he said, and he sat up and looked me square in the eye. "I can beat these fifth graders up if you want me to."

I have to admit, that was sort of what I was hoping for.

He went on. "But there's always going to be a fifth-grade bully and I think it's time you learn how to manage them yourself. I won't be able to beat them all up."

I remember thinking that I was pretty sure he could, but I let him finish.

"So, the next time, they corner you, you stand your ground. You ball up your fists and you tell yourself, *I don't get scared. I am not afraid of you. I will not get scared.*"

He paused and I waited.

"Then what?" I asked.

"Well, if you think you can take the biggest one, swing your arm back as far as you can and hit him with your fist below the belt, *HARD*," he emphasized.

I knew exactly where he meant.

"And then, you either take the whooping that's coming from the other boys standing around or you run as fast as you can until you find a teacher."

I consider this advice. "Which would you do?"

He looked at me with that real serious face and said, "Hey, how do you think I got fast enough to steal all those bases?"

And he elbowed me in the ribs so hard I fell over. And we laughed and laughed, but I never forgot his counsel, and the next week, I got the sucker punch in on Kevin Highsmith, the biggest bully. And when he dropped, I ran all the way home. I didn't even try to make it to a classroom where a teacher might be; I started running and didn't stop until I was safe inside the house.

I shake these thoughts from my mind. This is not fifth grade, not Kevin Highsmith, and I have nowhere to run.

I don't get scared. I am not afraid of you. I will not get scared.

"Lady bird, you all alone up there?"

I try to calm myself by thinking that this group of boys is just on the way to the lake or taking a shortcut to town; maybe, I try telling myself, they just stumbled upon my place. There's no ill will, I keep saying, just kids playing a prank. They'll go when they get bored.

And yet, even as I try to come up with reasons for why a group of young men have stopped beneath my stand, even as I pray my mantra and make myself believe they'll soon be gone, I am thinking I'm being targeted by a whole different brand of bully.

"Kate Davidson," the dominant one, alpha male, calls out. "We know who you are. You're the crazy forest ranger holding up progress."

Another member of the group—and I've now counted four—the smallest guy, skinny, wearing a denim jacket over his black hoodie and jeans, a pair of cowboy boots, steps out of the quartet and goes to the spot with the best view into my nest. When I see where he has stopped, the dimming evening light around us, I catch him grinning at me. It's unnerving.

"You got a bed up there in your tree house?" The guy who mentioned the turkeys is asking.

"Is it a double or a single?"

And they all hoot again.

"Say, when is the hunting season on park rangers? Is that in the spring or the fall?"

I'm not a park ranger; I work for the Forest Service, completely different entities, but I'm not bringing that up either.

"Well, we could just tranquilize her and tag her; isn't that what they do? It might be more fun."

The skinny one is still watching and I try to move behind the limbs to get out of his line of view.

"Lady bird, I bet we could make some money dragging you out of there, what do you think, fellows?" The alpha male again.

"I think Mr. Hatch would be happy to give us a sizeable reward for getting her out of that tree," the other one says, the third one standing with the leader, making sure he's loud enough for me to hear.

Once I hear that name, I understand this is not going to end with just a sucker punch.

Twenty-Four

"So, let's see, there's four of us, and . . ." he hesitates. I can hear the danger in his voice. "And just one of her."

"One little lady bird," another says.

"And how shall we get this little bird out of her nest?" The leader asks the pack.

"We could just lasso her, like a calf." And he laughs a menacing laugh and then mimics the move of a cowboy throwing a rope around his head.

"We could shoot her down," another one suggests.

The leader speaks again. "Or what if two of us fly up there and push her out of her little pine tree nest and two could stay here to catch her."

I see him reach up for the first step on the sweetgum. "Or maybe you'll just come down on your own, keep us from having to come up there and get you."

"Yeah, I bet she'll come on down right by herself. She don't have no mate up there, do you, lady bird? No gun? No officer of the law close by?"

They cackle again.

I don't get scared. I am not afraid of you. I will not get scared.

I decide it's time to speak to this murder of crows.

"I don't know why you're here; but this has nothing to do with you." My voice is high, stretched. I sound like a sand crane squawking.

"Well, maybe it has a lot to do with me," the leader replies. He comes back into my full view.

"I don't see how," I reply, my throat suddenly very dry, all the words sticking in my mouth.

"See, I might be losing money every day you're up there. You might be keeping me from doing a job I was hired to do."

Then it clicks. He's supposed to be tearing down the trees. He's one of the demolition crews hired to rip apart the forest.

"Are you employed by Winston Hatch?"

"Oh, the lady bird thinks she's smart now."

A rock flies up at me almost hitting me in the head.

"Well, maybe I do or maybe I don't. You see, that really doesn't matter."

"It turns out you got a pretty good bounty on your head," comes another voice. I think it's the skinny guy, now moved back to join the others; I think he was the one who just threw a rock at me.

"You're sort of like a rare frog or a spotted owl or something. We get a lot of money for bringing you to a collector."

"Yeah, and the funny thing is they didn't say whether you had to be dead or alive. Maybe they just want your skin."

I feel them getting closer to the trunk.

I look around my stand, trying to find something to protect myself. I realize that even if Charlene had given me a rape whistle no one would hear me way out here, and I doubt it would scare these guys away. I try to find the phone she brought, just to see if I might get a signal. I'm caught like a mouse in a trap.

Another rock comes in my direction and I dodge to miss it.

"We don't really have to climb up there, dude, we could just pelt her to death until she falls out." A couple more rocks make it to my stand.

I feel the trees on which I'm standing start to move.

"No, you know, I kind of like climbing up a tree." And the leader starts shaking the loblolly.

"Get a better view from up there, don't you?" It's the second in command. He's egging him on.

"Yeah, it's like being in a deer stand, I bet, except we ain't hunting deer this evening, are we?" He laughs and shakes the tree again. "We're hunting lady birds."

I don't get scared. I am not afraid of you. I will not get scared. I move around to the other side, trying to get out of his sight.

He's already off the ground in the tree and I hear the other guys, laughing.

"Go, dude, go!" the wild turkey guy yells.

"You should just stop, get down from there." I'm really shrieking now, flustered and alarmed. I am terrified.

"See, it's not really that hard." And he keeps getting closer. "Come out, come out, wherever you are!"

I reach above my head and move up from my stand and onto a higher branch.

"You can't run from me, lady bird." He's laughing and the boys beneath us are clapping and cheering and I scramble up, branch by branch, trying to get away.

I don't get scared. I am not afraid of you. I will not get scared.

"You need to get down!" I keep moving, higher and higher; but I feel him very close.

The crow is almost at my stand when suddenly out of nowhere I hear this loud swooshing noise and feel the hair on my neck stand up as wide descending wings almost touch me.

There's a scramble of needles and branches and the loudest, longest single screech I've ever heard. The climber falls through the limbs, yelling, a scream low and menacing, swish, swish through the limbs and the leaves rattle, the boys scuttle beneath me. And then I hear another sound, a loud pop, loud, that sets up an intense racket in the forest around me. Suddenly, there are all these birds flapping and flying out, leaving nests I had not seen, roosts I knew nothing about. The Cooper's hawk, the chickadees, the nuthatches, and warblers, they all squawk and flutter and leave. And then there is a terrible silence.

I am straddling the loblolly just like I did in the storm, my arms and legs wrapped securely around it, muscles tight and eyes clenched shut; and it isn't very long before I hear one of the boys telling the others to hurry.

I don't get scared. I am not afraid of you. I will not get scared.

I hear them run away, open my eyes, and suddenly understand the tragedy that has just unfolded.

Twenty-Five

"Oh . . . no . . . no . . . no." I say as I move from branch to branch, slide down the trunk of the loblolly, climb out of the sweetgum, until I reach a place where I am able to jump ten feet to the ground below. I land hard, biting my lip, twisting my ankle.

"No . . . no . . . no . . . no," I keep saying as I watch the bird flinch, the long feathered wings flapping, his hideous and unsuccessful attempts to get up, to get away, his instinct to rise, trying to fly.

"No . . . no . . . no . . . no," I repeat as I feel his talons grasping my arm, tearing into the flesh, his beak pecking at me. But I grab his body, trying to find the bullet hole, trying to see where I can stop the bleeding. He fights me hard and long and I see the terror in his eyes, his heaving white chest, his desperation, and I struggle with him, trying to do what I can to save him and then suddenly he stops the furious fight, falls limp, and he's gone. Mr. Delores is gone.

I gather him up, his fierce head, his dangerous beak, his thick wings, his fallen and strewn feathers, his ferocious talons, his bloody back, all of him, all I can hold of him, in my arms. He is almost as big as me and I hold him against my chest, leaning and rocking against the tree.

I cannot name this grief, but it takes no time to remember what I have known before.

Not long after my mother left I had a recurring dream. It started out harmless, even happy. The family, Mama, Daddy, Nathan, me, all climbing in the car for a vacation. I feel excited and it's some kind of surprise, our own "foursome adventure," our parents tell my brother and me. It's a road trip, a family excursion to somewhere fabulous. Nathan and I are laughing and high-fiving, and rolling down the windows, yelling to those passing by that we're the Sinclair family and we're off to our brand-new adventure.

The day is bright and sunny; the trees are full and green. We pass meadows and forests and pastures, the cows bobbing and munching their grass, lifting their lazy eyes to watch. Daddy's driving and Mama sits close, leaning into him as he has one arm loosely thrown around her shoulder, the other holding the steering wheel, guiding us to some place magical. People are waving as we pass, the world enjoying this day with us.

"Disney World," Nathan guesses. "Orlando!"

"The ocean," I chime in. "We're going to the beach!"

And our parents laugh and will not give us answers, only clues. "You'll need comfortable shoes," my mother calls out, twisting around in her seat to tease us.

"Hiking," I yell. "We're going to the mountains and we're going hiking. The Appalachian Trail!"

"You'll want to take a camera," my dad adds, peering at his children in his rearview mirror, the big smile plastered across his face.

"Europe!" Nathan yells. "We're flying to France!"

And we laugh and fall back in our seats, thinking how fun it would be to jet away to another continent, fly off together to a new place.

"You'll need sunglasses and a bathing suit!"

"White Lake," I guess, remembering a trip there in the past, the water so clear you can see your feet even standing waist deep. "Or the South of France!" I laugh so hard my sides hurt.

The riddles and the answers go on and on and we drive through the perfectly displayed scenery until we make a turn off this dreamy road and stop at a row of abandoned buildings. And in just a second, just a tiny passage of time, I can tell everything is changing, everything is different, turned from something wonderful to something ominous. From green to gray, from natural to apocalyptic. From trees and forests to steel and looming danger. And my parents, still acting in this happy mood, still behaving in this "giving us a surprise" mood, get out of the car, wave at us through their windows and walk away. And I watch as they head up a set of stairs and into the front door of one of the buildings.

I'm just sitting and staring in the direction they went, looking for them, trying to understand where they've gone, trying to understand how everything has changed so quickly, trying to figure out where they're going and what we'll do. And when I turn to Nathan to ask what he thinks, where they're heading, he's gone, too. I never saw him leave the car and I don't know where he is, but I do suddenly know

that I'm in the backseat all alone. No one around. Just this dead-end
stop with buildings and a dark sky. And when I try to open my door
so that I can get out too, run and join them, it's locked and I'm stuck.

I beat on the window. I pull on the door handle. I jump to the other
side, the side where Nathan had just been, and I do the same thing.
I beat on his window, try to lower it, pull on the handle. It becomes
more and more clear that I'm stuck in the car alone. I try to get in
the front seat, slide through the bucket seats, wiggle to the driver's
side, but everything's locked. Nothing can be opened or turned on.
And by this point, I am frantic. I try to see my mother or father, try
to locate my brother, yell and scream for them, but there's no one.
Just me, locked in the car.

Then, of course, it starts to move. It lunges forward and I'm stuck
behind the wheel, too short to reach the pedals, unable to stop it as
it picks up speed. And I'm screaming and yelling and beating on the
windows, trying to find the brakes but it goes faster and faster until
I guess I finally scream so loud in my sleep that my father runs in the
room and wakes me up before I know what will happen, before the
car runs into traffic or slams into a tree or plunges off a cliff.

I'm stuck and alone and out of control. It's not so hard to figure
out; but even understanding it as a kid, I could not stop the dream
from happening and I could not change the way it unfolded night
after night. I cried and cried every evening for months, fighting with
my dad, refusing to go to bed, to go to any bed, try any arrangement,
petrified of that dream and what was going to happen.

Finally, after a few doctor's visits, several sessions with a counselor
whose name I don't even remember, some pediatric benzodiazepines,
anti-anxiety drugs that helped me sleep, I was able to rest again, able
to go to bed without terror. I had the dream again a few times after
Nathan died but it didn't have the same power over me. In fact, in
the dream when I was older, I just watched it all happen and simply
stayed in the back seat, dispassionate and uncaring, just letting the car

go, always waking up before the inevitable crash or fall.

Still, it was never the same, never produced the same reaction; and I realize that until now I haven't felt the way I did when I was eight and dreaming that dream, so afraid, so desperate for something other than how it was, so completely unglued.

Until right now, holding a dead owl to my chest, his mate, Delores, calling and calling. I am shivering and I weep and scream, begging for it to be something different from what I know it is.

I don't remember how long I stayed like that.

It was dark and very late when I finally moved from the base of my trees, deciding that I needed to do something with the bird. I placed him carefully beside me and crawled around until I found an area nearby that seemed big enough to bury him. I felt around until I came across a stick that was thick and sturdy enough to help me dig, and that's what I did for hours.

With the stick and my hands, I dug and dug, clearing brush and stones, breaking roots of trees, opening wider and wider a place to lay the dead owl. When I thought it was deep and wide enough I made my way around the tree slowly, my foot and arm throbbing, my fingers reaching until I found what I was looking for, Marge's prayer shawl that had been left on the ground. I wrapped him in the shawl, slid into the grave, and placed him at the bottom. I pulled myself out, filled in the hole, handful by handful, finishing the work just before dawn.

Two feathers had been left where the body had fallen and I picked them up, stuffed them in my pocket, and crawled back up the tree into my stand.

I found the bottle of wine Jim had given me, the one from which I had taken only a few sips, and I drank every bit of it, every single drop, until I fell asleep, drunk and still weeping.

Twenty-Six

"Kate, Katie . . ."

I hear my name being called. I hear the voice, but I am groggy and unable to answer. Everything hurts.

"Kate, Katie . . . Wake up! Are you okay? Talk to me. Kate . . . Katie!"

I struggle to raise my head and as soon as I do, I feel the world spin and immediately drop back down. I'm pretty sure I am going to throw up. My stomach churns. I try digging my nails into the board beneath me but my fingers are so sore from the digging I can't grasp onto anything.

The trees start to shake.

"Kate!"

I slide over to the side of the stand, drop my head, and throw up.

"What . . . . oh, Ka— . . . oh . . . Ga . . ."

I pick myself up enough to see below. I think I just vomited on someone. I roll over on my back. I try to open my eyes. When I do, I see myself, my arms, my chest, and I'm covered in blood. Some of it, I suppose, is mine.

"Kate, what happened?"

"Ray?" I whisper his name.

"Move where I can see you. It's a mess down here, what happened last night?"

I slide a little, slowly, making my way to the edge again. I roll back on my stomach. He's trying to find me through the branches and finally we meet eyes. He's wearing a brown jacket, his Carhartt from work, blue jeans, boots.

I look away from him, turn over on my back and try reading the sky. I have no idea what time it is.

"It's one o'clock," he tells me, realizing what I'm doing. "I came on my lunch break. Charlene was worried about you, said it took you a long time to wake you up and then once you did, you just kept crying and talking about somebody getting shot."

I close one eye, thinking about the woman beneath the tree this morning, trying to tell her about Mr. Delores, but I kept falling back to sleep. I recall her tossing a bag up here. I glance over and see it at my feet. Breakfast, I suppose. And the thought of a biscuit makes me salivate but not because I'm hungry. I swallow hard.

"What happened? Are you okay? Let me see you better. Stand up."

I shake my head and then feel the nausea again.

"There's blood down here," he says. "Is it you? Did something happen? There's shattered glass."

"Blood," I repeat. I try to get up, putting the weight on my right arm but instantly cry out. It's a mess, bruised, cut, swollen. Then I move around, trying to get to my feet but feel the pain in my ankle, the throbbing starts.

"I'm going to come up there if you don't let me see that you're all right."

"I'm drunk," I say, no longer moving, no longer interested in changing positions. "Leave me alone. I'm just drunk."

I hear him sigh. A big one, long and drawn out.

"You don't drink, Kate."

"I do drink," I say, my words like cotton in my mouth, my tongue sore from biting it last night. "I drink a lot; I just don't do it in front of you because you're an alcoholic, because you might have a relapse." This comes out sharp, mean.

Another breath blown out. "Kate."

"What?" This time I yell. I hate this conversation. I hate this day. "Just go."

"Kate, tell me what happened."

"I said . . ."

He interrupts me. "I'm not going until I can see that you're okay."

I wish I could get up and show him my face since I'm pretty sure that's not bruised or scarred but if I move again, I'll be sick.

"I'm okay."

"Who was here last night? Did somebody come here?"

I close my eyes and think of the boy trying to get up the trees, the one throwing rocks, the cackles, the danger, the shot of a gun, the grand forest exit, the horrible silence that followed.

"Kate!"

"Some guys, Hatch's crew or something, I don't know."

"Did they hurt you?"

I feel the tears sting my eyes.

"Tell me, did they hurt you?"

"They shot the owl," I say softly. "They killed him," I whisper. "They killed the male," I say loudly enough that I'm sure he can hear me.

"Did they hurt you? Did you get hurt?"

"They shot the owl!" I say between clenched teeth. "It's the same thing."

"Kate!"

"What Ray? What?" And I sit up, holding back the nausea and the spinning. "I'm up. Now just leave! Just go! I've got nothing else to say. Leave me alone. I was drunk; I am still drunk."

"Let me help you," he says to me. He's standing closer to the base of the tree. I feel him closer.

"I don't want your help," I reply.

"You don't know that," he answers. "Just let me help. Slide closer to the edge and let me make sure you're okay. Tell me what I can do."

"You can go, Ray. Just go. I'm drunk and I want to be left alone. Why can't you listen to me? I want to be left alone. You remember that, right? You remember when you went home and locked your doors and how you just wanted to be left alone?"

I sit up a little because all I feel right now is just angry.

"And I did leave you alone, Ray, lots and lots of time. I took care of your little girl day after day, stayed with her in the hospital, by her bed, me, Ray, me, because you were too drunk to do it, and I left you alone when you were stupid, stupid drunk or getting over being stupid, stupid drunk. So, return the favor and just leave me alone now. Just go!"

And I drop back on the stand.

"Kate." A pause. "Kate."

"JUST LEAVE!" I scream and I reach over beside me and grab the other bottle of wine I had started to drink and throw it down at him. I hear the crash and I truly don't care if I hurt him or not. I just want him to be gone. I just want not to have to talk, not to have to answer another stupid question, not to have to think, not to have to move. I just want him to go.

And after a few minutes of silence, I realize he has.

Twenty-Seven

Hours pass and I honestly can't tell what time of day it is. I think it's raining but I'm not sure about that, either. I do know though that it's not the alcohol any more that's making me feel this way. I think I'm sick. At the place on my arm where I was grabbed by the owl, it hurts a great deal. More than it should. It feels hot, infected maybe; I don't know.

I sit up on the landing, slide over a little so that I can lean my back against the tree, be in a more restful place; but there's another reason, too. It's dusk and from this perch I have a clear shot at Delores, a good view, my first since the murder, and now that I get a good look, I can tell she knows that her mate is dead.

I can tell by the way she's moved closer to the opening of her roost, the way she sits, taller, emboldened, more defensive, careful, alert, more determined not to leave her eggs, not to be pushed away by predators or intruders, by grief, more determined to feed herself.

She stares at me for a minute, maybe more, and then looks away. I don't know if she realizes I'm the cause of his death or not, if she was a witness to what happened and if she's retained that information and is using it against me, that I am now the enemy. I don't know.

We like to ascribe human emotions to animals, to birds, but as a scientist I've learned that they don't feel the same way we feel. There may be emotional pain but it isn't stored within their brains like it is for us. They don't need to talk things over. They don't need an apology or handholding. Birds, owls, operate by instinct, by generations of survival lessons learned, by knowing how to preserve energy, moving only as much as is necessary, doing what has to be done to stay alive, to reproduce, to care for the eggs, to protect, to eat.

She somehow knows, with or without the grief, that she will need to feed herself now, and leaving the nest for any extended period of time will be detrimental to her young. If this causes her anxiety or sorrow, I don't know. I only know it makes me feel terrible and I try to think how I can catch a mouse or squirrel and get it near her so that she can take it back to the nest. I have never been very good at trapping or hunting. I don't have weapons or tools. I don't have bait. It will be hard but I see that it has to be done.

"So, you're up?"

The question startles me since I didn't expect anyone, hadn't heard anyone below me. The last conversation I recall was the one with Ray sometime this afternoon and remembering it makes me twinge. It would be better if I could forget it.

"When did you get here?" I ask, knowing the voice well.

"A couple of hours ago."

"You just sitting there, waiting?"

"Yeah, well, sometimes that's the best thing pastors know how to do, just sit and be still. Wait on the Lord, you know."

There's a pause, a moment where nothing passes between us but friendship. I close my eyes. It bolsters me and I speak.

"The great horned . . ." I choke a little.

"I know," Jim says before I finish. "Ray told me."

I keep my eyes closed and wrap my arms around my waist. My right one, the one that was injured and now probably infected rests on top of the other one. I feel my heart pounding, the heat rising inside my body.

"You okay?"

And I try to pull myself together, take a few deep breaths. I clear my throat. "I think I may have an infection. He got me with his talons."

"You came down?"

"He crashed into the guy who was climbing up here. He just flew out of nowhere and made the guy fall and then they shot him. I came down when they left. I buried him."

Jim doesn't respond.

"He fought you before he died? That's how you got hurt?"

I nod, feeling the tears again.

"You coming down again?"

I guess I hadn't thought that far ahead. I thought about hunting a rabbit or a squirrel but not leaving, not going to a doctor or emergency room. I know that if I come down and go out of the forest, Hatch and Brownfield will find a way to keep me from coming back.

"I can't." And I'm not sure what my answer means to him and he doesn't reply.

Then finally, "I got some antibiotics for Mama. I have them in the car. I just picked them up at the pharmacy. I'll get them and come back."

His answer surprises me. I thought he'd argue with me or tell me that I need to leave the tree but he doesn't. He tells me this instead.

"That's illegal, Jim."

"Yeah, well, I'll deal with it if it comes up."

I hear him rustling around below me, getting up to leave, I suppose.

"Wait," I say.

And it's quiet.

"Just don't go yet," I add, and I hear him sit back down.

He doesn't speak or make a sound. He is good at this pastoral thing.

I hear the robins and the chickadees and know it must be late in the evening; there's always a ruckus just before the last feeding of the day.

"I said some pretty terrible things to Ray."

There is no reply and I imagine this is more than just a good pastoral response. I imagine that Jim knows, that Ray told him what I said, how I acted.

"I was mean."

"Is this some kind of confession, because you know I'm Lutheran; we don't really believe you need a priest to do that."

"I know," I answer. He's trying to be funny, I can tell, but I'm not feeling very funny.

"What do you want me to say?" he asks.

"I don't know," I reply.

"Well, here's something. I think Ray can take it," Jim replies. "I think his skin is a bit tougher than you give him credit."

"Maybe," I answer.

"He didn't say anything like that when he came to tell me about you."

This time I'm waiting.

"He was worried, not mad; concerned, not hurt."

I nod even though Jim can't see.

There's another pause.

"Is there anything else?" he wants to know. I did ask him to wait.

I shake my head.

"Are you shaking your head?"

This makes me smile. "No, there's nothing else."

"Then I'll go to the car and get the drugs. I'll be right back."
And I peek over the side and watch him as he leaves, knowing I lied, knowing there's a whole lot more.

Twenty–Eight

"Delores will be fine," Jim says, watching me raise and hold my binoculars in the direction of her nest. "She's quite a capable survivor. I watched her while you slept and she's had plenty to eat and she hasn't had to be away from her eggs more than ten minutes at a time."

Jim knows I'm worried about her, that I even thought I should help her find her food.

"She goes out and she comes back, always with something in her mouth."

"She's building a cache for leaner times, I guess."

"I guess," he answers. "Also, I said a few words over the grave. I don't know if Mr. Delores was Lutheran, but I read from the Bible that was beside the tree, from Psalms. I didn't think you'd mind."

I put down my binoculars and glance down at him. "Thank you," I say, and then watch him nod in that pastoral way I've seen him do so often.

I turned my view back to Delores and feel a sense of relief to know that she's managing, that she's a lot better than I am, in fact. She's smart and strong and fast. I see now that she'll do well. And the eggs should be okay, too. It's warm tonight just like it has been all this month; they will certainly not freeze or probably even suffer from an absent parent or a chilly spring season.

"It's Azithromycin," Jim explains when I put down the binoculars and take the bag out of the bucket. "It's prescribed for an upper respiratory infection."

I guess there has been another pneumonia diagnosis for Mama Stallings or maybe her infection is from something she's picked up from living in a new environment. He doesn't speculate about the origins.

"It's used for cat scratch fever, too," he informs me. "Maybe an owl swipe is no worse than a cat's."

"Maybe," I answer. I find a bottle of water in the bucket and take my first dose.

"It's also used for syphilis in case you have a venereal disease."

I finish my drink and place the bottle at my side, pull the blanket around me again. "I don't think they use that word, *venereal* anymore."

"Really?" He seems surprised. "I always liked that word."

There is a pause. He's thinking about the word, I guess, and I'm thinking about how chilled I have become.

"I put a few painkillers in the bottle," he says. "They're the heavy hitters; so be careful when you take them. No swinging from the limbs."

"Thanks," I answer. "You know you can't tell anybody that you've given me these. It could get you into a lot of trouble. Those hospice nurses pay attention to drug diversion, so you be careful about what you say to them."

"Yeah, I know, but don't forget that I'm pretty good at keeping secrets."

"Right," I reply.

"So, how are you feeling now? Still hurting? Your arm still swelling?"

I can tell my arm is swollen; I don't have to see that to know it and I still feel like I have a fever. I don't tell Jim this though because I don't see any good reason to make a list of all my aches and pains.

"The hangover is mostly gone. I don't have a headache and I'm not going to vomit again." I decide to name the positives.

"Can you eat something?"

I think I can, now that he's mentioned it. I reach into the bucket again and take out the crackers he's sent. They're saltines, probably also meant for his mom; but at least diverting these isn't a felony. "Thanks for the crackers."

"No more wine," he tells me. "I think a drinking woman in a tree is a liability."

"True," I answer.

I sit and rest, drop my head back against the tree, close my eyes, pull the blanket tight around me. We are quiet for a few minutes.

"I think I'm finally coming out of my drunk stupor."

"Yeah? Is that a good thing or bad?"

I ponder the question. "Both, I guess."

We listen to the crickets starting up.

"I learned you can't really deaden the pain of grief with alcohol."

"That's true. But you can hide it a while."

"Says the Lutheran pastor," I add. He's right, I suppose. "It stings," I say.

"What? Your wound?"

"No, death, grief. It stings. I know I've heard you read that passage that asks the question, 'O death, where is your sting?' Like there isn't one. But there is. There is a sting."

"Yes, you're right, it's much too optimistic to think it doesn't hurt. The apostle was trying to be hopeful, I suppose. But the sting does have a certain clarity, don't you think?"

"What do you mean? Like you suddenly understand the great mysteries of life, comprehend the problem of evil?"

"No, nothing like that. That would take more than grief; that would take, well, faith."

I look down at him, wait, listen.

"What I remember about grief is what becomes perfectly clear in its wake, this perfect knowledge that nothing about the life we live, nothing about the story we write for ourselves, nothing about what we have taken for granted regarding waking up and being alive is ever, ever the same."

I close my eyes again and think about the deaths, about the clarity of the sting, realizing he's right.

When Nathan died every thought I had about what my life would be was ripped away, taken in like one snap of the fingers. I mean, Mama's leaving was hard, there's no doubt about that, and at eight years old, it was completely unsettling, but more like an earthquake than a sting.

I think about how it was that I started to lean on things back then, how I didn't run down the stairs at school anymore, skip steps on our front porch, but rather how I held onto the banister, how I always felt a little shaky.

But Nathan dying, Nathan driving home to celebrate my birthday and running off the road, the road we live on, the road we walked and drove and biked down a thousand times, to run off that road and crash and burn and die. Well, that's not just hard or unsettling or difficult to understand or accept. That was the moment my life changed. That was the moment I knew that nothing was ever going to be the same for me again.

And I can actually say that I can look back on everything I have done or seen or thought about since and see that it is directly tied to what happened to me on that night. I see now that his death colored everything then when I was young and it never stopped; it's doing it even now.

"You're right, Pastor," I say. "Nothing's ever the same."

"Amen," he adds. "But I still read the passage. I still think it helps."

I don't respond. I'm not sure it helps or not. All I know is that death does sting and to pretend it doesn't is not something I want to do anymore.

"Maybe that's the real reason you're so interested in birds." He suggests. "Maybe it's not because you're actually curious or passionate or even think of studying them as some vocation."

There's a night song somewhere close by so he stops.

"So, what it is then?" I ask when the silence returns.

"Maybe it's envy. Maybe you're envious of them because you don't think that they have that emotion. Maybe you have a deep longing for how it must be not to have to feel this kind of pain."

I listen.

"An egg is taken; you lay another. The nest is destroyed; you build a new one. A fledgling falls and is taken by a stronger, swifter animal; you keep on caring for the others." He hesitates.

"Your mate is shot and killed by careless humans and you search the forest ground for your next meal." I add. It's true. In the natural selection process, in survival, there is no place to sit with grief, perhaps not even a place for that experience at all. Maybe I am envious. I had never thought of this before.

"So, maybe evolution isn't so great after all. Maybe, it would be better to be a bird."

Jim and I sit together on this night, me up here, him below, and we make the same decision without speaking. We both reach for our binoculars and turn to the nest in the tree beside me. The light of the moon is bright and we get a good look.

It's empty and I'm not sure about Jim but I keep my eyes focused on the spot. We wait and in just a few short minutes Delores returns to the nest with dinner in her beak. I observe her with just a twinge of sadness and remorse, but mostly satisfaction, as she tears apart the flesh of a vole she just found.

With this perfect glimpse I do not see wrath or anger; she's not doing something because she's upset or broken. All I see is the instinct to survive, a will to live.

And as Jim and I watch together, I have a heightened sense of this mother's abilities to overcome what I'm confident she witnessed but perhaps unlike me no longer feels. I put down the binoculars, reach into the bottle of pills Jim brought and find a painkiller. I take it, chasing it with water.

I am not a bird. I want to hide again what hurts.

Twenty-Nine

There is a sound, a call. Not a bird, though. Human, I think. I slide my body to the edge of my board in the tree and try to focus on the visitor beneath me. Jim left an hour or so ago and the pain pill has kicked in. I feel a little like I'm flying, a little like there is more than just one of me.

"Who's there?" I ask, glancing around the trunk of the loblolly. The moon is still bright enough to shed light on things, but I can't see anyone.

There's a sound, a rustling in the leaves. I grab my lantern and hold it up. Finally, I see a figure, light brown, white with dark streaks on one side. It looks exactly like the brown thrasher but I cannot see its eyes. Seeing yellow eyes would confirm the sighting.

"Kate?" It knows my name, the bird of a thousand songs, it calls out my name.

I blink hard and focus again.

"Kate?"

I turn off the lantern. I don't want them to see me.

A beam of light shines in my direction and I'm almost blinded when it hits me in the face. "Kate, it's Deputy Massey. Are you okay?"

"Franklin?" I respond, when he puts down the flashlight and I can see him, causing me to realize it isn't the brown thrasher at all. It's the thornbill.

"Kate, what's going on?" He turns his flashlight in my direction again and I back away from the beam of light.

"What'd you mean?" I respond, setting the lantern down, falling on my side so that I can rest. I am so sleepy.

"We got a report that you had some trouble."

"Trouble," I repeat, the image of the owl flying through the branches, a wing almost touching me.

"What's wrong with you?"

"Wrong with you?"

"Why are you repeating everything I say?"

"Why . . ." I stop when I realize I'm about to do it again. I roll on my back, my good arm crooked under my head.

"Do you have something you want to report? Some guys harassing you?"

I consider the question, close my eyes and remember the group of troublemakers standing at the trunk of the trees, one of them starting to fly up here.

"Crows," I answer. "Hooded crows; they're not native to these parts."

"What?"

"Hooded crows, they're in Europe, Iran, Russia. Dressed in gray, black feet, eyes, juveniles have a red mouth."

"Kate, Kate Davidson, are you okay?"

"No." I shake my head. No, I'm not okay.

"Have you taken something? Are you high?"

This makes me laugh, me, living in a tree. Of course, I'm high. I laugh again.

"What happened the other night?"

"The other night?—" How many nights has it been?

I recall the gathering, the stones pelting my stand, the cheering as one of them started to climb.

"Do you want to press charges? Are you hurt?"

I roll on my side and peer over the ledge. Franklin lowers his flashlight, giving me a better view of himself. Maybe he does look more like a brown thrasher than a thornbill. The buffy underparts, his rust-brown feathers, his khaki uniform, the one I remember Daddy wearing in spring. I study Franklin and recall one birder writing that the thrasher is, 'a large sulking bird of thickets and hedgerows.'

"Do you sulk, Franklin?" I roll on my back, careful with my wounded arm.

"What?" I hear him blow out a breath, and I close my eyes, letting the spin take over me. "What are you on? Did somebody give you something?"

"Jim," I answer. "Jim gave me a pill. It helps. Helps with the pain."

"Do you want to file a report about what happened? Do you want us to press charges? I heard they shot an owl."

"Us?" I ask. "Who's us? Did the sheriff send you out here?"

"Of course, the sheriff sent me out here. Do you have a report to file or not?"

"The hooded crows are scavengers, opportunistic," I tell him, filing my bird report. "*Corvus cornix*, they steal eggs from gulls and cormorants, even puffins, if you can imagine that."

He makes no reply.

"Did you know they use to think of them as fairies? Shepherds used to make offerings to them to keep them from killing sheep. Hooded crows—not carrions, not rooks."

"Kate."

"Jethro Tull wrote a song about them, a Christmas song. Have you heard it? 'Jack Frost and the Hooded Crow.'"

"All right, I'm leaving if you aren't going to talk sensible. I'll tell the sheriff that you don't want to file a report. Have you got the carcass?"

I open my eyes; the spinning stops. "The what?"

"The carcass? The dead owl. If you've got the dead owl, I can take it as evidence, get the bullet, check around for the matching gun."

I close my eyes again. "No, there's no body, no carcass, as you call it. Tell the sheriff not to worry."

"Tell the sheriff not to worry." Now he's the one repeating.

I don't respond.

"What is it with the two of you anyway? Why can't you talk to him? What did he ever do to you?"

"The sheriff?"

"Yes, the sheriff, your father. Why is he sending me out here to check on you? Why won't he come? What happened between the two of you?"

I shake my head from side to side.

"I'm fine. And I don't have any report to file. I buried the evidence. So, there's nothing to show you." My voice is low; the words seem to flow together.

I hear him blow out a breath.

I roll to my stomach, lean my head over the side so that he can see me.

"Just don't come anymore, Franklin. If he tells you to come out here, just make something up. I don't need a babysitter, and we don't need any family intervention." I pause, look at him, trying to keep my eyes from falling shut. "Tell him to arrest me if he needs to just don't come here for him. Okay? That clear enough for you?"

"Yep, that's clear." He casts his flashlight directly on me, in my eyes, and I wince. "But you need to get things straight with him, the sheriff, I'm talking about, and you need to do it soon. He's your father and this is stupid. You need to talk to him."

I slide away from the beam of light and reach for my blanket. I pull it over me, covering my head and immediately fall to sleep. I don't know if Franklin stays or goes.

Thirty

I wake up. I don't think I slept for very long. I'm still groggy from the pain pill, still feel sick, feverish, but I'm restless. I change positions as much as I can without lying on my arm. One side, on my back, on my belly, nothing is comfortable.

Maybe it's the crows, thinking they may come back to finish what they started; maybe I'm anxious that one of them will return, knowing now how to get to me.

Maybe it's Delores, her dead mate, her single parenting. Maybe it's what I said to Ray earlier, how I'm sure I did hurt him even if Jim doesn't see it. Maybe it's me sitting in a tree without any idea of how I can come down from here. I don't know what it is. I know I just can't get back to sleep.

I sit up and feel my ankle.

It's sprained, I'm sure. It hurts now almost as much as my arm. I feel around for a bottle of water and take a few swallows, sit up, lean back against the tree, close my eyes, pull the blanket to just below my chin. I try to figure out what's bothering me, what thing is sticking in my brain, and suddenly I think about Franklin, what he said, that last thing about the sheriff.

What was it? That I needed to get things straight with the sheriff? And then he used the word, soon? Why soon? What did he mean?

And Marge? What was it she said when she was here all those days ago? How did she phrase it? *Why he keeps looking for some reconciliation, wanting some word of relief from you.*

Is there something wrong with him, I wonder. Is he sick?

I slide down and start to turn on the side where I am most wounded, but as soon as I land on my arm, I fall to the other side.

This isn't comfortable either, so I roll on my back, throw my good arm across my eyes.

What if he is sick? Do I care? Does this change anything for me? Would it make a difference?

I glance up through the branches of the loblollies and see the constellations. I find the Big Dipper, name the seven stars: Alkaid, Mizar, Alioth, Megrez, Phecda, Dubhe, Merak, and remember that he taught me those. I could spell every one of them before I was six years old, before I was in first grade.

My father taught Nathan and me the names of all of the constellations and the stars when we were both very young. I learned them before I learned the birds. He quizzed us about them, bought us books about the sky. Because of him, I knew everything about the sky, and I think about the late nights we camped in the backyard, when we lay beneath the blackness and he pointed them out, had us say the names back to him.

It was a perfect time. Perfect.

I learned that the Big Dipper is circumpolar in most of the northern hemisphere, that it doesn't sink below horizon at night. He taught us that as a result of the earth's rotation, Ursa Major, which is the name of the constellation, the third largest of all eighty-eight, isn't the same thing as the Big Dipper. That group of stars is known as an asterism and is just the most visible part of the Ursa Major.

He showed us how the Big Dipper can be seen in different parts of the sky at different times of the year. In the warmer seasons of spring and summer both the Big and the Little Dipper are higher overhead, and in fall and winter they are closer to the horizon. "Spring up and fall down," he would tell us, that's the rule of the Dippers.

I envision the three of us, sitting so close together at the door of the big tent we slept in together, how I could feel both my brother's and my father's breath on my neck. I think about how he'd throw his arm around me, laugh when I'd tell him what I knew, what I had learned from the night sky, when I could point to a star and name it. And then, well, it was suddenly different, and I don't actually even recall when it all changed, when the tent was blown away by spring winds, the sleeping bags and mats given to a thrift shop or sold at a yard sale. I don't remember when I got mad and quit talking to him, quit asking him the names of the stars, quit thinking of him as strong and heroic.

I know when Mama left and he made up some lie that she needed to visit her cousin up north, help her take care of some ailing relative, and then weeks later just said she was staying longer than she thought; I knew then that I thought he could have done something to stop her, that he could find a way to bring her home. I remember saying that he should take the squad car up to Delaware or New Hampshire or wherever she was and make her come back, charge her with neglect or something, and make her come home. But he wouldn't. He'd just say, it's more complicated than you can understand. And finally I got so tired of hearing his excuses I quit asking the questions, and I got accustomed to the new way we did family. I even learned to like it: me, Nathan, and him.

And then there was the car wreck, Nathan almost home, walking distance, really. And he wrecks? He tries to avoid an animal, or so they say, and he runs into a ditch and dies? Why couldn't the sheriff do something about that? Hadn't people complained about Mr. Temple's cows getting out all the time? Shouldn't he have charged him or made him fix the fence before he realized Nathan was driving home? Didn't he understand the dangers of having those cows on the road?

And I see now that it wasn't that one big fight that my father and I had, it was this series of disappointments, this list of grievances that I had, these charges I made against him and he wouldn't even defend himself. Little by little, the older I got, the smaller he became, and the less I felt that I could count on him, the more I held him responsible for everything bad that happened to us.

Then when I did find my mother, when we had the big fight after I ran the computer searches and found out she wasn't in Delaware or New Hampshire but rather in Florida, when I found out that she didn't leave us to take care of a sick relative but instead ran off with a salesman, that she left her family and started another one. He had nothing to say about that, either. No defense for himself for lying to us.

She was completely surprised to see me when I showed up in Panama City more than two decades ago, her other daughter's pictures on the mantle, and she finally asked me hadn't I read the letter she left. She asked me hadn't my father told me that she fell in love with this book salesman from Wilmington—Kenneth, she called him, not Ken or Kenny, but Kenneth, this man she met on a trip she took to the beach with a friend, this man who took her to Florida, got her pregnant, and then died.

She told me that at the time she asked my father to share custody, to let her be with us, let us visit her in Florida but he had told her no. He told her that if she left him, she left the family, and that if she tried to reach us, he would have her arrested and charged with "Alienation of Affection," a law then still on the books in North Carolina that aimed to punish adulterers.

And when I heard that story, I didn't know what to say. I had never seen any letter. He had never told us about the affair. He never said anything about what had really happened. And I was mad at her for not trying harder to see us, mad that she was the mother to another child. I was certain that I would never go back to Florida to be with her again, and I was infuriated with him for keeping the truth from us.

That was when we had the huge falling out, the fight of all fights, the cherry on the sundae of arguments, and I haven't talked to him since. He married Millie and started his whole new life without me. And then Dwayne and I got married and Charlene stood with me as my only witness. Dwayne's parents bought us dinner, and I never even told my father when it happened. And really, if he is sick, if he is waiting for some reconciliation or is in need of some relief from me, as Marge phrased it, I don't have it to give. Too much water under that bridge.

I close my eyes, the pain pill starting to wear off, and decide to take another one. I know it won't stop the memories. It won't make me feel better about how my life has turned out, about the busted-up relationships with my parents. It won't change what happened to the owl. But I feel too broken and hurt to try anything else.

I just want to sleep tonight, just close my eyes once again and sleep.

Thirty-One

"So it's better, then?" Charlene has returned. It's more than a couple of days now since the incident. The hours are running together but I'm pretty sure that she was here yesterday and then this morning, and now she's back after work. She's worried about my arm.

"I think so, yes," I tell her, even though really I don't think it's much better than it was eight hours ago. I do feel better, though, stronger, more like myself, less achy, so I'll just go with that.

"Were you able to get it cleaned?"

"I did, and thank you again for the water and soap." Maybe the shower is part of why I feel better. After all, it's been a while since I've washed my hair or the rest of me, for that matter. Charlene sent up three buckets of water, a bottle of hydrogen peroxide, a fresh towel. Today was a very special morning up the loblollies.

"You're welcome." She pauses. "Is your fever gone?"

I rest the back of my hand on my forehead. It's still warm. "I think so," I lie again.

"Did you eat some soup?"

"Yes, Mama, I had soup and three bottles of water. I had an afternoon nap, and I'm taking the antibiotics."

"Okay, okay," she replies, taking the hint. "I'm just worried about you."

I wait.

"Well?" I ask.

"Well, what?" she answers, sounding sincere.

"Well, aren't you going to ask me about keeping a Taser or a semiautomatic weapon? Don't you want me to have your rape whistle? Aren't you going to tell me that I need to come down?"

I can see her shaking her head and this throws me.

"You're going to do what you're going to do about staying up there," she tells me. "I can't change your mind about that."

I slide closer to the edge of my stand. "Wait, I'm sorry. I was talking to Charlene Davidson a few minutes ago. Charlene Davidson who hates that I'm up here by myself, who only just found out a couple of days ago that a random gang of misanthropes came out here at night and scared the living daylights of me, the Charlene Davidson who thinks I need some protection . . . where did she go? Who are you and what did you do with my friend?"

"Hahaha," she replies. She sits down next to the trunk of the tree. "You're a big girl, Kate. You know the dangers of being out here. Besides, I think killing the owl scared those guys. Franklin and I talked and I'm thinking they won't come out here again."

I return to my perch, pull the blanket up. I am shocked at her ability to let go of her fears for me. I'm actually happy, since I had dreaded the conversations I expected after that night. Still, I have to say, her acceptance of everything leaves me feeling a little distrustful.

"Winston's backed off, too," she adds, giving me an extra dose of good news.

"How did you hear that? Eugene playing ball with him again?"

"No, I asked him myself."

"What?"

"Yeah, I saw him at the gas station and I just asked him whether or not he was aware of the guys who showed up at dark saying they were there to get you down."

Charlene can be such a brute when she wants to be.

"And how did he act?" I wondered too whether Winston Hatch was behind that little venture.

"All squirrelly, claiming he didn't know anything about it and if they said they he did, they're lying, that he can't be held accountable for anybody else's actions regarding what you're doing."

I imagine the scene of Charlene confronting Winston Hatch at the pumps in front of the Piggly Wiggly. "Do you believe him?"

"I don't know. I guess."

"Did he say anything about going to a judge to have me committed?"

"Yep. I asked him about that, too, and he said he and Mr. Brownfield were working on another project at the moment and that you'd have to come down out of there eventually and that he didn't have time to deal with your lunacy."

"Lunacy?" I repeat the word. I kind of like it. I know Winston Hatch meant it in a derogatory fashion but I also know that it has the same roots as lunar. I know that it derives from *lunaticus*, which means, *of the moon* or *moonstruck*, and therefore it doesn't offend me, rather it kind of makes me feel proud.

"Lunacy," she says again. "So, I don't know, but I guess he's backing off," she repeats.

"Or he could just not be telling what he's planning next."

"Maybe."

"You are unbelievably calm this afternoon," I comment.

"I know, it's nice, right?"

"It is nice."

We sit for a while quietly and I think about Winston Hatch, whether he's really backing off.

"So, what's going on with you?" I ask.

"Nothing," she replies.

And once again, there's this weird way in which she's not saying anything but telling me something.

"Work okay?"

"Yep."

"You and Eugene?"

"Okay, too."

"Then what?" I ask her. "What are you not telling me?"

She moves around beneath me so I get to a spot where I can see her.

"Dwayne's getting married this summer."

"Oh," and I move back.

"I didn't know how to tell you."

"Well, you did it just fine." I feel kind of funny hearing the news, not sad really, or mad, just funny.

"Debbie wants to have children."

And oddly enough, this changes the feeling just a little.

"Oh."

I thought Dwayne didn't want children. This is what I think but I don't say it. Why should I? What Dwayne wants or doesn't want has nothing to do with me any longer. But still, I can't help myself, so I say, "I thought Dwayne didn't want children."

"He said he does now. He said he's changed."

"Well, that's something, isn't it?"

"Yep."

And just hearing that and then thinking about Dwayne and Debbie, how he finally found his one true love, how he now wants to have children, well, it's like walking away from a grave.

This thing is really dead, too.

Thirty-Two

"They shot the owl?" Tiffany arrived just before Charlene left. She's brought me a small pillow, more protein bars, and water.

She's just now learning about the incident. Charlene told her some of the story while I tried to get her bug display out of the hiding place where I was keeping it safe. My sprained ankle makes standing difficult; my infected arm makes yanking and pulling almost impossible. I did my best trying to retrieve the glass box but finally I just stopped.

I can't really get to it and I'm afraid I might break it. I'll just have to send the bucket down empty.

"Yeah," I say. I sit down. I feel faint, woozy.

"Well, did you tell the police?" I see her peeking around trying to get a better look at me. Charlene's gone. Tiffany leaves the bucket on the ground where it landed.

I lean forward so she can see me.

"No," I answer. "Not really able to make a 911 call from up here."

"Oh, right, the signal."

"Or lack thereof."

"Well, did they hurt you?"

I lightly rub my wounded arm with my other hand. I had to take off what I had been wearing and put on a sweatshirt Jim had in his car. My elbow and forearm are so swollen it was the only thing that fits.

"No, the owl swooped in before they did anything, scared them off."

"And somebody shot him?"

"Yeah."

I see her glancing around. I know she's looking for the body.

"I buried him."

I watch as she keeps searching.

"Over on the other side," I direct her and watch as she moves there. She finds the plot of freshly turned earth. I see her bow her head slightly and wonder if she's praying and I recall Jim saying that he said a few words at the grave while I slept. It makes me feel as if I missed the funeral, so watching Tiffany like this, bowing at the grave of the martyred bird, seeing her from up here doing that, well, it seems a second chance to pay my respects, so I bow my head, too.

There's a cardinal calling nearby, the benediction sung.

"How's the female?" She walks to the place where we can see each other. I sit up, try to sound alert.

"Okay," I answer, glancing over to the old leaf nest where Delores is still sleeping. She's been there all day, exhausted from all her work from the previous nights, I'm sure.

"I read up on them since I saw you," Tiffany tells me.

"Oh? Left your bugs for a bit?" I reply, teasing her a little.

"Yeah, well, I had a few hours to spare."

I wait to hear her report.

"The average weight of an owl's egg is about two ounces, and they're about two inches wide and two inches long. The incubation period averages about thirty-three days. And the owls vary in size, tend to be smaller on the west coast."

"That's what I read, too," I respond. "Hollywood diet," I add, trying to be funny. "Thin is in."

"Right," she replies, without a laugh, making me think she really doesn't get my humor.

"Do you know how long they've been there?"

I shake my head and try counting the number of days I have been in the loblollies but it's all running together now, days, nights, visits ... "More than a couple of weeks, I would say."

"So, you might see them born?"

I had not actually thought of this, bearing witness to great horned fledglings, something I've never seen. As I think about it I feel excited at first but then immediately there is sadness. Delores having to bear the weight of being a single parent, tending to them alone, guarding the nest, feeding them, alone, it's a sobering thought, and it draws me back to the pain in my arm and the ache in my chest.

"I guess I will," I answer.

"Oh, I have some other things for you," she notes.

I watch as she walks over to her backpack that she had dropped on the ground. I knew about the pillow and water because Charlene had commented on it before she left.

She pulls out a strap and something I can't really make out.

"It's a flashlight for your head."

And it is.

"Wow, okay," I respond, wondering if Tiffany thinks I come down after the sun sets and forage through the woods like the nocturnals.

"You can wear it and read at night. I used it when my sister was home and made me turn off the light when she was going to sleep. We shared a bed and she always wanted it quiet and dark."

I guess it makes more sense than I first thought. "Thanks, Tiffany."

"What do you do now when it's dark?"

"I have a lantern," I explain.

"Oh," she replies, sounding a little dejected.

"But that headlight is a great idea. The lantern doesn't really give me a focused view. I can't read by it," I say, hoping this raises her spirit. Tiffany needs more than a little encouragement.

"Well, you can use it if you want; it's okay if you don't." She places it in the bucket with the other things she's brought.

"It's perfect," I say, mustering up all the enthusiasm I can in my fatigued and feverish state. "Really. Thank you."

"Okay," she says softly, and it's easy to see that something's bothering the vice president of the science club.

"Do you need help with studying?"

"No, I'm ready for the test."

"Okay."

There is a long pause; I almost fall to sleep.

"I got accepted at Lenior Community College," she says, startling me.

"Oh, well, that's good, right?" I can't recall which two-year school she was most interested in.

She hesitates. "They have good science labs."

"Well, there you go," I respond, feeling my energy draining.

"Yep, there I go," she says.

My eyelids are so heavy, my body so fatigued that I drifted off and don't even know for sure when Tiffany left. When I awoke she was gone and the bucket, filled with supplies, was at the bottom of the tree, the rope tied tight, ready for me to pull.

Thirty-Three

It's strange. This place at night. The sounds. The silence. The black sky dotted with so many stars.

It was slow going, but I was able to bring up the bucket from Tiffany with my good arm. There were protein bars, water, the small camping pillow, and her special gift.

I attach the reading lamp over my head and turn it on, but casting light around every time I move feels intrusive to what I now know is home to so many. My being here has already caused so much damage to their protective shelter; I think I need to honor the darkness instead of trying to break it.

I've had more than a couple doses of antibiotics and I think I'm better. I still feel feverish, unsettled; my ankle hurts like crazy and I still can't wear my shoe, but I no longer feel as if I need to talk to Jim about my funeral plans. I'm confident that some progress has been made.

I punch up the pillow Tiffany brought and spread the blanket over me, feeling more comfortable than I've been in days. I am very glad to have the little camping accessory, a soft square of polyester fill and foam to lay my head on, and I remind myself to tell her that when she comes back.

Delores is out and about. I've watched her come and go several times now. She found one meal, a small rabbit, but maybe she's still working to fill a storehouse or maybe she's just out looking for information, trying to find the details of what happened to her mate, or searching for a new one.

I wonder how she knows what to do. How does an owl understand the connection between a missing mate and a new requirement to secure her own food? And when does it happen? The first night when she doesn't get dinner? The first few hours without return calls? When did Delores understand she is all on her own?

I close my eyes, listen to the night breeze rustling the dead leaves along the ground. I hear a few scurrying animals, see a few flashes of white eyes, raccoons and possum more than likely. I think they've gotten used to me now, or maybe that's just what I want to imagine. Maybe what I really want is to think I've blended in, been accepted. Probably I'm just being tolerated. After all, what else are they going do? I don't think any of any of the animals I've seen or encountered are big enough to run me off.

There are a lot of black bears in these parts, a healthy population, and they could move me out. In fact, I'm surprised I've not had one of them rooting around the trees, mothers with babies in tow, but maybe it's still a bit early. Maybe they're still sleeping in their caves or secret hiding places or maybe they've been warned by the others in this neighborhood to stay away. Humans are their only predators in Jones County, and there are plenty of other places for them to roam.

The deer are fairly active in the wee morning hours. They pass beneath me, with their tender twitching ears, their light careful grazing and tight-knit families; but if they know I'm here, they are not afraid. They walk right under me, never stopping to peer above. They're lucky, I suppose, living in a stand of trees without a recent history of hunters. They have no stored memory of snipers above their heads. They don't think to raise their eyes.

The Garvers, the family who owned this land for as long as I've known, about five hundred acres in all, used to permit hunting. My dad told me that on the opening day of hunting season, Mr. Garver gave out a two-hundred-dollar reward for the biggest kill. There was a community cookout with all kinds of food and entertainment. Apparently, Mr. Garver loved to take photographs of the prize trophy. It was a kind of badge of pride, Dad said, and Jones County men loved to hunt here for deer and turkey, even quail. And then a boy, Jacob, was born to the Garver family, and after his birth the Garvers immediately prohibited anymore hunting on their property.

Jacob was my father's age and he was born with some damage to his brain, something that happened during the delivery. He died when he was ten, but the story goes that when they brought him home from the hospital, they soon learned the sound of gunfire frightened him, made his screams unbearable. So they put up the NO TRESPASSING signs, putting an end to the annual hunting contests and community dinners.

Ten years later when Jacob went into a coma and never came out, Mrs. Garver wouldn't allow her husband to change things. Whether it was the grief of losing her son, the gunshots reminding her of what had been taken from her or her own unrevealed dislike of hunting, she forbade her husband to permit shooting anywhere on the property. She wouldn't even allow target practice at the edge of the farm.

The Garvers had a daughter, Teenie; she's the one who eventually sold the farm to Hatch and Brownfield. She moved to Raleigh, married a senator, and never came back to live in Jones County. She was three or four years younger than Jacob, maybe, and she was petite, hence the name, and smart and comely, or so Dad always liked to say. And he said she wanted out of this place, told people there was too much sorrow in the tobacco fields, too much hurt in the farmhouse.

A few years before her parents died, she picked them up in a rented van and moved them into a nursing home in Wake County. She left the house exactly as it was, refusing to rent it or the land for farming. The Garvers lived maybe only three years in the facility, and when they died, months apart, Teenie sold all five hundred acres to Thomas Brownfield, never even giving anybody else a chance to bid.

Dwayne said it was an arrangement that had been in the works for years, that he saw the paperwork at the bank after Mr. and Mrs. Garver went to the nursing home. He said nothing could be finalized until they were both dead because of issues concerning Mr. Garver's will, but that as soon as both were buried and gone, the land was Teenie's to do with as she wanted. And what she wanted, apparently, was to sell it to Hatch and Brownfield.

I recall Dwayne also mentioned that her husband, the senator, helped tweak a few bills on behalf of the development Brownfield was planning. As I think back about this, something else suddenly comes to mind. Why is it that I never hear anything about Mr. Brownfield's reaction to what I've done?

I know about Hatch and his plans to have me committed. I think those guys from the other night were paid by him or at least encouraged by him to come out here. But I never hear anything about Mr. Brownfield, the senior of the two partners.

This puts me in mind of Charlene's last comments that they've moved onto another project. I punch up my pillow and think that with all the time already spent waiting for the Garvers to die, and with all that needed to be done to buy this property, it seems improbable that they're suddenly uninterested in how I'm holding things up.

This thought gives my pulse the slightest rise and I find myself listening even closer to the sounds of this night. I am suddenly more afraid than Charlene, and for reasons I can't explain I look over to the edge of the forest, in the area of the large black willow tree, where I saw the man with the binoculars standing a few days ago. There's no one there, but I have a weird feeling I'm being watched.

I am not so sure those crows won't be back.

Thirty-Four

"Well, hello, my little chickadee!"

I feel much better today. The infection is clearing up. The swelling in my arm has gone down. My ankle is strong. I think I have finally come out of the woods; metaphorically, of course.

"Hey, Katie." It's Lilly Carol.

I slide over to the end of the board and let my legs hang down. I'm happy to see her and I'm looking for Ray. I'm happy to see him, too.

"Hey there, you." It's Charlene. She's driven Lilly Carol out to see me on one of the Forest Service ATVs.

"Well, hey, Charlene? What's going on?" I try not to sound disappointed.

Lilly smiles. "I got to ride in the mule."

"I see that." I wave at Charlene.

She waves back. "We were in the neighborhood and just thought we'd stop by and check on the pines before heading back to the station. Need to check for tree damage," she says with a wink.

This is code for *I've taken the four wheeler out for personal reasons* and means of course that I shouldn't mention to anybody else that she was driving an unauthorized Forest Service vehicle.

"Tree patrol," I reply with a smile.

"Yes ma'am," Charlene responds, stepping out of the ATV.

"And speaking of work, how is that invasive non-native plant maintenance project going? You and Phil doing okay?"

"Phil." And she rolls her eyes which makes Lilly Carol laugh. "It's fine. It's the fine citizens of Jones County who are driving me crazy."

"Yes?" I wait.

"Even though I have explained more than once that it will bring down the trees it seems as if the ladies at the Methodist Church are mad that we're yanking the wisteria from the oaks near the library." Charlene is taking out a bag from the rear of the vehicle. I think she's brought me a change of clothes.

"Your sister has started a petition to stop the project and I think maybe she and the other Methodist women are planning a prayer meeting on the library grounds."

"Well, there's one reason for quitting your job and sitting in a tree," I reply. "And she's not my sister," I say, referring to Marge.

"I brought your mail," she tells me, holding up the bag. "And another sweatshirt, pair of socks."

"Mail?" I hadn't even thought about mail. I haven't thought about bills or withering houseplants or starting the Jeep so the battery won't die. I suppose my power has already been turned off by now, probably the water, too, and the yard must be a mess.

She shrugs. "Yep, mail. I thought you might enjoy reading your magazines and the Forest Service newsletter. There's a good article this month about the geochemical reference standards that I think you might find interesting."

"We're such nerds, you know," I say.

"Yes, but we're well-informed nerds," she replies.

"Daddy's at work so Charlene is spending the day with me," Lilly Carol pipes up.

There's a twinge of remorse; I should be spending the day with her. Everybody, it seems, is picking up my slack.

"And how lucky for you," I reply, trying to sound pleased.

"I brought you something else," she smiles. "A surprise."

"A surprise?" This piques my curiosity.

"Yep, and I drew you some pictures," she says, and I watch as she slides around in the seat of the all-terrain vehicle.

"Well, it is almost as good as my birthday," I tell her.

"And we stopped and got you a hamburger." Charlene holds up a small bag.

"What! Maybe it is my birthday!"

And she laughs.

"Did you go through the drive-thru with the mule?"

"No, Charlene drove the truck."

"Oh, right."

I move over on my stand and to where I stash the buckets. I think about asking Charlene to empty the toilet but decide I'll wait until she comes by herself. I lower the supply bucket and watch as she stuffs inside the bag of mail, another brown bag—the surprise, I suppose— the extra clothes, more bottles of water, and the small white paper bag from Johnny's, the hamburger joint on Main Street.

Lilly leans out of the ATV and hands her the pages of drawings; Charlene places them inside and then gives me a thumbs-up signal that I can pull the bucket up.

"Wow, this is a lot of stuff," I say, the bucket heavy from everything they've brought. I strain a little because of my arm.

Charlene watches as I pull it all the way up and then takes her seat in the driver's side. She reaches in the back in the cooler, pulls out some water. She opens a bottle and hands it to Lilly and then takes one out for herself.

"These are beautiful," I say to Lilly Carol as I unfold the pictures she has drawn. I leave the mail in the bucket along with the clothes and food. I hold up the first one.

"*Cyanocitta cristata*," she says, sounding the words perfectly. "It's a passerine bird from the Corvidae family."

"Otherwise known as the blue jay," I respond, proudly.

"And this one?" I ask, pointing to the second picture, a robin.

"*Turdus migratorius*," she answers, pronouncing the words slowly. "Passeriformes, the family Turdidae."

"You are an aviary rock star!" I tell her.

"Open the bag," Lilly Carol shouts.

"This one?" And I hold up the small one, the one from Johnny's.

"No, the other one," she responds.

I pull out the other bag and look inside. It's a suet, a large seed cake, homemade, I think.

"Wow, how great. Did you and Charlene make it this morning?" I don't really know how long they've had together today.

"We made it last night," Lilly Carol answers.

"Ray did it," Charlene tells me, for clarification, I suppose.

"We bought all the ingredients from the grocery store yesterday and we made one especially for the woodpeckers," the little girl added.

"That's great, Chickie. I will put it right up above me and I know I will soon have some very special guests."

I see the big grin plastered across her face. She thinks this will bring the red-cockaded to me.

There is a pause as I turn the suet over in my hands. I am touched by the gift, touched that Ray would help her with it.

"I'm sorry, but we can't really stay long," Charlene tells me; I know she has to get the mule back to the office and out of sight before somebody sees her. She's taken a great risk coming out here with Lilly Carol riding in it.

"Oh, sure," I respond, putting the suet back in the bag and moving closer to the edge of the stand. "Thank you for everything. Thank you for the mail and the clothes, and lunch. Thank you for the pictures," I add. "And the bird food; that was a great idea."

The little girl nods and I watch as Charlene puts the ATV in reverse, backing away from where I sit.

Thirty-Five

"Ms. Davidson."

I hear my name from below. I've flipped through the magazines and now I'm reading the Forest Service newsletter that Charlene brought. She's right, the article about the geochemical reference standards is interesting; reading it makes me a little homesick for my job. I miss the science. I put down the reading material and slide to the edge. I can't see who's calling me. I stand up.

"Ms. Davidson."

I look up the path and then around the trees.

"Ms. Davidson, I'm over here."

And I turn to where I think the voice is coming from and there's a young man standing beneath a red maple, about twenty yards away from my perch. I can't tell from this far away but he appears young and not anybody I recognize.

"Yes? Who's there?" I ask.

"Ward Thomas," he answers.

I don't place the name.

"I write a blog for an environmental website. You don't know me. I live in New Bern."

"Okay," I respond, not sure why he's here or what he wants. "You can come closer," I tell him. "I'm not going to throw anything at you."

"Oh, all right," he replies and I watch him move under the loblollies.

"But step out some. Now I can't see you because of the branches."

He steps away and I get a good look at him.

He is young, a teenager, I think, and he's wearing a bright yellow shirt, white pants. He has black hair and he's thin, small, reminds me of a goldfinch.

"Can you see me now?" he asks, bending and looking.

"I can. What can I do for you?"

He scratches his neck and twitches a bit.

"I'd like to write about you," he answers.

"Yeah? Why?" I sit down.

He shrugs. "Oh, I don't know, I guess I think you're interesting."

I shake my head. "Ward, I'm not interesting."

"Well, maybe what you're doing is interesting then," he says. "Living in a tree, that's interesting. I think my readers will want to know about you. I'd like to interview you."

"Okay."

"Okay?" He sounds surprised. "Does that mean I can ask you some questions?"

He sounds so tentative. He's not a goldfinch; he's much too nervous and fidgety for a goldfinch.

"Fire away."

He pulls a notebook from his back pocket, a narrow one like the newspaper reporters on television shows and movies use. He clears his throat.

"How long have you been up there?"

I count back the days; but truthfully, I don't know. "Ask me another one."

He glances up in my direction like he doesn't know what to do next.

"I can't remember exactly," I explain.

He nods. "Um, what are you hoping to accomplish by staying?"

It's a good question but I shake my head to that one, too. "Don't know."

"Is the loblolly pine a species we should be concerned about?"

This one I can answer. "Ward, we should be concerned about all the pines, all the maples, all the oaks, all the willows. The trees need us to be concerned."

He nods as he writes. "Would you call yourself controversial?"

That's an interesting question and I truly don't think I've ever thought of myself in that light. "No," I reply.

"Have you ever done anything like this?"

"Like climb a tree and hang out?"

He smiles and nods.

"I lived in my car once," I confess. "When I was in college I spray-painted an obscenity on a big sign marketing pesticides." I don't tell him that I was one of three who did it and that I went along mostly because I had a crush on David Larkin, a senior biology major, the one who organized the graffiti party.

Ward writes this down.

"Has there been any surprises since you've been up there?"

I think about the past few days, the nights. I glance over at Delores's place, but I don't want to tell that story. "You're a surprise," I answer.

He writes that down, too, and I think that maybe I ought to set him up with Tiffany. Neither of them seems to get my humor.

"Will you come down if they promise not to develop this property?"

That's another good question. What will bring me down, I wonder. "Maybe," I answer.

"What are your demands?"

"Demands?"

"Yeah, don't you have a list of demands for the landowner?"

"No, not really." I can't say as I thought of this. "I'm not involved in kidnapping," I tell him. "I don't really have demands."

He shrugs, writes that down, too.

"Is your family concerned?"

I think about Dwayne but then realize he really isn't family any more. He's ex-family. I just shake my head.

When he doesn't hear a verbal response he glances up and I shake my head again so he can see.

"How do you get anything to eat?"

"Friends bring me stuff," I answer, looking over at the hamburger wrapper.

"Do you have a sponsor?"

"A sponsor?"

He stops writing and looks back in my direction. "Yeah, like someone paying you to be up there, somebody you're endorsing?"

"No, there's no sponsor. No money has exchanged hands with anyone." I pause. "No endorsements. But maybe after this blog, well, who's to say?"

Again, nothing.

"Why haven't you been arrested yet?"

Now, there's something I wasn't expecting.

"I don't know, Ward. I guess you'll have to ask the powers that be that one."

He flips a page in his notebook. "Well, actually I did."

"Yeah?" I wait to hear what he learned.

"I asked the sheriff."

I flinch.

"Do you want to know what he said?"

I don't answer.

"You're related to him, aren't you? He's your father, right?"

"Ward, you have certainly done your homework. Yes, the sheriff is my father."

"Right." He glances at his notebook. "He said that you're related to him does not stand in the way of the job he is commissioned to do as sheriff and that he sees this as merely attention-seeking behavior."

I don't respond.

Ward hesitates; I don't know what he's waiting for. He's just watching. Finally, he clears his throat. "Do you think he will arrest you? Are you just doing this for attention?"

I hear someone singing, coming in our direction, and I have never been so happy to hear a Lutheran pastor arrive.

Thirty-Six

"Well, what is going on here?" Jim is smiling. He's not in his pastoral get-up today. It's Saturday; he always takes off on Saturdays.

"Ward here was doing an interview; but now he's not," I answer. "Thank you, Ward," I say and watch as he hesitates, makes no noise at all, and then just flits off.

I wait until I'm sure he is gone and then sit down. "I hate the show-offs," I say to Jim. "The ones with all the bright feathers, the ones that somehow think they're better than the other guys at the feeders, the plain ones, the average joes. Did you know hummingbirds are actually the most aggressive species? Same with blue jays and cardinals?" I pause. "All that color. Show-offs."

"Well . . . well . . . isn't somebody in a *foul* mood?"

I don't respond even though I know he's trying to use the word *foul* as a way to make me lighten up.

Jim takes a seat beneath the tree.

"How's Mama?" I ask.

"She will probably not qualify for recertification; the hospice nurse told me yesterday. It seems she's improved in the last few days."

"Is that right?" I try not to sound sarcastic.

"So it is," he replies.

"If they don't recertify her, who's going to look after her?"

"Bernard has offered to come."

"Bernard?" This surprises me. "He can't leave his job in Charleston."

"He says he will, for me, for Mama."

This guy, this selflessness, I can't understand.

"Well, what does Mama think of that?" I don't really know how Jim explains the relationship when Bernard is with the two of them.

"I haven't told her."

Of course, you haven't, I think but don't say because I don't need to.

"Just stop," he says, reading my thoughts. "I'm not going to let Bernard quit his job and come be a nurse to my mother. Although . . ." he hesitates. "It is a beautiful offer."

"Beautiful, but unfair," I say, deciding that's it for my two cents worth.

"I know," he responds. "I've got a few weeks to consider my options. The church board has agreed to give me family leave if I need it."

"That's nice."

"It is," he agrees. "But the job is probably the only thing keeping me sane right now."

"It does help to have a place to go, doesn't it?"

He nods.

"Why did you bring her here, Jim?" This is the question I have wanted to ask for days.

"Why?" My question seems to stump him.

"Yeah, why? You could have gotten a home health nurse to check on her in Charleston, pay somebody to stay with her. You could have even put her in a facility."

"I couldn't do that," he answers.

"But why not?"

"Because she's my mother."

"And she's been terrible to you," I reply, remembering all the awful things he told me about her when he was a boy, the way she taunted and punished him, her unique ways of being cruel.

"I've forgiven her for all that," he tells me. "She's old and frail; she's not that same woman she was when I was a boy."

"She still seems to have the same hold on you as she did then. And you forgave her?" He never told me that. "Did she ask to be forgiven? Did she even admit to the things she did?"

He doesn't answer because of course, she didn't.

"I forgave her for my own well-being, not for hers. I had to forgive her, had to let all that stuff go or I'd end up . . ." And he stops.

"You'd end up how?" I move closer to the edge. "You'd end up how, Jim? Like me? Like a crazy person standing in a tree?"

He shakes his head like he doesn't plan to answer; but it's too late. This cage door is open. "How long are you going to punish your father for the sins of your mother?"

"Wow . . . what?" I feel the heat rise to my face.

"Your father, Kate. Why are you mad at him? What did he ever do to you except try to take care of you when his wife left? When your mother left? How long are you going to stay mad at the man?"

"I'm not mad at him anymore." Although hearing the quote from Ward's little interview didn't help matters.

"No, but you won't see him. You won't talk to him. He's the only family you got."

"Well, I didn't really think that before, since I've always thought of you as my family. I guess I was wrong about that."

He peers up at me and I back out of sight.

"We are family," he says softly.

I stay hidden.

"But you brought this up, you're the one who always tells me to push my mother out of my life, let her spend her last years alone. You're the one who thinks that if I punish her the way she punished me I will somehow be released from all that history, all that drama. But it doesn't work that way; if anybody should know that, it should be you."

"I'm perfectly happy with the way my life is at the moment."

"Yeah?"

"Yes," I answer.

"Then what is this you're doing?"

"What?"

"This little tree-climbing exercise. Your divorce. Your unwillingness to speak to your father. Your refusal to forge a relationship with Ray."

"Ray?" I almost wish the goldfinch hadn't left. "What's Ray got to do with this?"

"Kate, don't sit up there and pretend you don't know that Ray has feelings for you."

"Ray doesn't have feelings for me," I say adamantly. "What has he said to you?"

"He hasn't said anything to me, but I'm not blind. I just don't know how you don't see it."

"We're not talking about Ray."

"No, you're right. We're talking about forgiveness and about your father and my mother. And it seems to me that neither of us has it exactly right, so let's just let it be."

I don't respond. What else is there to say?

"I got to go work on my sermon. I'll come back Monday."

"Fine," I reply, and I don't even watch him when he gets up to leave.

Thirty–Seven

"What's this, a lover's quarrel?"

Who is that? I never heard anybody else arrive. I glance around, move over to the other side of the stand, trying to get a better view.

"You and the priest? Is there some disagreement?"

I step out on a limb.

"Maybe he's not happy that his lover climbed a tree? Maybe he's threatened by such a public display?"

"Who's there?" I ask, straining to see who is standing under the trees.

Wait. I know that voice. That screechy vulture voice.

"Hello, Kate."

The lammergeier is back. She moves to where I can see her, smiles, and then steps behind a tree.

"Hello, Tonya."

"You're still here," she says, matter of factly.

"And you're still trying to think of a way to get a byline."

"No, not a byline really."

"No? Then what? A check? A job?"

"That's cute," she replies.

"I thought you had filed your story and gone away for good."

"No, but I'm close to being finished. Just a few more details to add."

"And you're thinking the lover's quarrel is the best way to go?" I stand near the trunk of the loblolly, out of her line of sight. If she can hide, so can I.

"It's got potential," she answers.

Then she steps out, giving me a good look.

She's wearing the same black overcoat, buttoned up this time so I can't see her clothes. She has on a different scarf, different boots, but there's no disguising herself, she's still the same bird.

"There's no lover's quarrel, Tonya," I tell her, keeping my place hidden.

"No?"

"No."

"No pastoral concern for your well-being? No frustration with your unwillingness to come out of the woods?"

"Nope, none of that."

She is quiet, and I watch as she glances around the loblollies, around the pine tree stand.

"I heard there was an accident out here."

"Yeah, what kind?"

"A shooting."

I rub my arm, the wound healing but still sore.

"I heard you were injured."

Where is this vulture getting her news?

"Not really, no," I tell her.

"An owl is dead."

I glance over to Delores but she's on her nest in the tree cavity, out of view. I'd like to keep it that way.

"Tonya, there's really no story of interest to report to you. I don't know why you keep coming around."

"Well, see that's where you're wrong. I think there is a story of interest. I think there's a great story."

"Yeah, how so?"

"I'm not quite sure yet," she answers.

This makes me chuckle. I want to ask her if she's acquainted with the goldfinch since their styles seem to be so similar, birds of a feather, so to speak. But I don't ask her since I don't want to have any more of a conversation than I have to.

"I'm sorry, Tonya, I'm really not that interesting. The fact that I've climbed a tree and stayed put is not all that interesting. Surely, there's some public official skimming off the top of a county budget or some great celebrity diet to write about. Some sex scandal, perhaps?"

"Well, that's certainly a possibility," she responds and then she's quiet again and I lose her through the branches.

I hear her walking around and I find her again. She stops at the grave of the great horned owl. I watch her kneel down.

"Get away from there," I tell her. "Leave him alone." And I think the lammergeier might just dig him up, suck his bones dry.

"Would you come down and stop me?" She peers up through the branches, catches my eye.

"I'll throw my toilet bucket on you. It didn't get emptied today and I've got a great shot from where I'm standing."

She grins and stands up, steps around the trunk of the loblolly.

"Do you know the men who did it?"

"How do we know they're men? I've met some pretty hotheaded women in my time. Any fool can fire a weapon, doesn't require a Y chromosome."

"No, they were men. I read the police report."

"I didn't file a police report."

"No; the deputy definitely wrote a report. No charges were made, no arrests, but there's still a report."

"I didn't recognize any of them," I say, deciding to take another strategy. Maybe if I answer her questions truthfully, she'll leave sooner.

"You and the pastor, have you been friends a long time?"

"Yes, a very long time," I answer.

"And he's never married."

"Nope."

"But you have. Been married, I mean."

"I have indeed. But you already have all that information."

"Yes."

"So, is that it? You got any more questions or are you satisfied with what you have?"

She squints and looks at me again.

"Because I've got a couple of questions for you."

"Yeah?"

"Yeah. I do."

"Then for heaven's sake, fire away."

"How long have you been working for Mr. Brownfield?"

If the question surprised her, she didn't show it. She sticks her notebook in her coat pocket and clears her throat. "I think I've got enough for my story now, but you know, I'll bring it by before it runs." She pauses.

"How's that? I'll break my rules and actually let you take a look at it before giving it to the publisher. And then, you can decide if I'm missing something."

"That'll be just fine. You be careful walking out. The woods can be dangerous if you aren't paying attention."

"Oh, I'm paying attention, Kate. I'm paying very close attention." And she turns away and, like a bird startled by an intruder, she's gone.

Thirty-Eight

"But isn't that anthropomorphism?"

Tiffany is back. The twins went to a birthday party so she has the afternoon off. After the visits I just had from Jim and the vulture, I'm glad to see a friendly face. She takes a seat on the ground beneath the trees.

"Well, I suppose defining it as inventive could be called anthropomorphic; but what would you call it? She recognized that she was not able to get the meat with a straight wire so she used her beak and bent into a hook. And then she stuck it in the vertical tube, pulled up the tiny bucket and had a very good supper. She was forward thinking and resourceful."

Tiffany just read the report about Betty, the New Caledonian crow that was witnessed making a tool. It was a research study from

2002 and it was groundbreaking. No one had ever reported the craft of toolmaking by birds until this study.

"I just know Mr. Billingsley, the biology teacher, is always warning us not to think that animals have emotions or human inclinations. He's always showing us those videos you see on Facebook and YouTube of the cute animals and telling us what we're seeing is not friendship or despair, that we're just humans trying to pretend what we see and feel is seen and felt by all animals, that we're ascribing our emotions onto creatures who do not have the ability to emote."

"Todd Billingsley is a biology teacher?" I remember Todd Billingsley. We were in the same class. He played tuba in the marching band, ate lunch by himself out in the parking lot. It's funny; I don't ever remember Todd liking science. He sat in the back of the classroom, never had much to say.

"I don't know his first name, just Mr. Billingsley."

"That's too weird," I say, thinking of Todd trying to walk through the doors at school while he was carrying the tuba. He must have broken the glass panels once a week. He was a clumsy adolescent, hard to imagine him as a teacher.

"Forget about Mr. Billingsley," Tiffany says. "What do you think? Do animals feel sadness? Is what we see between two monkeys cuddling, affection, or just a means of finding warmth?"

I glance over to Delores's nest, think about the conversation I had with Jim when he suggested that the reason I liked the birds was because I was envious of them, envious that they didn't feel emotional pain. I think about the magpies and their funerals.

"I don't know, Tiffany. Sometimes I think I've got it all figured out regarding animals. I've studied birds all my life; but they still surprise me with their behaviors, how much they seem to be like us, seem to share a mutual experience with us; but I don't know if they feel the same emotions we do or not." *I honestly don't.*

She sighs. I can hear her from up here. She wanted an answer.

I slide closer to the edge.

"What do you think of when you think of loyalty?" I ask.

She shrugs. "A dog."

"And what about valor and pride?"

"An eagle?"

"Yep. And agility, strength?"

"Tigers, cougars, the big cats." She looks up and smiles. "Courage, a lion. Evil, a snake. Freedom, a bird. I get it."

"It's hard to shake those anthropomorphic glasses. Even the most rigid scientists that I've ever come across get stumped from time to time. Like Betty the crow. Nobody saw that coming. Everybody knew birds, especially crows were smart, but nobody figured they could display the quality of insight and know-how to make a tool. I mean, that's not really an emotion but it's certainly a quality humans thought animals were incapable of displaying. So maybe Mr. Billingsley is simply trying to convince himself about animals and human emotions because he prefers believing that animals don't have emotions. Maybe it makes him feel superior. But in reality, nobody really knows for sure. It's like Thich Nhat Hanh says, "If you tell me you already understand, I feel a little pessimistic. If you say you do not understand, I feel more optimistic."

"Tick Not . . . who?"

"Thich Nhat Hanh, he's Buddhist, smart."

"So, you're saying that being certain about something is not always best."

"I'm saying that science opens up a world of 'not understanding' and that if you need solid answers, complete proof to verify your hypothesis, then maybe you should go into math or accounting."

"Two plus two will always equal four."

"It's that way for a mathematician, yes," I respond.

"So, you think animals are more like humans than most scientists want to say."

"I just don't think that a crow making a hook is just following some random instinct. That took insight. And after losing its mate, an owl that no longer displays the same social behavior as it did before the death, no longer sits outside its roost watching the activity in the forest every evening at dusk, or the fact she continues to call for her mate even though he does not answer, may in fact be based in emotions."

"You think Delores feels grief?"

I look back over at the nest, Delores roosting with her back to us and nod. "I didn't at first, but I know now it's because I didn't want to. I absolutely believe now that she knows he's gone, but how that translates into emotions, I don't know. I don't think we'll ever know."

"Well, this all kind of disappointing to me," Tiffany says.

I turn to her. "Why's that?"

"Well, I can't figure out people at all. I think Stanley likes me, but he's just using me. I don't have a clue as to why the popular girls are so mean to each other, and my sister tells me I'm clueless about how to flirt, so I just thought going into biology, studying science, would be easier. I guess I've been wrong."

"No, you've not been wrong. Studying animals and animal behavior does help you understand people. You're heading in the right direction, I think. Still, I have to say, I've been doing this a long time, and I certainly don't understand people. I don't even understand myself half the time."

She nods but a cloud blows across her face.

"What?"

She shakes her head. "It's nothing."

"What, Tiffany?"

"I just thought the older you got, the more you know, that things make more sense, but you're telling me that's not true. From your view, it seems like the older you get the less you actually know."

"Yes, young grasshopper, I would say that is exactly how I see it from my view."

"Grasshopper?"

"Oh, you're so young. 'Grasshopper,' it's from a television show. The mentor calls his student that."

"Huh." She's thinking, I guess.

Tiffany twirls a strand of her hair; she still looks troubled.

"What's really going on?"

She shrugs.

"No, what is it? What can't you figure out about yourself?"

She takes a breath, crosses her legs at the ankles, leans back on her elbows. "The prom is coming up in a couple of weeks."

"Okay." I never went to my proms, never wanted to. "And?"

"And nobody's invited me."

"Do you want to go?"

She looks up at me as if she's afraid she won't have the right answer. "None of the other girls in the science club are going."

"That's not what I asked."

She shrugs.

"It's your last chance, right?"

She nods.

"Well, if you want to go, you should go."

She shakes her head. "I don't really know if I want to. I know I don't want to go by myself."

"Then ask somebody to go with you?"

She looks at me like I'm a hawk in a hummingbird's nest.

"You can do that, you know? You don't have to wait to be asked. You can do the asking."

"I don't know," she says quietly. "I wouldn't know who to ask at school."

"Does it have to be somebody in your class?"

She shakes her head. "They just can't be over eighteen."

"Do you know anybody outside of school that might want to go, somebody not over the age limit?"

I can see the wheels turning. There is somebody, I can tell.

"He lives in Trenton. We met at the science fair. He's homeschooled."

"Bingo. There you go. You got his number?"

She nods.

"You got a pink frilly dress?"

She laughs. "I got my sister's."

"Then what are you doing out here in the woods? You know what you want. Get home and make the call. Show that homeschooled boy what he's been missing."

She stands. "Yeah?"

"Heck, yeah."

She turns to walk away then turns back.

"Thanks, Kate."

"You're welcome, Tiffany."

She stands there like she's got something else to say.

I wait.

"I know this might not be scientific to say." Her face is a bright happy light. "Mr. Billingsley would kill me if he heard it. But I feel just like a bird, flying, I mean. I think this must be exactly how it feels."

I watch the little fledgling leave the nest, scared and exhilarated and brave, .

"I think so, too. Now go!"

She nods and waves, and I've never seen the vice president of the Jones County High School Science Club move so fast. She practically flew out of these trees.

Thirty-Nine

"I wasn't sure if I should tell you. That's why I didn't come yesterday; I was trying to decide if I should let you know."

"Well, of course, you should tell me; I want to know these things."

Charlene is my only visitor today. It's Sunday; I guess I shouldn't be surprised not to have any other company. I think the novelty of a woman in a tree is starting to wear off. Most folks aren't so interested any longer. Still, I think I was hoping for someone. And somehow, the news Charlene brings is not what I wanted to hear, either.

Ray's ex-wife showed up Friday night.

"She was there when I took Lilly Carol home," she tells me. She's sitting under the trees in the chair Jim left. She's wearing shorts and a sweatshirt. She brought me a milkshake and has one of her own. We're sipping them while she tells me the latest gossip. She started with news about the Forest Service having to cut some of the work force, then moved on to Eugene's mother having a facelift, and has just now gotten to this little tidbit.

"Just out of the blue?" I ask. I never saw this coming, never.

She shrugs. "I guess."

"Did she say where she's been?"

"Not to me." She takes a big slurp from the shake.

"Well, how did he seem?"

"Surprised, I think."

Lonnie Marcus, home, back in Jones County. I can't stop shaking my head.

"Did she say anything to you?"

Charlene pauses; she's thinking, I guess. "Just hello. She was pretty focused on her daughter at the time."

Her daughter, I think. Lilly Carol is Lonnie's daughter. I shove the straw into the milkshake, try to stir it a bit, pull it out, shove it in. I feel Charlene watching me. "What?" I ask.

She shrugs. "I just wasn't sure how you'd take it."

"Take it?"

"Yeah. You never really liked Lonnie."

"Why do you say that?"

"Because it's true. You must have told me every day after Ray married her that you thought he was making a mistake, that you didn't like her."

"Well, that was a long time ago," I answer in my defense.

"Not that long."

"Well, how did Lilly Carol seem?" This must be really confusing for the little girl. And what if Lonnie shows back up only to leave again? I shake my head again, shove the straw in the cup.

"Surprised, happy . . . I couldn't really tell."

"Hmm."

"Lonnie cried when she saw her."

"As right she should."

"See?"

"What?"

"You don't like her."

She's right. I don't like her at all. And not just because of abandoning her family; she was just too happy when I first met her, too perky, too clingy to Ray. He always told me he didn't like clingy girls; I don't trust perky people. "She's just . . ."

"Too perky," Charlene interrupts. "I remember."

"Yeah, well, she was."

"Well, she was also mostly manic when you saw her."

"Yeah, I know, the bipolar thing." I circle a finger beside my head, gesturing that she's crazy.

"I don't really think bipolar is a thing," she says, startling me.

I bring down my hand and place it in my lap, feeling chastised.

"Anyway, she's not so perky now," she adds.

"No?" And for whatever reason, this brings me a little comfort, but I don't smile or let on.

"She seemed nervous, a little beat down, I'd say." Charlene pauses, looks up at me, eye to eye. "I sort of felt sorry for her."

"Great," I say, not sure why.

"I know you don't like her, Kate, and I know you think she did wrong by walking out on her husband and daughter . . ."

"You think?" I ask, sounding bitter and I drink some milkshake because I really don't like that taste in my mouth.

"She has a mental illness. Cut her a little slack."

"Cut her a little slack? I don't begrudge her for her mental illness. I feel for her because of that; it's a terrible thing. But she could have seen a doctor here. She could have gotten her meds here. She didn't have to run off. She should have stayed home and been here for Ray and their daughter. Just because she's depressed or mentally ill doesn't give her the right to walk out on us."

"Us?"

"What?"

"You said, 'walk out on us.'" She sits up, tilts her head.

"No, I didn't." I'm sure I didn't.

"Yeah, you did. You said, 'just because she's depressed doesn't give her the right to walk out on us.'"

"Well, I don't think I did."

"Uh-huh." She sits back in her chair.

We don't talk for a while. A squirrel is running from tree to tree around Charlene and she watches him. I hear a warbler a couple of trees over.

"Is she staying?" I ask, breaking the silence.

"I don't know," she answers. "You'll have to ask Ray."

"I might not be able to do that," I say.

She looks up, waiting for more.

"I was sort of mean to him the last time he was here." And I start thinking about the days, counting back, and realize it's been almost a week since I saw him.

"I suspect he can take it," she replies, and I recall that was almost the same thing that Jim said after I made the confession to him.

Still, I'm not proud of my behavior, and I need to tell Ray so.

"Thanks, Charlene, for telling me. And you're right, I'm mixing my stuff up with Lilly Carol's stuff. I got my own abandonment issues that I need to keep to myself and not drag them all over everybody else's family reunions."

"Don't worry about it," she says, waving off the apology. "We're all just doing the best we can with what we got, right?" She smiles up at me.

"Right," I say. But I still feel awful.

Forty

Really, what do I care if Lonnie Marcus has come back to Maysville? What does it have to do with me?

I try focusing on a magazine Charlene brought, *Orion*, a nature journal, and particularly on an article by Sy Montgomery about an octopus. The writer was arguing about the very same issue Tiffany and I were discussing yesterday, only instead of birds and emotions, Montgomery was writing about the intelligence of the mollusk, an invertebrate. It was interesting, personal and touching, a lovely article, and I tried to stay with it, reading the same lines over and over. But I could not get Charlene's news out of my mind.

Lonnie Marcus is back.

I close the magazine and put it aside. I lie back on the stand and look into the branches above me, into the piece of sky that I have deemed as my very own. I watch the clouds like visitors, come and go, drift in and out of my little realm of vision.

He can't take her back, I think. But then, why can't he? She's the mother of his child. She's been sick, not negligent. It appears as if she's getting help, getting better. Maybe they'll pick right up where they left off.

Maybe he'll bring out those boxes of her things that she left, unpack them and return them to the shelves that they'll share once again, the blouses and skirts on the rack in the closet, her clothes on one side, his on the other. Maybe he'll put her hairbrush in that first drawer under the sink, the one she always used for her toiletries, bring out the His and Hers towels that somebody gave them for a wedding gift, hang them on the towel racks. Maybe he'll take his books from the nightstand drawer, making room for hers.

Maybe this is exactly what Ray wants, and more, what he needs. Lilly Carol has a family, has a mother and a father, her very own family, and I suppose it is a perfect homecoming and the perfect reunion.

Introducing the happy, reunited Marcus Family: Ray and Lonnie and Lilly Carol.

"I don't know" is what he said when I asked him years ago if he still loved her. It was two weeks after she left, and it appeared she wasn't coming home, that this time she was gone for good.

Lonnie had left and come back three times before. She'd get manic, buy things, take Lilly Carol, then just a little girl, and go shopping. She'd spend thousands of dollars on clothes and make-up and jewelry, all of which had to be returned. She and Ray would consequently fight about what she had done, fight about the money, about Lilly Carol. And then Lonnie would just pack up and leave, no note, no explanation.

She'd be gone a few days, hit a wall, and then end up calling Ray to come get her. And then, he'd bring her home and she would stay in bed for weeks. It was a crazy ride for them in the beginning and I wasn't really in the picture in their early years. I was on my own merry-go-round with work and dating and then marrying Dwayne and trying to manage my new little nest.

I called Ray when I heard she left the last time. I think Dwayne had found out about it at the bank. Somebody's brother knew his sister or her mother told his father. News travels in a small town, sometimes with twists and turns making it not completely reliable, but it travels just the same. So I called him, "just checking in," I told him, and the next day I met him for coffee and he explained the state of things. I asked if he'd take her back, if he loved her enough to take her back, and he claimed he didn't know.

"But that was like seven or eight years ago; how could he take her back now?" I ask the question out loud and then I look around to see if anybody heard me.

I've found that now that I'm up a tree I talk to myself more than I used to. Maybe this is how the real "crazy" starts. A person is alone for so long they start saying things out loud to just to remember how to have a conversation.

"Lonnie Fay," I say to the warbler sitting on the limb above me, "just showed up out of nowhere and wants to settle back into the little Marcus nest."

I don't really know Ray's ex-wife. I actually only met the woman a couple of times. She grew up in Raleigh, a city girl. Her family moved here after we were all out of school. And they moved right beside Ray's folks. And one weekend she came home from college and they met at the mailboxes and apparently fell in love. And then she got pregnant and they were married before I even knew they were dating. I didn't find out about them until I came home for the summer after my first internship with the Forest Service, and they were already on their honeymoon.

I had dropped my stuff off at home and driven right over to his house. I was excited to see him, tell him about my research, but I found out from his mother, Mrs. Marcus; she already had pictures from the wedding to show me. And I didn't see them all summer, not until Christmas, which is when I met Lonnie and found out that Ray was going to be a father.

After that, I just stayed away, took jobs out of state and didn't come home much. And then I got the job in Jones County, met Charlene and then married Dwayne, and then, well, Lonnie left and Ray started drinking, had the accident, and I stepped in to take care of Lilly Carol. And then, it was just the three of us sort of rolling along, days into months into years, doing it all together.

And now, Lonnie is back. The mother bird is back.

I close my eyes, drifting a little; when I open them again, the sun has dropped low in the horizon, and dusk has fallen. I look over to see if Delores is coming out; I haven't seen her just sit and watch from her perch like she used to, but for the first time since her mate was killed she's there at the nest. She finds me in the branches, peering at her, and she stares at me for the longest time.

I feel ashamed for what happened, responsible for what happened, and I keep looking away and then back at her. I don't know what to say or do, how to explain. And she never takes her eyes off me.

"I'm sorry," I say, to myself and to Delores. "I'm sorry about your husband's murder. I'm really, really sorry."

Delores just watches.

"Your eggs okay?"

She blinks.

"Can I do anything?"

She blinks again.

"I kept two feathers," I tell her. "It's against the law, but I kept them. I put them up there," I nod above me, the owl feathers stuck in the crook of the fat limb. "I kept them for you, in case you wanted them."

She doesn't move.

"He saved my life," I say, like she doesn't know what happened.

"He swooped in like some knight, no, like some brave bird, and saved me."

I turn away and I hear her flutter. She stands at the nest and shakes her wings a little and I notice she's looking above me now. Her line of vision slightly above my head.

I glance around and see what she sees.

The man who has been watching me for nights is standing just at the edge of the woods. I take out my binoculars and catch him following my every move.

Forty-One

I turn to Delores and she has moved further into the nest. She's no longer watching me or the intruder. She's leaving this to me. I look again at the edge of the woods and he's gone, but I just have this feeling that he'll be back. For some reason, I just think he's going to show up tonight. And this time I will be ready.

I glance around my stand, trying to decide what I should have close to me, what weapon I might use if he tries to climb up like the last guy, what I have that's most threatening, but I realize that I'm no better off than I was when the murder happened. I should have asked Charlene for a knife or something, but I was too messed up from the whole experience and didn't. Why didn't she offer me anything? It's odd that she was so worried about me before the incident but actually seems less so after it happened. Maybe she really does think that nobody will bother me again, but that seems terribly naïve.

Why isn't she concerned? But then I know I've caused her enough anxiety. She's probably just tired of worrying about me and really has left me to whatever happens, which is exactly what I told her do. I'm fine, I told her time and time again. Don't bring me a gun, I told her. So, she listened. I really am on my own out here, I realize.

I shake those thoughts of loneliness starting to creep into my mind and keep looking for what I can use as a weapon. I have the long-lens camera that could probably do damage with just the right swing, but that's an expensive means of defense that likely would only stun. I have Tiffany's bugs. I could smash that glass case on top of somebody. But with my arm still healing, I'm not sure I can lift and hold it long enough for the necessary force that would be needed to break it over a head.

An ink pen? Pen knife? Lantern? Nothing I have up here can protect me. Then out of the corner of my eye I see the rocks that Hatch's boys threw up here. I had just rolled them to a corner and stacked my clothes on top of them.

I slide over and pick them up, hold them in my hands. The four good-sized stones are plenty big enough to hit a target yet small enough that I can hold them in my right hand. I feel a rush, and I stick them in my pockets and then think about what else I have up here that I could throw at my enemy. I have a thermos and a phone that doesn't work, shoes, the buckets; I'm not as defenseless as I first thought.

And I have this view, I think. At least, I can see him when he comes. I won't be surprised like the last time. I will take a position, wait until he is out from under the branches, a perfect standing target, and I'll aim for his head. I won't get caught empty-handed again. All I have to do is get ready.

I stack the magazines, wedge them between the buckets, fold up my blanket, stash it in the corner, and tidy up the place as if I'm planning on company coming but it's not company I'm expecting. I just want to have adequate space if I need to strike from every angle of the stand. I give myself plenty of room and then I squat near the trunk and wait.

Until darkness falls, I sit on my perch and wait. If he comes tonight, I am not afraid. I will be ready.

I sit and prepare myself for battle, prepare myself to face him, realizing that I have no idea who the man is or what he wants. I don't understand why he keeps showing up but doesn't come to the tree, doesn't make himself known, doesn't try to scare me down like the crows. He just stands there, watching, far enough away that I cannot see who he is, but close enough for me to know he's there.

I don't know if he works for Brownfield or for Hatch or for somebody else. He could be some weirdo just here on his own, waiting for the right moment to get to me, or maybe he's just trying to intimidate me, watching me, making sure I see him, just hoping I'll get so frightened I'll come down.

I think of how easy it would be to start a fire and smoke me out of the woods. I think about kidnapping, pulling me out of my perch and taking me to some torture chamber. I think of a chainsaw cutting down the trees. I think of lots of things that a predator could do; but the truth is, all this time out here alone, all that I've seen and heard and gone through, all that grief and fear and facing down evil, I am not scared any more.

I don't even have to repeat the mantra. I really am no longer afraid. Maybe it's like how Ray described getting over being nervous playing the catcher position. I asked him how he did it, how he didn't shut his eyes every time the batter swung, which is what I did when I practiced with him and Nathan. I hated being behind either one of them when they batted.

He said they wore equipment and that he'd been hit once before and hardly even felt it and that the bat wasn't as frightening as a runner heading to home plate, right at him.

"So, how do you do it?" I wanted to know. "How do you stand there and let him run into you?"

"I just decide it's going to hurt but it has to be done. I'm the protector of home plate and I ain't letting nobody just walk right in here and take what's mine."

"That's crazy," I remember saying.

"Nah, Katie," he said, grinning, "That's baseball."

I remember watching him play, how he stood his ground, did his job, how he'd take the brunt of attempts to score and never flinch, never move. And every time, he'd jump up, shouting, "That all you got?" And Nathan would look up from the pitcher's mound, find me in the stands, and the three of us would just howl. God, I love those memories. And just thinking of the two of them makes me strong.

"Bring it on, Mister," I yell.

I hear a flutter underneath me but I know it's just the nuthatches. I guess by now they're used to talk, but they haven't really heard much yelling.

"I'm not scared of you," I sing out. "I've been through storms and gunshots. I've faced down a whole lot worse than you. So come out where I can see you! Come over here and show your face! Let's play ball, sucker!"

I don't know if he can hear me or not. He's a good three hundred yards out. But I don't care, I'm screaming at him just the same.

"I said, you don't scare me!"

I decide I want to climb higher. I want to stand on a limb, not a piece of plywood. I want to be as high as I can be. So I step up to the next limb, feeling my sore arm tighten up, and I pull myself up and decide to go one more. I reach for that one, pull up, and I think, this is just right, this is just high enough. And because it's dark, I fail to see that there's another branch higher, a fairly big one.

I stand up, yelling as I do, "Try to take my home away from me . . ." and just as the words are out of my mouth I slam into the limb above my head, knocking myself unconscious, causing me to fall all the way back down to my perch.

In a second, everything goes black.

Forty-Two

"You shouldn't be here," the voice tells me, but I'm too groggy to respond.

"I said, you shouldn't be here."

"Nathan?"

I feel light-headed, drunk. I feel the same way I did when I was sick, except this is like me outside of me. "I'm in a dream, right? I bumped my head and now I'm having this dream."

"Yes, that's exactly what this is, a dream. And in a little while you'll wake up and you won't really remember it. Some of it, but not everything. You can't remember everything because if you did, well, you'd want to come back. And you can't come back. Not yet anyway. You know that, right?"

"I don't know." I try to see where I am.

"There aren't any markers," he says, knowing that I'm trying to find something familiar. "You've never been here before; it's all new. Only, well, it's not. You have been here . . ." He hesitates. "Never mind, it's too hard to explain."

"Okay."

There is blue and there's yellow. There are streaks of red. Purple. It's like a painting and it's beautiful. It's color but it's also light; but it's light like nothing you can explain. It's something your heart knows but you don't have words to describe it. Nathan isn't really here, either. It's his voice; but he's not embodied in any way. He's the blue or he's the yellow. He's speaking from the light. Well, I mean he is the light.

"How are you?" he asks, like we're meeting on a bus, like we're having lunch or talking on the phone, like he's alive, like he hasn't been dead for more than twenty years.

"I'm okay," I say, not very convincingly. "Nathan, where are we?"

"We're here," he answers, like I ought to know what that means.

"Well, where's here?"

And I see him smile, but not him really; I just know he's smiling. Maybe I'm making that part up.

"You're living in a tree," he says. It's not a question, more of an observation.

I nod and then quickly stop, afraid my head will hurt; but it doesn't. I don't feel the pain in my head. I don't actually feel anything in my body. I'm in the light, too.

"Not very practical," he adds. "You're not really meant to live in a tree, not this time."

"What does that mean?"

"Nothing."

"Why are you so mad?"

This surprises me. "I'm not mad."

"Oh, yeah, you're mad all right."

"I'm not mad."

"Uh-huh."

"Well, even if I were, how do you know? You're gone. You've been gone."

"How's Ray?"

"He's okay. He misses you. I think he's missed you a long time."

"We were brothers. Before."

I don't know if he means metaphorically or literally, like brothers in this light he's in, this light I'm in.

"Lonnie came back," I tell him but then realize that he doesn't even know who Lonnie is. She came into the picture after he was dead.

"Yeah."

So, he does know.

"She's been working a long time on that relationship."

"Which one? Her and Ray?"

"No, her and Lilly Carol."

"Wait. You know Lilly Carol. You know their daughter?"

"Yes. I know a lot."

"Like what?"

"Like Ray, how he tangles himself up in a web."

He means the guilt, I suppose. "He punishes himself."

"Yes. It's time for him to stop."

Okay, I think. "You want me to tell him that?"

There is no response.

"You're alike, you know?"

"How's that?"

"Neither one of you does well with the curve."

"What?"

"The curve. The hitter moves because he thinks the ball is coming at him but the catcher doesn't change his position. He keeps his mitt right where he always does. He knows what's coming because he signaled for it."

"I'm lost. I don't know what you're saying with the baseball talk."

"You've both moved away because it's a curve; but it's actually right where it's supposed to go."

"I don't understand the baseball metaphors. I do birds."

"Okay, the red-cockaded."

"How do you know about that?"

He sighs.

"Sorry, I get it."

"Do you think he just showed up this spring?"

"You're saying he was here but I never saw him."

"Forest for the trees, yep, something like that."

"I still don't know what that has to do with Ray and me."

Another breath from above me or around me, somewhere close.

"How's Dad?"

I shrug.

"You seem to know everything, you tell me."

"Okay."

I wait.

"He's troubled."

"Yeah, well, we're all troubled, Nathan."

"No, this is different."

"Right."

"That's him out there at the edge of the woods."

"What?"

"Yeah, funny right? All this time you thought it was the boogeyman and it's just your dad."

"What's he doing?" And I don't know why but I try to see him. Of course, I don't.

"What do you think?"

"Waiting to arrest me?"

"Nope."

"Acting like he's working so somebody will think he's going to arrest me?"

"Nope."

"Then I give up."

"Oh, come on Katie, think."

"I don't want to think. Not about him. I don't want to think anything about him."

"Well, you're going to have to."

"No, I don't. I've gone a long time not thinking about him and I can keep going."

He doesn't reply.

It's so quiet I forget where I am.

"Nathan?"

"Yeah, I'm still here."

"Why do you think I'm going to have to think about him?"

"Well, you're right, I guess, you don't really have to; but you should."

The silence again.

"You going to tell me why?"

"Because he's not who you think he is."

"And who's that? Who do I think he is?"

"See, that's the thing, I can give you clues; but I can't give you the real answers. You got to do some of the work for yourself. That's just the way it is."

I don't respond.

"You want one?"

"One what?"

"One clue."

"Sure." And I start to feel something, a tingle like when you fall asleep on your arm and then you wake up about the same time as your arm.

"He's not Superman."

"Well, duh, Nathan, I know that." Then it's not just my arm, it's my face and my feet, my spine. And then I start to feel the top of my head, where I remember smacking it on the limb. It starts to ache, just a little.

"Do you?"

"Nathan," his voice is smaller. He's drifted away.

"I'll see you, Katie."

"Wait." My head is really starting to hurt now.

"You got this. I know you got this."

And just like that, this blue and yellow light, the streaks of red and purple, this airy feeling I had, this dream or vision, it just slips away, slides right away, and my head is killing me and there's someone kneeling over me.

"Kate, Katie, are you okay?"

All I know for sure is it ain't Superman.

Forty-Three

"Kate, Katie . . ."

I feel the hand on my shoulder, the breath, hot against my face. I open my eyes and there is my father, kneeling over me. I almost forget who I've become, where I am. I feel like a child, my dad waking me from my sleep, calling me to life again, my protector, my guardian.

"Hey," he says when I open my eyes and blink. "You had quite a fall."

The lantern is on, there's a small amount of light in the stand but it's dark, must be late. I can't quite think of what day or time it is.

"You okay? You feel sick or dizzy?"

I start to get up, lift my head, slide away from him. I know I need to figure out where I am, what's happened.

"No, no . . . just stay where you are. You probably have a concussion, so just stay put for a bit."

When he says concussion, I reach for my head, where it hurts the most, right on top; just to touch it makes me wince. It was a hard hit. It was from above. I was climbing higher, forgot the limb above the stand.

"Yeah, you smacked yourself pretty good and then you fell about six feet. I'm going to lift your head up just a bit and put my jacket under you." He studies me. "Will that be okay?" he asks.

I nod and he raises my head gently and does exactly what he said he was going to do. "That okay? You feel nauseated or dizzy?"

I shake my head and I do feel better now in this position. He waits, remains silent, watches me closely.

My back is sore; my ankle is throbbing again. I lift my arm and then drop it back down. I don't know when I've hurt like this before. Everything seems to be impacted by the fall; my whole body aches.

"Is this the arm where you got the infection?" He holds up my elbow and looks at me. "That hurt?"

I shake my head just a little. It doesn't hurt like it did a few days ago. I don't think I reinjured it.

He holds out my arm, straightens out my elbow, so easily, so carefully; and it doesn't feel terrible, sore, not terrible.

"That okay?"

I nod.

He places my arm by my side and he starts to feel around; my shoulders, behind my head. "Feel okay?"

I nod.

"Any tingling or pain in your neck?"

I shake my head.

He touches my other arm and waits to see how I look with each touch, no pain. My hips, my legs, one at a time, slowly, moving them to lay side by side, making sure nothing is broken, I guess.

He gets to my ankle, I grunt, pull it away. He looks me in the eye. "This the one you sprained jumping down last week?"

I nod and wonder how he knows about my past injuries and I watch him in the dim lantern light as he gently, so gently, removes my shoe and slides off my sock.

He makes a funny face. "Kate, it may be broken."

I close my eyes and then open them again, remembering I'm in my tree on the plywood, and it occurs to me suddenly that my father climbed the trees.

The sheriff is in my stand.

I see him kneeling over my feet, checking the bruising on my ankle. He's wearing one of those flashlight headbands like Tiffany gave me and he's looking all around my foot. He's careful, making sure not to hurt me. He shakes his head from side to side, displeased, I think, with what he sees. And watching this, seeing him caring for me, handling my ankle, nursing my wounds, I do not even anticipate what's about to happen. All of a sudden, I start to cry.

It's Nathan and it's him and it's me and it's Delores and it's Ray and it's just more than I can bear. The river, without a dam holding it back, flows.

"What is it, Katie? What's the matter? Are you in a lot of pain? Did I hurt you?"

And I slowly shake my head from side to side, my face wet with tears. He slides up from my feet, turns off the flashlight, holds my chin in his hand.

"You're okay. It's going to be okay," he tells me, and that just makes me cry more. And he slides his arm under my shoulders and pulls me closer.

"It's okay," he says again, and I don't know how long we sit like this, me cradled in my father's arms. Me, sitting in a tree, broken, wounded, weeping, so unbound, so untethered, loosed, gathered up in his arms.

And I watch as a wall of pain crumbles between us.

When I finally get myself together enough to speak, I pull away from him, and he releases me, drops his arms from around me, slides over a little, giving me room. I sit up, get my bearings, remember where I am, what has happened between us.

"I saw Nathan," I say. "He was here; well, his spirit was here. He told me I needed to talk to you."

"Yeah?"

"Yeah."

"He tell you what about?"

I shake my head. "No," is all I say, and we are silent, the two of us, for a long time.

"Come here," I tell him. "Lean against the trunk; it's better." So he moves over and we sit side by side, our backs against the tree.

"You feel okay?"

"No nausea, no dizziness," I report. "Head hurts though."

"Yeah, you're going to have a pretty nasty bump."

I nod and then wince. It hurts to do that in this position.

"You remember when you built that tree house for Nathan and me?"

He nods. "Your mother was so mad at me for that. She just knew you were going to fall and hurt yourself."

"But you told her I was a tough kid and that if I fell I'd probably bounce right off the ground."

He laughs a little, remembering.

"I never did," I add. "Fall, I mean."

"Nope, you never did. You always were a good tree climber; you'd go higher and faster than your brother."

"Yeah, well, he had a thing about heights. So, then we got the tents."

Another moment of silence. I'm thinking of me sitting in the tree above Nathan. I don't know what he's remembering.

"Those were good times," he finally says.

"The best," I reply, and I lean into my father just a bit.

"I was probably wrong to treat you like another boy," he says, surprising me.

"What?"

"I just didn't know what to do with a girl," he confesses. "After your mother left, I was at such a loss and all I knew to do was just treat you the same way I treated Nathan."

Well, this is certainly a surprise. "Are you kidding me? I loved my childhood with you and Nathan. It was the best."

"Really?"

"Yes, really. Why would you think I was unhappy about that?"

"Well, you were unhappy about something," he replied; and I suddenly realized some of my father's place.

Forty-Four

"I wasn't mad at you because you treated me like a son," I say.

"No?"

"No."

He waits.

"I loved what the three of us had. I loved that you let me do the same things that you let Nathan do. I felt special because of that."

I think about the ease with which I played, the way boys expect and are expected to fall and get back up. Nathan punched hard and I learned to punch right back. He threw wild pitches at me and I learned to get out of the way. He taught me to wrestle and run and spit and I loved the things I learned, loved how I did what made me afraid, and loved that my father never made him stop, never handed me off to female relatives. I love that he made us a threesome. I always felt like I belonged.

"I was mad because you lied about Mom; you didn't tell us that she left you, that she had an affair. You didn't tell us that she wanted to see us after she moved."

He doesn't speak for a few seconds. There's a light forest breeze around us. My head and ankle throb and I move a tiny bit, trying to get comfortable.

"Do you need something? Can I help you in some way?"

I think about the pain pills but decide I want to feel all of this, even if it hurts. "No, I'm okay."

He takes in a breath, nods like he knows what he needs to say.

"I was wrong about that. I was wrong to lie; but the truth is I was so angry when she left me, so hurt and angry that I wanted her to feel the same kind of pain. I realized later that I was trying to punish her by keeping you away from her but by then it was too late. I know now that I punished you when I only wanted to punish her. That was wrong. I'm sorry."

And just like that, like falling from a tree through branches that cannot stop them, through wind and air, there they are. The words I had longed to hear, now spoken. Right there, out in the open, between us.

And somehow I thought there would be more to it than this, more emotion, more sentiment, more drama. Instead, it's just the two of us sitting in a tree, telling the truth like it's the easiest thing in the world. It turns out that it's not really that complicated.

I wait to say anything more, and I remember my trip to Florida a few years ago, meeting my mother all over again, seeing her in her home, seeing who she had become, who she loved and leaned on.

"She has another daughter, another family," I say. "She has grandchildren; she's made her own place, has a nice little nest."

He nods, but I can see he still holds himself responsible for all that has happened in my life. I go on, "If she had really wanted to spend time with Nathan and me, she would have made that happen."

I think about Lonnie Marcus, back in Jones County, back home, wanting her family again, fighting for the right. I think about how I have judged her, the unfair way I have thought of her. She came back, I think. She left, but she came back.

I say, "She could have fought a little harder."

He shrugs. "She was afraid of me. She was afraid of what else I might do to her. I wielded my authority over her." He hesitates, recalling the past, I'm sure. "No, I was wrong. I was to blame. I should have told you the truth when she left and I should have let her see you. I shouldn't have kept you from your mother and I shouldn't have kept a mother from her children. You were a child; Nathan was a child. You needed her and I kept her away."

And what he is saying is exactly what I have said a thousand times. I have said it; I have screamed it; I have used it as a weapon for decades.

And yet, now, to hear him say it, to hear him confess it, I see that it no longer bears any weight, not really.

"Because you were afraid of losing us, too."

I cannot believe I know this; but I do. I absolutely know this.

He's not superman. That's what Nathan said. And of course, it makes perfect sense now.

"I was, wasn't I?"

I nod.

We are silent. The moonlight grows brighter. It's so peaceful in the forest tonight.

"I blamed you for everything," I confess. "I blamed you for Mama leaving. I blamed you for Nathan crashing his car. I blamed you."

It was easy, the low-hanging fruit, and I just fell for it. I just plucked it and claimed it and kept it like it was the gospel. I see that now, and I'm sorry that it took all of this for the insight, sorry that it took me climbing a tree and him sitting night after night at the edge of it all. I'm sorry it took a head injury. It seems like such a waste.

"Well, I certainly gave you reason for that. I blamed myself; I have for a long time. So, when you did get mad and quit talking to me, when you started to hate me, I felt it was only fair. I would have hated my father, too. You had that right."

"No, I didn't," I tell him, sitting up a little. "I didn't have that right. I still don't."

"You were a kid, Katie."

"Yeah, well you were a father who lost his son."

And just like it happened to me, it happens to him. The river, again; it flows. He weeps and I pull him to me. I hold my father who mourns for his only son, dead, and his only daughter, lost.

Time passes. He slides away, takes out a handkerchief, blows his nose, wipes his eyes, pulls himself together. I move over, find a bottle of water, take a sip, and hand it to him. He takes a swallow, gives it back to me, and all I feel is holy.

We sit in the silence, everything said that needed to be said, and we watch as Delores stands at the edge of her nest, peering across the way at us. I don't even have to show him. He sees her, too.

"We're all just doing the best we can with what we got," I say, remembering Charlene's words from earlier in the day.

"I suppose that's about right," he answers. He reaches for the bottle of water, takes a long swallow and then gives it back. He wipes his mouth and I see he has something else he needs to tell me.

I brace myself because I think it has to do with everything I've heard from the deputy and from Nathan. I prepare to hear the bad news that my father is sick and dying and is about to tell me this for himself.

Forty-Five

"Something's wrong, isn't it?" I ask.

"What makes you say that?"

"Just a feeling."

He reaches in his pocket and pulls out a letter, a folded page. He turns on his headlamp so that I can read.

"What is it?" I ask, thinking it must be from a doctor or a hospital. It must be some medical report about heart disease on incurable cancer. I watch as my hands, shaking, take it from him.

I unfold it and see immediately that it isn't a medical report; it isn't from a doctor or clinic. It's written on letterhead from the sheriff's office. I know this because I've seen this stationary since I was a child. He keeps a stack of these sheets at home. I remember finding them in boxes in his office.

Dear Jones County Board of Commissioners:
I glance up. He keeps his head down to give me light to read.
It is with regret and sadness that I hereby resign my position as Jones County Sheriff effective immediately.
"What's this?"
He reaches up, turns off the headlamp, and looks at me. "It's a resignation."
"I see that."
I wait.
"Why are you resigning?"
He shakes his head.
"Are you sick?"
"No."
"You don't have terminal cancer?"
"Why would you think that?"
I shrug. "Just the way people have been acting, the way you're acting."
"I don't have cancer."
"Then why are you resigning?" I fold up the paper, grimace a bit when I try to move my foot.
He reaches down, places the blanket, the jacket, under my ankle, trying to elevate it, I'm sure to keep the swelling down.
"Just seems like the right time," he answers, satisfied that he's got my foot raised properly. He sits back beside me.
"There's a right time to resign from a job you've had all your adult life?" I shake my head and it hurts.
"We really need to get some ice on that," he tells me, and I'm not sure whether he means the lump on my head or the ankle that was injured in the fall.
"Sorry, no ice in the tree."
"Tylenol? Advil?"
"Percocet."

"I don't want to know how you got that," he replies. "So, don't tell me."

And I think that's an odd response.

"I'll take a half," I reply. And I slide over ever so carefully, find Jim's pills and break one in half. He hands me the bottle of water, and I swallow.

We don't speak again for a few seconds.

"Are you retiring?"

"I guess that's what this would be."

"But that's not what you want to do?"

He doesn't respond.

"Are you in some kind of trouble?" I try to see the expression on his face by the light of the moon and the lantern on the stand.

He glances away.

"Is it Mr. McDonald?" I have known for a long time that Daddy never got along with the County Manager. I'm thinking that maybe he's holding something over my father's head, a budget cut, a misuse of county funds; I know how politics can work.

"No, it's not Leroy. Leroy, I can handle."

"Then, what?" And as soon as the two words escape my lips, I know. I understand. "You're being forced out because I'm up here."

He turns to me and my guess is confirmed.

"But how?" I want to know.

"I'm tired of the job anyway," he says, without answering my question. And I know this is not true. My father loves being the county sheriff. He loves law enforcement. He loves the people in this town. He loves the authority the job affords him. He was made for this work.

"No, you're not."

He doesn't answer.

"Is it Winston Hatch?"

He shakes his head. "No, I think we both recognize that Winston has the heavier hand."

I realize he knows about what happened with the owl. He knows just like I did that Winston put those crows up to that.

"It's Thomas Brownfield. Seems like he's done a lot of homework about trespassing on private land."

"Because you won't have me arrested, is that it? Because I'm breaking the law and you haven't done anything about it?"

"Brownfield and Kathy Moore's husband are tennis partners at the country club."

And I understand what he's saying. Kathy Moore is a county commissioner. Her husband has told her to start proceedings or whatever it is they do to deal with county employees who don't do their jobs. My father was threatened and he has refused to arrest me.

"Why didn't you do it? Why didn't you serve a warrant? You sent Franklin out here, why didn't you just have him arrest me?"

He blows out a breath. He thought about it, I can tell.

"You ever see Deputy Massey try to climb a tree?"

Although this is not a real answer, it does make me laugh.

He continues, "I actually admire what you're doing. I think it's courageous and I never liked Winston Hatch or Thomas Brownfield. They build all these buildings just to erect monuments to themselves. They've destroyed the river at the other end of the county with their strip malls and dollar stores. Now they're doing it down here for a retirement village that nobody from Jones County will be able to afford. Nah, I was never going to arrest you and they know it."

"But you do know that I have to come down sometime." It seems weird to me that I'm the one saying this.

"Yeah, I guess, but it doesn't have to be me or the law that makes that happen."

He's right.

"But there's something else, something worse, and my resignation isn't going to make this go away."

He reaches in his back pocket and pulls out another piece of paper. I take it from him but wait before I open it. "So, just to make sure, because I do have a head wound and might be somewhat altered, you're not sick?"

He shakes his head. "No, not sick, just unemployed."

"Good." And I really do mean it. I know that we can fix the unemployed part. He will not need to resign.

I hold the paper in my hand and I know, just by the way it feels, just by the way my father has given it to me, it carries a burden.

"I'm sorry," he says, turning on his headlamp again, and I unfold it.

Forty-Six

"Where did she get this information?" I ask.

I feel myself start to tremble. He's absolutely right; this is worse than the resignation. I'm chilled and he takes off his jacket and throws it around my shoulders.

He turns off the headlamp because he can tell I'm through reading. I see him shake his head. "I don't have any idea."

We pause to listen to a song sparrow. It's late and I think the call must be urgent. Three sweet notes, a lower one, and a trill. It must be the hawk.

"I knew she was bad news." And I did.

Tonya Lassiter is a lammergeier. She breaks bones for food. She sucks out marrow. She drops tortoises from the sky. She picks them up from among the rocks with her sharp claws, then flies high above the tops of trees, and then drops them, shattering them into pieces so she can have a few bits of meat.

Now she has grabbed Jim right out of the pulpit, right away from his mother's bedside, has dangled him above everything he loves, and now she's going to drop him, smash him, right at my feet. All for a small reward or some personal vendetta.

I have no idea what she's getting for this but it can't be as much as the damage this information will cost.

"He'll have to leave his church," I say, only imagining what the Lutherans will do when they read this. "He'll have to leave Jones County."

My father doesn't respond but he doesn't have to. He agrees; these accusations mean death for a man of the cloth.

"It's not true," I say, even though he hasn't asked. "We have not been having an affair. He was not the cause of my divorce." But even as I state this I understand that the truth is worse for Jim than the lammergeier's lies.

"I know," he replies. "Not all of it is true, of course, but there's enough here that can be proven to cause your friend a lot of damage."

"The drugs," I respond.

She has proof that he gave me his mother's prescribed antibiotics and the opiates, which I just consumed in front of an officer of the law, putting my dad at risk as a witness to a crime. Now his earlier comment about not wanting to know where I got the Percocet makes sense.

He nods. "He probably wouldn't be prosecuted because it's such a meager amount, but it could still become public knowledge. It just depends on what the prosecutor would want to do, and unfortunately he and Thomas Brownfield also . . ."

I interrupt. "Play tennis together."

"Golf actually. It is a small town, Kate."

"Yep."

I think about the report, Tonya Lassiter, this news.

"Why did she give you the letter? Why didn't she just bring it to me herself? She's been out here enough times to know where I am."

He waits, thinking about the question, I suppose. "She saw me sitting at the edge of the woods, knew I was here every night since the incident with the owl. I think she wanted me to see it, too, and she knew I'd bring it to you."

"And you did."

He doesn't respond.

I sum it all up. "So, if I don't come down from the tree, she's going to publish an article about Jim taking pain medicines from his mother, a hospice patient, and diverting them to me, the woman whose marriage just broke up." I pause and then continue. "She claims to have a paper trail to prove the drug theft and if I refuse to vacate the premises she's threatening to dig deeper into our relationship."

Of course, I know she won't discover proof of an affair, but it is highly likely that she would stumble upon even more damaging information. In fact, I'm surprised she hasn't already found out about Jim and Bernard, and maybe she has. Maybe this is just her way of letting me know what she's capable of doing.

He hesitates. "I'd say that about covers it."

"Do you think anybody else knows?"

"I can't say."

I figure it out for myself. "She didn't need to tell anybody else. She only needed to let me know. Jim has no idea."

"That's what I thought, too."

She's smart, I give her that.

"It's not true," I tell him again. "I'm not having an affair with Jim Stallings."

He nods. "Yep, I found that a bit farfetched."

There's something about the way he says it that gives me pause. "Wait, you know?"

"What?"

He's waiting for me to say it but I don't.

"You mean do I know that Jim is gay?"

Yep, he knows. "How did you find out about that?"

He hesitates, measures what he's about to tell me. "There was an incident. . ."

I wait.

"It wasn't long after he came to Maysville. There had been reports of indecent behavior going on at the park. He was picked up."

And I already know how this story played out even though Jim never told me about this run-in with the law, and my father has never broken confidence with the new minister in town.

"You didn't press charges."

He shakes his head. "What would have been the sense of that?"

A moment passes while I really take in what happened between my father and my best friend, Jim's embarrassment, the sheriff's refusal to make an arrest.

"Thank you," is all I can say.

"It was a stupid witch hunt implemented by the mayor. I never intended to use the law to enforce his bigotry. I was just sorry Jim had to go through what he did."

"Well, at least it was you and not Franklin who was on duty that night."

"I have an idea that Franklin would have done the same thing."

I think about the deputy, how many times he's been out to my tree, how many times he could have but didn't arrest me for trespassing. It makes me feel a little bad for saying the things I've said to him over the past few weeks. I realize that I'll have to think of a way to make it up to him.

We are quiet for a bit and before long I nod off.

When I wake up, dawn is breaking, and I'm heavy with the knowledge that today is the day of decisions.

Forty-Seven

"How's your head?" He asks when he realizes I'm awake.

I touch the top of it and it's not as sore as it was last night. "Okay," I answer.

"The ankle?"

I glance down; it's about twice the size of my other one. He looks at it, too, and I see that I don't have to reply.

I try moving around. I'm stiff; my shoulders, my back, I can tell I've fallen. He slides away, giving me room. He's straightened up my stand a bit. My food is stacked. The buckets are neatly placed near the trunk of the pine. He's folded my jacket and sweatshirts, cleared away the leaves and needles from my fall.

"Breakfast?" he asks, holding up protein bars, a bottle of water.

I nod and take my spot again, finding the pillow and punching it as I put it behind my back. He sits across from me and we open the packages and start to eat. I'm not very hungry.

"You sleep any?"

He shakes his head. "No, but I'm glad you did."

I take a drink of water.

He doesn't ask me anything about what I plan to do, and it's a good thing because I don't really know. I'm sure that I can't let Jim suffer the consequences of my actions. I'm not going to let my father resign even if he claims it's his choice. I know I have to come down; I just hate that it's because of Thomas Brownfield and the lamb vulture.

My father is glancing around. He's smiling. I can tell he likes it up here. He stops and catches my watching him.

"What?"

I shake my head. "Just you," I answer.

He shakes his head, waits for me to continue.

"You just look so young sitting there, cross-legged in a tree house." He grins.

"Well, I'm not young anymore," he responds.

I stretch my back, feel my ankle as it starts to throb again. "No, neither am I."

We eat in silence.

"You know your brother would be over forty if he was still living."

I take a bite of protein bar, think about Nathan as a grown man, wonder what profession he would have chosen, how many children he would have had.

"I always thought the three of us would live close to each other, get together on Sundays with your families, play ball, cook out." He finishes his breakfast, rolls up the package, tosses it into the bucket.

I don't think I ever thought much about us being older; I never moved beyond our youth.

"He seems to be happy where he is," I say after a long pause while the morning birds are waking and starting to sing.

He nods, but I'm not sure if he believes me. And yet I realize that it doesn't matter whether he does. I see now that we have our own ideas, make up our own stories about what happens to those we love when they die. Besides, I don't tell him this because I need confirmation about what I saw and heard. That was real for me and nobody can take that away, not that I think he would.

"Are you happy? I mean with Millie. Are you happy with her?" We've not spoken yet about his other family.

"She's a good woman, and yes, we're happy."

"I'm glad," I say, finishing off my protein bar. "Does she know you've been watching out for me all these past nights?"

He nods. She knew. She probably even encouraged it.

"You and Dwayne?"

I shake my head, not really sure how much to say to my father about that. I pause but he doesn't ask for more.

"I'm going to come down," I tell him. "It's the only thing I can do."

He nods. I think he knows this too.

"You shouldn't resign," I add. "So tear that letter up."

"Kate, I . . ."

But I won't let him finish. "Just stay sheriff a little while longer; this thing isn't over and, well, let's not let them take every battle."

"Are you going to tell Jim?"

I shrug. "Not sure what good that would do."

"So, that's it, then, Hatch and Brownfield win? They tear down the pines, build their village?"

I shake my head. "I don't see any other way, do you?"

He glances away. He doesn't. I'm sure he thought about this a long time before he even brought me the letter. He knows the same thing I do: they got me. I would never do anything to bring harm to my friend.

"You know I didn't even get any photographs while I've been up here," I say, noticing the camera placed near the buckets. "Jim brought it a few days ago but with the murder and everything that's happened since, I've not gotten one shot."

He reaches over and pulls out the camera. He takes a look through the lens. I watch him as he checks out our surroundings.

"See what's going on with Delores," I tell him, and then I remember that he doesn't know the owl's name, but he focuses right in the direction of the nest.

"The eggs have hatched," he tells me. "Looks like three baby birds."

"What?" I can't believe it. "When did that happen?" I hold out my hand and he gives me the camera.

Delores is out of the way, standing on a limb right above the fledglings. I can see them so well. "They're healthy," I announce.

"Sure looks that way."

I bring the camera down. "Well, at least something turned out okay."

"You take a picture?" he asks.

I shake my head, knowing that I feel protective of Delores' family, that I don't want to take away from her what this morning means. She's giving me this view but still, I have no right to photograph the young birds. It's too sacred for that.

I glance above the nest and look at Delores for a long time. She stares at me, too, never blinking, and just as I'm about to lower the camera, having seen all I need to, I catch one last glimpse of the nest. Near the front of the fledglings I see a feather and realize that Delores has taken one of her mate's feathers from the limb above my head. I put the camera down and see there is one left, one she has left for me. When I look back at the nest, she has taken her place with the young, satisfied it seems that I have noticed what she intended.

"It's too bad the owls aren't endangered," my father says.

"What?" I'm still trying to figure out how Delores would know to do such a thing, to take one feather for herself, place it in the nest, and leave the other one for me.

"The owls," he repeats. "If the owls were endangered we could stop the development."

As he says the words, I catch a flash of red just at the corner of my stand. He's back. The red-cockaded is back, headed for the suet Lilly Carol brought, and I raise the camera to my eye and snap that perfect shot.

Forty-Eight

"I think that's everything; I'm going to go down and get it ready for pick-up."

I nod, hang onto the limb, lean against the trunk.

Dad has managed to take all the stuff from the tree, Tiffany's collection, my clothes, the books and magazines. He left the plywood, a little food and water, my pillow and blanket, so that I can be as comfortable as possible until he gets back. At first, he tried to talk me into going out with him; but when I said it would just be too hard with my ankle injured as it is, he agreed. He's going down and out of the woods, make a few calls, and come back shortly on the four wheeler. He's going to drive me out.

While he worked, I traveled up a couple of limbs, lugging the camera and dragging my injured foot behind me. I'm taking more pictures, saying a few goodbyes. I was instructed to stay out of his way and simply watch once I had filled up the supply bucket, managing to get it down to the bottom of the trees before almost falling again.

The toilet bucket was dismantled; most of the food wrapped and sent down, every piece of trash, every shred of evidence wiped clean from the loblollies. Now I'm just sitting on the limb taking one last look from this place I've called home for the past twenty-one days. I keep an eye on Dad, making sure he doesn't trip or hurt himself; but mostly I watch Delores and her babies. She hasn't paid me any attention since I woke up this morning, but I've taken the feather she left and stuck in my hair.

I know that her young owls will be helpless for several days. They won't open their eyes for a week. It will take up to six more for the fledglings to achieve maximum size and eight to nine weeks for their feathers to develop, finally equipping them to set out on their own. I know Delores has her hands full. She alone has to feed and fend for her family. But I also know that she's resourceful and has a cache; I'm certain she and her babies will be fine.

I wedge myself in between the limbs, put my weight on my good leg, and lean against the trunk. Once steady, I go through the pictures I took of the woodpecker with Jim's camera. Although unsure at first that this was the way to go, I now have the proof of an endangered species in this pine tree stand, and I have an officer of the law as my witness. Without either of us needing to explain, we are both well aware of the environmental laws put in place to protect the birds I love.

Federal penalties include a fifty thousand fine and up to thirty years in prison if a habitat of red-cockaded woodpeckers is destroyed. I know from my research that in other places in the state, a Safe Harbor Agreement is typically entered into by landowners with the Wildlife Resources Commission. This agreement allows private landowners to continue their current land-use practices while agreeing to restore, enhance, and maintain habitats that benefit species listed under the Endangered Species Act. In return for their proper management of the land, these owners are guaranteed that no additional land-use restrictions will be imposed on their property.

Since a clan of woodpeckers needs at least five thousand pines ten inches in diameter surrounding the nesting site, it's a pretty sure bet that the government won't interfere with Hatch and Brownfield's present use of this bottomland but a retirement village will not be built. It takes anywhere from sixty to five hundred acres to provide enough trees. Hatch and Brownfield may have gotten me out of their sweetgum and loblollies, but they can't do anything about the red-cockaded. They can't do a thing about the endangered species. That lucky bird and his clan are here to stay.

I was able to follow the lone male this time. I kept him in my line of sight for almost forty minutes after he left the suet above me, finally finding the nest. With binoculars and the long-lens camera, Dad and I watched the three adults, the mating pair and the helper, tending to the nest that sits in a cavity in another loblolly less than fifty feet out. There are several cavities in several trees, some longleaf, even a slash pine, all of them live. The red-cockaded is the only woodpecker species in North America that excavates its nests in living pine trees instead of dead ones. That was what threw me before, why I hadn't seen the nest. I kept looking for woodpecker cavities in the snags, the dead trees near the water. Now that I've found the small clan of reds, I remember their unique nesting places.

I glance over to the nest again. It's active. Like Delores's place, there must be newborns, there too. In fact, on this early date in April, this morning of my departure, the forest is brimming with life. Despite my sadness in coming down from the stand, I know that it's a good day to leave. I know the days of brooding and late winter storms are over. Better times are ahead for everybody.

I turn the camera below me so that I can see my father. He's placing everything I had in small piles beneath the loblollies. He's careful with Tiffany's collection, as careful as he was with my science projects, when I was her age. He has already emptied the toilet bucket and placed it in the garbage bag with all the trash I had accumulated.

He orders my belongings, sets them aside, and I know he will retrieve every single item. He's meticulous that way; he was the one who taught me how to pack in and pack out when camping. He was an environmental nerd even before it was popular, and I'm glad of the things I learned from him, glad for all that he instilled within me about taking care of the earth. Even when I was mad at him for all those years, I was always grateful for those lessons.

I put down the camera and watch him without a zoom. He's aged, seems slightly shorter than I remember, his hair thinned, a little balding on top. But he moves the same, still stands and rests his hands on his hips, still lifts his chin, glancing around, smelling the air, the same. It makes me smile. This was the way I saw him when I was a child, when I climbed trees in the backyard and he worked and rested beneath them. I always loved him from here.

He glances up, catches me watching him. "Hey."

"Hey."

"You okay?"

I nod. I am.

"You going to be able to make it down to the stand?"

I nod.

"How about when I get back? You going to be able to come down by yourself?"

I check my ankle. It's not going to be easy, but I can manage. I can slide a lot of the way. "Yeah, I think so," I answer.

We listen as the warblers fill the air with their songs, the cheerful *sweet-sweet-sweet-sitta, sitta, see.*

"You got enough pictures?"

I check the counter on the camera; I have taken more than thirty. I have close-ups of the male who has been flitting around me for twenty-one days and I have long shots of the nest, the clan, and the fledglings. I nod. I know that I have more than enough.

"You'll be famous now," he tells me.

"Yeah, I don't want really want that," I reply. "And I'm not sure they'll want it either," I add, talking about the woodpeckers.

I say this because I was around in 2004 when everybody with a pair of binoculars and a video recorder headed to the Big Woods in Arkansas looking for the ivory-billed woodpecker. I know that announcing the discovery of the red-cockaded will surely save the forest, decimate any ideas of development by H and B Construction Company or anybody else for that matter, but it will forever alter our bottomland surroundings.

A report of this magnitude will bring in the Croatan Forest Service pinheads, the boys from Swansboro, maybe even a higher-up from Raleigh, and the birders will come from everywhere. It'll be aviary mayhem, but there's nothing I can do about that.

"Well, you did find the bird. You are the one with the pictures. I imagine there's even a reward for this discovery."

As he says this, something comes to mind, something almost as important as saving the bottomlands from development.

"You're probably right. I bet there's a monetary reward from the Sierra Club, the Audubon Society. I bet there's even money from the state for something like this. They're always giving birders incentives to locate endangered species."

He nods. "Yep."

He tilts his head, trying to get a better view of me, trying to look more closely into my eyes. "What are you going to do with it?"

"Tuition," I decide. "I'm going to pay tuition."

"You're finally heading back to school," he responds, saying it like he approves.

I don't answer but the decision I've made liberates me.

He waits a bit and I wonder if there's something else he wants to say. "I'm proud of you, Kate."

And of all the things I would have thought he might say, this surprises me the most.

"I love you," I tell him and even from way up above where he stands, I can see what it means to him.

He nods and I know he loves me, too.

"I'll be back in just a little while."

Carefully, I step down from the limbs and land on my stand one last time.

Forty-Nine

"So that's it, then?" Charlene is the first one to show up today, the first to appear in the woods since Dad left. I've told her about the fall, about my ankle, about the letter from Brownfield, about the resignation.

"That's it," I answer. "He'll return with the four wheeler and I'll be going home."

"After you go to the hospital?" She obviously talked to the sheriff on his way out.

"Well, yeah, I guess," I say, glancing at my foot.

"I don't understand. If you're not having an affair with Jim, what does it matter?"

"There's the drug issue."

"One bottle of antibiotics, a few pain pills? That's not really a huge offense."

"It's still an offense," I respond. "And I don't want my dad to resign over this. I don't know what I thought would happen when I climbed up here; to be truthful, when I got up here I didn't really care what Hatch and Brownfield would say or do to me." I look over at Delores's nest, see her feeding the babies, feel the remorse. "But I don't want to cause trouble for the people I love. It's not worth that." I glance away.

"You and your dad?" she says. It's a question and when she asks it, something dawns on me.

"You knew the whole time he was out there, didn't you?"

She shrugs.

"That's why you weren't nervous for me after all that trouble. You knew he was watching."

"He showed up the next night. He was sitting out there at the edge of the woods when I left right after they were here, after you got the infection. We never even spoke about it, but, yeah, I knew the sheriff wasn't going to let anything bad happen to you again."

"Well, we got it all worked out," I say, answering her question from earlier. "I bumped my head, had a kind of 'coming to Jesus' experience."

"That's good, right?"

"Yeah, that's real good."

She smiles and glances around. "So, everything down from there?"

I look at the empty stand and nod. "Everything but a protein bar and a bottle of water." I reach over and open the package. "You know,

I don't think I'm going to ever eat another one of these as long as I live." I take a bite.

She sits on the ground. "You going to tell me about the bird?"

I guess the sheriff must have mentioned that as well when they passed each other.

"Red-cockaded," I answer.

"That's quite a find."

"I know."

"Lilly Carol will be excited."

"Lilly Carol was the first to spot it," I tell her.

She hesitates, as if she's thinking about something. "Well, that explains it," she replies.

"Explains what?"

"Why she wouldn't go with Ray and Lonnie to the beach this week."

I put down the protein bar. I'm suddenly not hungry. I reach for the bottle of water, take a sip. I don't want to ask but can't help myself. I clear my throat. "Ray and Lonnie went to the beach?"

She leans forward to get a better view of me. "I thought you knew."

I shake my head. No, I certainly didn't know.

"I'm sorry," she says, and I can tell she's embarrassed for breaking the news.

"It's okay," I reply, trying not to sound wounded. "So, who's taking care of Lilly Carol then?" I try to sound upbeat, positive, unaffected.

"She's staying with his mom; she came in from Asheville to visit and then I'm going to get her tomorrow, keep her until they get back, just a couple of days, I think. She wanted to come out here. Ray tried and tried to get her to go with them, said she'd enjoy it; but she was determined to come and stay the day with you. He told me that she said something about needing to get a picture of a bird and so he let her stay."

"Oh," is all I can think to say.

"But now, I guess we won't be coming out after all. And it sounds like you already got the pictures so I guess we'll be visiting you in the hospital."

"Oh."

"Because that's where you'll go, right?"

"Oh."

"Kate?"

"Huh?"

"You keep saying, 'Oh. Are you okay?"

"Right, yeah, no, I'm fine."

"But you're going to the hospital when you come down? Probably going to have surgery on your ankle?"

I guess that's right, I think.

"Kate?"

"Yeah, what?" And then I remember the question. "Yeah, that's probably what will happen. I'll come down and go to the emergency room; I don't know if I'll have surgery, just planning on the X-rays first."

"So maybe we'll come to your house. We can have a party, get pizza, watch a movie. Hey, we can stay the night with you. That would be all right, wouldn't it? When you're home, even though it's a school night?"

"That sounds great," I reply, mustering up as much enthusiasm as I am able.

"Yep, maybe that's what we'll do." She stands up. "Well, is there anything you want me to do before tomorrow? You want me to take some of this stuff with me?" She looks around at my father's tidy stacks of my possessions.

I shake my head. "No, we'll get it later."

"Okay. Well, I probably should get to work. Don will be waiting." She pauses. "Do you want me to ask him about getting your job back?"

I hadn't thought about the job. I'm coming down from the tree and I don't have a clue as to what I'll do when I land.

"No, don't say anything to anybody. I want to take care of some things before we file the paperwork about the woodpecker. I want to make sure they don't start tearing down trees when I leave; so it's best if everybody just thinks I'm still up here for a while."

"Okay, makes sense." She stuffs her hands in her pockets, stares up at me. "I'm glad you're coming down, Kate. I've missed you."

"You're a good friend, Charlene. I'll call you when I'm on the ground."

And she nods, waves, and heads out. She hasn't a clue as to how hard the news she brought just fell.

Fifty

"I thought you were mad," I say when I see him walking up.

He's wearing his black get-up, his collar, the binoculars strapped around his neck. He glances up at me. "I told you I'd be back, didn't I?"

He had. He told me he'd come on Monday and it is Monday. It feels good to see my friend.

He cranes his neck. "Why is it so empty up there?" He looks around the bottom of the trees. "Why is everything out of the stand?"

"It was a pretty eventful weekend," I tell him. "You missed quite a show."

"Where's my chair?" And then he finds it, opens it, and sits down. "I need to be comfortable to hear about this."

"How's your mom?"

"Mama Stallings is just fine last time I checked, but I don't want to talk about her. Tell me what's going on."

The warblers are still singing and I can hear the cardinal's whistle from a couple of trees away.

"The sheriff was here." I decide to start with that.

He doesn't respond, just waits for more of the story.

"He's been watching. Ever since the night with the owl, he's been out there at the edge of the woods, keeping guard."

Jim nods, and I can't tell if he knew this or not. It doesn't really matter, of course.

"And when I spotted him, I was fearless. I was spitting mad because I thought it was one of Hatch's guys returning. So, I climbed up a few limbs, screamed and yelled at him like a crazy person, and I banged my head and fell. My ankle's probably broken."

"Wow."

"I know. It was not my finest hour."

"I love it," he tells me. "I can't believe I missed all of this. And then what happened?"

"He came up here, stayed with me."

"He climbed up the trees?"

"Yep. When I came to, he was sitting right beside me."

Jim nods, just taking it all in.

"I had a vision."

"And?"

"And Nathan told me, well, he didn't really tell me, I just knew when I woke up."

"Told you what? Knew what?"

"That you were right."

He's grinning. "Is that so?"

"You don't have to be so happy about it."

"Sorry, it's just that I don't hear that a lot."

"Well, you were."

"You talk to the sheriff?"

"We talked a good long time and I realized now that I was wrong to be mad at him for so long."

"And all is forgiven?"

"It seems that way."

He doesn't respond and this puzzles me.

"What?"

"It seems like it happened kind of fast."

"Well, if you think that twenty-five years of being mad and twenty-one days up in a tree, sustaining a head injury and a visit from the dead makes it seem fast, then yeah, I guess so."

"Huh," is all he says for a while. "And now what?"

"And now I'm coming down."

He leans forward in his chair. "What? Why?"

I really don't want to have to tell him about the blackmail, about Tonya Lassiter's report, but I'm afraid he'll find out somehow. I already told Charlene. Still, I think I'll start with the other news.

"I saw a red-cockaded."

"You did not!"

I nod, knowing he can see me. "I did. Well, actually Lilly Carol did."

There is a pause.

"Twenty-one days ago." He sits back, figures it out.

"I'm sorry I didn't tell you."

He shrugs. I know he would have wanted to share in that knowledge, share in that discovery. "Is that why you climbed up there?" He's trying to make sense of everything, even though that's not really all of it.

"Well, yeah," I say. "It was the woodpecker; it was the loblollies. It was Hatch and Brownfield's development. It was the divorce. It was everything."

"Uh-huh," he says, like he doesn't believe me, like he's hurt I didn't let him in on this sighting.

The nuthatch below me sings.

"There's a nest, two mates, one or two male helpers. The eggs just hatched." I watch him. "You can see them from there." I slide over, try to show him where they are.

He doesn't look.

"I'm sorry."

"It's okay," he tells me. "I understand." But I can see that he doesn't.

"So, you're coming down because of the Endangered Species Act, because they can't tear down the forest if there's a red-cockaded nest here."

I nod.

There is another pause.

"Wait. I don't understand. If you saw the red-cockaded twenty-one days ago, why did you climb the tree? You could have just made the report then."

"I didn't have proof," I say, hoping he'll believe me. "I was waiting to get a good picture. I used your camera." I think maybe this will help.

"You don't have to have proof." Clearly, it doesn't.

"I thought I did."

"But you didn't have to climb up a tree and stay there. You could have stopped the destruction, had somebody from the Wildlife Commission or Forest Service or somewhere come out and verify the discovery." He's shaking his head, trying to make sense of it all. "So, why are you coming down now? What's going on, Kate? Is it your ankle? Are you badly hurt?"

Before I can answer, I hear the sheriff approaching. The four wheeler is loud and Jim doesn't ask another question. He turns his attention in the direction of the vehicle.

Fifty-One

"Does he know?" Jim asks about the sheriff. "Does he know about you coming down?"

I don't answer as we wait until he cuts off the engine.

"Does he know about the woodpecker?"

He walks in our direction.

"That was fast," I say, glad for the interruption, glad I can change the subject and don't have to say anything more about the real reason I'm really coming down.

He doesn't speak and I wonder if I should give my father a clue, some message so that he won't mention Hatch and Brownfield's blackmail strategy. Even though Jim's feelings are slightly bruised for not being told about the red-cockaded I'd rather not tell him the entire truth; I'd like to keep things just as they are.

"Hello, Reverend." He walks over to Jim and doesn't respond to my comment. I'm about to say something else when I notice that the sheriff seems bothered, upset about something.

I worry that the lamb vulture has already broken the news, that she's already made her claims about Jim's drug diversion and our alleged affair public. Maybe she's already done the damage. Maybe he has to arrest Jim for giving me the medicine. He doesn't glance up, doesn't look in my direction so I can't get a good read on what's going on.

"I've been trying to find you. I've been to the church and your secretary thought you might be at the nursing home."

Jim stands up from his seat beneath the tree.

I don't understand unless Hatch and Brownfield have gone ahead and filed a report. They haven't waited for me to make a decision to come down.

"Oh." Jim obviously doesn't understand either.

"And then I thought you might be here, might be out here seeing Kate."

Jim nods. He can see that the sheriff has something that needs to be told, so he doesn't speak.

"I need to get you into town," he says. "Right away."

"Wait a minute," I say. "You're not going to arrest him now."

"Arrest?" Jim wants to know. He looks up at me. "Why am I being arrested?"

"Because that reporter found out about you giving me the medicine. She said if I don't come down she's going to make that public, have you arrested for trafficking a controlled substance."

"What?" Jim asks.

My father shakes his head. "No," he says.

"It's true," I tell Jim. "That's the real reason I'm coming out of the tree. They threatened to have you arrested and to tell your parishioners that we're having an affair."

"An affair?"

The sheriff keeps shaking his head. "No, Kate, that's not what this is about."

"Of course, it is. Just tell him the truth. Help me down and we'll get this all straightened out."

"No, Kate," my father says sharply. "This is something else."

"What?"

He turns to Jim. "There's been an incident."

"What?" I ask. "What incident?"

"I need to get you to the hospital," is what my father says next.

Jim waits. I wait.

"There was a 911 call."

"From the church?" Jim asks.

My father shakes his head.

"Then where?" I follow up.

"The first responders went out but there was nothing really to be done."

I slide over to the edge of the stand, straining to hear.

"What?" Jim asks. "Is it someone in the parish?"

My father drops his face.

"Who is it, Sheriff?"

I can see my father struggling with the news he has to tell.

"I'm sorry."

"What? Who are you talking about?"

"It's your mother, Jim."

"His mother?" I interrupt.

"What? What about her?" Jim asks, stepping back a pace.

"Like I said, there was a 911 call from your house."

"Did she fall?"

"No."

"Well, was there some accident?"

The sheriff shakes his head.

"What?"

"I'm sorry to tell you this, Jim, but she's dead."

Jim pulls away, holds up a hand in protest. "No, you're mistaken."

Dad reaches out, touches Jim on the shoulder.

"You're wrong. I was just there. I just left from there. The nursing assistant was coming in when I left. She was going to give her a bath."

Dad is nodding. "I know."

"We had breakfast together. She came to the table. She ate breakfast. No, you're mistaken."

"I know this is really difficult to hear."

"No, no, this is not right. We were planning to discharge her from hospice again because she was doing so well. What's this about? Why are you telling me this?"

Dad keeps his hand on Jim's arm.

"Did the nursing assistant call?"

Dad nods. "She had gotten her in the shower and was getting her out. She was just drying her off and she collapsed."

Jim keeps shaking his head. "No, she was fine this morning."

"I'm sorry, Jim." And then he looks up at me like he needs help or reassurance, but I don't know what to do.

"She fell?"

"No, not fell really, just collapsed."

"After the shower?"

Dad nods.

"They took her to the hospital because she didn't have a DNR. They tried to resuscitate her in the ambulance, but they were unsuccessful. She died, Jim, I'm sorry." He looks up at me again. "I'm going to take him to the hospital, and then I'll come back and get you in a little while. Is that okay?"

I nod. "Do you want me to come, Jim?"

He just keeps shaking his head and even though I'd like to come down, like to go with him, need to explain about what I just told him, I know with my injury it will take too long for me to climb down. He needs to go without me. I think of something.

"Call Bernard," I tell the sheriff. "Look in Jim's phone contacts and call Bernard."

My father waits for a second, trying to understand and then nods. "Okay," he says. He turns to Jim who keeps shaking his head. "Let's go then. I'll take you to my car and then I'll drive you over there. Okay?"

Jim stumbles towards the four wheeler. He doesn't reply and I don't say anything because I know the words are meaningless.

I watch as Dad helps Jim into the passenger's seat. He walks around to the other side and stops just before getting in the seat. "I'll be back soon," he tells me.

I nod and slide to the trunk. He cranks the engine and drives away, leaving me alone once again.

Fifty-Two

In the commotion I haven't noticed my ankle. Until now. It throbs. I'm out of Jim's pain pills, out of water. I try to keep my mind off it but I can't. I change positions, move from side to side on the stand, trying to get comfortable, trying to find a place where I can rest. I look at my watch realizing only fifteen minutes have passed since they left which means I may be here for another hour or so.

Finally, I fold up my jacket, the pillow, and blanket and elevate my foot; and that seems to help some. I slide around, lean against the loblolly and close my eyes. I know I won't sleep but I'm glad to have some time alone, time to figure out how to say goodbye to the forest, say goodbye to the trees, conclude this time I've had resting in the lap of the loblollies.

I think about my father's news. Jim's mother is dead. Mama Stallings is gone. And I realize that Jim is finally free; he can finally make a life with Bernard. All this time, all the plans they made, and now he can move on with his life. And yet I also know that if his path is anything like mine, the death can hold him back. It's a long road ahead of him.

I take in a deep breath, exhale, try not to notice the pain in my lower limb. Instead, I think about grief, the way it hangs over everything, and I hope that Jim will be okay. I hope that he doesn't mix up the other stuff that is so easy to get lost in, the other emotions that feel as if they carry more weight, possess more energy.

I learned a long time ago that people like to be mad when somebody they love dies, so it must be the simplest path to take. Having someone to blame, something to direct the helplessness towards, a banner to wave as the cause of all sorrow, for some reason that seems to quell the tide of loss.

"It's easier to be mad than sad," I remember a friend in college telling me. She was a rebel, always protesting some statute or rule. She organized sit-ins and hunger strikes, refused to pay tuition hikes or live with discriminatory processes towards women in pay or hiring that the rest of us, without ever entertaining a thought of injustice, just accepted. For the four years I knew her, it seemed she was always fighting, always up in arms about something, always finding offense at books to be read or tests to be taken.

I recall the last semester in school when she told me her boyfriend had broken up with her. They had dated for almost three years; we all thought they would marry. The girls on the hall and I were drinking margaritas, celebrating our upcoming graduation; and out of the blue, she said that he told her he was breaking it off. She said he explained it was because she exhausted him, wore him out with all that rage, all that anger.

"All I can say is that it's a good thing he's gone," she said as she threw down another shot of tequila, slamming the glass on the table, "because if he can't handle the anger, he'd never be able to handle what's really beneath it." Then she passed out, leaving the rest of us uncertain of what she meant. And even though I wanted to know the real story, wanted to ask when she sobered up what she was talking about, what was really beneath it all, I didn't. I wasn't sure that I could handle it, either.

I take in another breath, steady the exhale, and think about myself and the way I was led to anger. I was never as demonstrative as my college suitemate, somehow keeping it hidden even from myself. I never threw things or was a rabble-rouser or troublemaker at work or in school. I never yelled or screamed at anybody, but I realize now that doesn't mean there hasn't been this undercurrent of fury that I have kept at bay for over twenty years. It doesn't mean I resisted choosing my father as the easy target. I see so clearly now that being mad is the simpler choice because sadness is so hard to hold, so hard to keep a grip on, so impossible to wrangle. Anger has handles; if you want to carry it you just slip your arms around it. The bad thing, though, is that it's easy to strap on but there's always more trouble when you want to let it go.

I open my eyes, watching the light curve and bend around limbs and leaves, and I sincerely hope Bernard is up to the challenge of being Jim's partner because I'm pretty sure that he doesn't have a clue as to what is about to hit him.

This then leads me to think about Ray. About Ray and Lonnie. The two of them going off to the beach together. The uncomplicated way that he must be able to forgive her and take her back, the way he seemed to welcome her home. He never blamed Lonnie for anything, and as far as I've seen he was never bitter about that loss, never harbored any grudge. Truthfully, I have never understood that kind of grace. Maybe that's why I never really gave Dwayne or our marriage a chance. Maybe I just never knew how to love that way.

I think back to Saturday night, to Nathan's voice, the vision, and what he said when I hit my head and fell to the stand, how he knew that Lonnie was back, that she was still working on the relationship with her daughter and how he said Ray tangled himself in a web. I figured then he was talking about the guilt over Lilly Carol's accident, his drinking problem; but now I remember something else he said, the thing about baseball and how Ray and I are alike.

I remember he said that Ray and I both missed the curve. At the time I wasn't following him. I was still trying to make sense of where he was and what he was doing here. But now I think I understand. I think I know about the curve ball and how I, like a rookie hitter, stepped aside to miss it and how Ray, an unsuspecting catcher, isn't looking in the right place.

We both missed the curve, and now it's too late. The forest for the trees. The red-cockaded, here all along.

I glance over at Delores; she appears to be sleeping, somehow making room for herself even though the nest is full. The baby owls are still, and I suppose they're already learning to work those internal clocks, to adjust themselves to sleep in the light and wake to the darkness. Somehow as the days pass they will learn how to be quiet, to wait as their wings feather at the ends in fringe, making for the nocturnal silent flight.

When they finally open their eyes, they'll see so clearly, move their heads around so easily, figure out how to stand and wait until night falls and then know exactly how and when to capture their prey. They'll find mates and old unused nests to build for their own families. And Delores doesn't have to teach them any of this. All she has to do is keep them alive until they're big enough to trust what is wired within them.

"I think we've evolved so far we don't know our wiring anymore," I say to Delores and the loblolly, the fallen sweetgum, and the chickadees, to all who are nearby. "We've figured out ways to get around those basic instincts but I'm not so sure it's made us any better for it."

I peer in her direction again and see that Delores has raised one eye in my direction. I guess I'm keeping her from much-needed sleep and I nod at her, whisper my apologies, and she closes it again, making me smile.

I'd like to know how to tell her 'thank you,' how to let her know what a difference she's made in my life because of who she is, what she's done, how she overcame the tragedy, how she's raising her young.

In truth, I'd like to thank all the birds and trees, the clouds, the dusk and morning skies, the needles that cover the ground, sailing so needlessly from where they were attached, the river flowing down to the ocean without need of guidance, flowing in narrow streams and wide dark bodies.

I'd like to tell the loblolly what it means to me that she let me stand so long in her arms, rest against her trunk, sit in her lap, see what she sees from up here. I'd like to thank the red-cockaded for outing himself, showing me his flash of red that will now keep the forest in place. I'd like to thank the whip-poor-wills and the warblers, the chickadees, the nuthatches, and even the Cooper's hawk. I'd like to thank them all. I wish I knew how.

"Why are you up there?" That seems to be the question everyone has asked. Maybe even the question I have asked myself. And I know it's redemption. I know it's forgiveness and letting go. I know it's friendship and healing but I also know it's them. It's this place. It's the simple way of the bottomlands, the White Oak River Basin, it's this, season after season, storm after storm, nest after nest.

This is why I'm still alive. This is why I hope. This is even why I pray.

I close my eyes, reach behind me and touch the feather in my hair, and try but I know I can never say it all.

Fifty-Three

Within the hour Dad came back and without too much fanfare I was able to hop out of the loblolly. Carefully, I went limb by limb until I managed to find and hold onto the trunk. I slid down the sweetgum and landed on one foot like Kerri Strug in the 1996 Olympics. I even threw my arms over my head like I had just completed the vault but I don't think the sheriff caught the reference. Once I made it down, he busied himself gathering up my belongings. I stood against the sweetgum until he was done, limping over to the grave to pay my final respects.

Twenty minutes or so passed, and I heard him clear his throat. It was finally time to go.

"You can always come back," he said.

I nodded. "Won't quite be the same though."

"No, I guess not."

I looked up, saw the place where I had lived, where I had been hurt and helped, where I had seen and been seen, the place where I called home for three weeks.

"You want to take the plywood down now?"

I shook my head. "Maybe later."

He stood near the four wheeler and waited without pressing me to leave, and I suppose that I will remember this scene as clearly and with as much meaning as I recall the best moments I cherish from childhood. Of all the things I might have lodged as complaints against him, my father has never been an impatient man, and I have always known him to wait on me without displeasure or irritation. I realize now that his greatest span lasted twenty-five years and I'm just grateful he never gave up.

We got into the vehicle; he turned on the engine, kept it in park, giving me one last long look. I took the feather out of my hair, held onto it so as not to lose it, and glanced around. The forest was alive and busy; fittingly, the birds went on with their morning as if I had never come or never left. A breeze blew across the scattered leaves and I turned to him, smiled and nodded. He put the vehicle in gear and we backed away.

At the edge of the woods I got out of the four wheeler and into his car and was taken first to take care of the important matters and then straight to the hospital. Twenty hours later, I am awake, rousing from the anesthesia for good this time, and I find only one person sitting by my bed.

"Hey, you're alive!"

I blink, try to remember where I am, how I got into such a soft bed, what has recently occurred. I glance down at my foot, raised high in a sling, wrapped in a cast covered in white gauze. I feel sleepy, groggy; but I understand my place.

"You've been asleep for like twenty-four hours. The sheriff went to get breakfast or lunch. He's been here, well, like the whole time."

I nod.

"You want something to drink?" she asks, and she gets up to find the cup on the table beside my bed. She holds the straw so that I can take a few sips. She waits until I pull away, having had enough, and then she takes her seat again.

There are bouquets of flowers, balloons, stacks of cards. I think I must be sharing the room but when I glance around I see that I am the only patient.

"You're kind of a rock star," she says. "Well, I guess we both are."

I can't imagine who would be sending me these gifts, all these well-wishes. I didn't realize anyone knew I was in the hospital, or even that anybody knew I had come down from the loblollies.

"They're from your co-workers, the Wildlife Commission, the Sierra Club, the Birder Association of Eastern North Carolina, the Nature Conservancy, even some group from the Woodpecker Trail down in Georgia. Who knew they had their own trail?" She laughs.

I turn to the young girl, able now to see her face to face, eye level. She's pretty, has soft features, fair in skin tone. She looks a little like a mourning dove, slim, a small head with sandy brown hair. "You got the pictures?"

"I still can't believe you did that." She rests her elbow on the arm of the chair, drops her face in her hand. "Why did you give them to me?"

"Did you call the number I had Dad give you?"

She nods.

I have a contact at the state Fish and Wildlife Service, a special agent at the Washington office. Bill Hughes is an old friend and I thought that would be the best call to make first. I knew he would be able to tell Tiffany what she needed to do, where to send the photographs.

"He came out and I went exactly where the sheriff said, right near your stand. They marked off the territory, called the newspaper and, well, it was a big deal. You should have been there."

I smile. *I have been there. I have been there a long time.*

"And Hatch and Brownfield?"

"They showed up later, I even got my picture taken with them. They act like they're really happy about the sighting, about the nest, but I know it really peeves them. This morning Stanley's dad told him Mr. Brownfield threw his tennis racket at another player yesterday afternoon. They called the police and there was some big drama at the club." She shrugs. "I guess even rich people can have the cops called on them."

"I guess so."

"I'm going to get a reward," she tells me.

"Yeah?"

She is smiling. "Yeah."

"Enough for tuition at State or East Carolina?"

She nods. "Actually, it's enough for Duke."

"What?" I hadn't even heard that she applied, much less that she was accepted.

She grins. "I helped Stanley with his application and I just thought I'd see what would happen if I applied."

"Well, Tiffany Bowers, you are going to Duke!"

She nods. "I found out a couple of weeks ago. I didn't say anything because I knew it didn't matter. There was no way I could afford to go there."

"Well, aren't you something?" I cannot believe the news; it's even better than I could have imagined.

I'm still enjoying this latest report when the nurse comes in, introduces herself, checks my toes, my blood pressure and IV bags, explains the pain meds, how I can press a button and get what I need, asks me if I want lunch. When I tell her yes, that I am a little hungry, she promises that she'll call it in and it should arrive within the hour. She writes her name, Jenny, on a whiteboard and heads on to her next patient.

Tiffany and I are quiet for a bit. I close my eyes, still trying to believe the fact that Tiffany is going to Duke.

"You never told me why you did it," she says, causing me to open my eyes. "You never told me why me, why did you send the photographs to me?"

I take a good long look at the young high school student. "Can I have some more water?" I ask.

She gets up, pours more water in the cup and hands it to me. I hold it myself this time, place the straw in my mouth, and drink. I hand the cup back to her and she places it on the bedside table, takes her seat again in the chair across from the bed.

"There's nothing wrong with getting an associate degree. I applaud the community colleges; they provide a wonderful education for lots of young people. You would have done well at Lenoir or Craven County or any two-year school around here."

She nods.

"But you also deserve the chance to leave home, to know what's it like to go to college, live in a dorm, get a four-year degree, study Biology. You deserve the same right to go to a university, Duke University it seems, as anybody else. You've helped your mom and taken care of your brothers for a long time and now it's your turn to try out those wings. I just felt like you're too big for that nest. It's time for you to see if you can fly."

She nods and looks away, slides her fingers across her face, wiping away the tears, and I still can't believe it. The shy little mourning dove is going to Duke!

Fifty-Four

"Kate, this is Bernard."

Jim is standing beside my bed. He's dressed in casual clothes, a T-shirt, bright yellow, tan pants, and he's wearing a red hat. He looks like a tanager, the male.

I turn to the man next to him. He is exactly like his pictures. Tall, kind face, dark-skinned, a crimson shirt—he's a blackbird, a western red-winged blackbird—and he smiles looking down at me.

"Hi, Kate," he says, placing his hand on top of mine and I see everything that Jim does, and more. He will not leave his mate.

"Hi, Bernard. It's really nice to meet you."

He squeezes my hand, steps back, giving Jim room.

"So, you jumped down?" He's referring to my injury and we both glance down at my foot still hanging from the top of the bed.

"I was trying to fly," I answer and look carefully at him. "Turns out I'm a land animal after all."

We pause.

"You okay?" I ask.

He nods and takes Bernard by the hand. The public display of affection both surprises and warms me.

"I'm going to get a cup of coffee," Bernard says. "You want anything?"

I shake my head and watch as he gives Jim a kiss. We wait until he's gone.

"Well, he's definitely a keeper," I say.

"So he is," comes the reply. "He's been with me since she died. He took a leave of absence from his job and he's not left my side."

"Good man."

"We're going back to Charleston tomorrow," Jim reports as he takes a seat. "That's where Mama wanted her ashes to be scattered."

I nod. I've lost track of the days but I suppose they've already had the memorial service. "And?" I don't know his plans.

"And then I'll come back, pack up everything, and I'll be moving in a few weeks."

I don't respond. There are so many questions and I don't know where to start.

He goes again. "So, you decided you had enough of civil disobedience? Don't want to start a tree-climbing campaign?"

"I sort of missed a mattress, and lucky for me there's a red-cockaded flying around out there so I don't have to stay up in a pine tree anymore."

There is a pause. He glances around at all the flowers, all the expressions of well-wishes.

"It wasn't the woodpecker that brought you down, we both know that."

I don't respond. I wait to hear what he has to say.

He's leaning forward, his elbows on his knees, his chin in his hand. "I know you came down because of me."

I shake my head. "Not true. I had a broken ankle. I had to come down."

"Okay," he replies, sounding very much like he doesn't believe me.

"So, Bernard?" I say, changing the subject. "Very cute."

"I'm a lucky man," he responds.

"Yes, you are." I smile, glad to hear that things seem to be going well for the two of them, glad that my worries were ungrounded.

"I met with the church board."

I wait.

"I met with them last night, after the funeral. We had a called meeting."

He takes in a breath, sits back in his chair.

"I told them about Bernard, about us." He hesitated. "About me."

And suddenly, the move to Charleston, the casual clothes, the willingness to be in public with his lover, it all makes sense.

"They fired you," I reply, feeling the anger start to rise, the disappointment. I think about writing a letter or making a call.

He shakes his head no. "Craziest thing. They said they knew."

"Yeah?" This is a surprise and I wonder how they found out, why they never approached him about it, why they didn't fire him before.

"Yeah."

I wait.

"And they said it didn't matter."

"What?" I sit up in the bed.

"It appears as if the Jones County Lutherans are a bit more progressive than I gave them credit."

"They want you to stay?"

He nods. "They do; but they also know how hard it would be for me and Bernard, for them as well. They want to come up with a strategy to tell the congregation. They want to prepare for the worst. There's still a lot of hate, you know."

He's right. I know this.

"And in the same spirit in which you would climb down from the loblolly before you'd let me suffer the consequences of a mean-spirited landowner, I want to spare the church from what it would mean for them to have a gay pastor."

I feel a twinge of sadness. I hate to see my friend go.

"Besides, I can always preach and read theology when I want, but if I really want to do this Bed and Breakfast, I need to do it while I can still paint the walls and pick out furniture. I'm not getting any younger, you know."

"It's true, and that clergy get-up, all that black, well, it only makes you look older."

He laughs.

"I do look better with a little color, don't I?"

"I always knew you weren't a magpie."

"Or a penguin?"

"Or a penguin."

He slides his hands on the tops of his legs, stretches them out, makes himself comfortable. "So, what about you?" he asks.

"What about me?"

"What are you going to do when you get out of here?"

I shrug. "I guess I'll go beg for my job back."

"I wasn't talking about your job," he replies.

"No?"

And as if on cue, the door opens and I'm so surprised, so unprepared for the visit that I don't even notice when Jim gets up and leaves.

Fifty-Five

"What are you doing here?" I pull up the sheet to cover me, try to fix my bedhead, run my tongue across my teeth, hoping I don't have breakfast stuck there. I feel caught, unprepared. I feel like a mess.

He shrugs and suddenly seems uncomfortable, as if he has appeared uninvited. "I just thought I'd come see you." He stands at the door.

I didn't mean to sound like that. "I'm sorry, I'm just surprised. I thought you were out of town. Come in, it's fine. Come in."

He enters the room and that's when I notice that Jim is gone. I suppose they had some interaction at the door, one leaving while the other arrives, but it's like I lost some seconds there or something. I realize I haven't seen Ray in almost a week, and I feel different somehow now that he's in the vicinity, close, practically right beside me. Everything feels new between us. Everything's changed.

"Are you all right?" He comes closer. "You seem weird." He glances over at the I.V. "Morphine?"

I nod, but I know it's not the drugs making me feel this way. "I'm fine, just surprised. Have a seat," I say, and he does.

He looks around at the arrangements of flowers, the balloons and stuffed toys. "I was going to say that I'm sorry I didn't bring you flowers but I don't think you could even notice if I did."

I glance around, too, seeing what he sees.

"I know. It's crazy, having all this. I don't even know most of the people who sent them." I wave it off like I get flowers all the time and they mean nothing.

"Lilly Carol says you're trending."

"Is that good or bad?" I ask, since I have no idea what it means.

He shrugs.

"How is our girl?"

He nods. "Great. She loves the photographs you sent, took them to school, got to show them to the entire fifth grade at an assembly."

This makes me smile. I love the thought of Lilly Carol being the center of attention for something other than sitting in a wheelchair.

"I was worried that she might be upset."

"I don't know why."

"I know. She's amazing."

"She told me about you coming to the school, about you asking for her permission."

When I got out of the woods, Lilly Carol was the only person I went to see. And I have to say, the sheriff driving me there really helped make that happen. The secretary at the school office found her right away and I was able to explain everything to her. She really didn't seem to mind that Tiffany was going to get the credit.

"She did spot the bird first," I say, thinking about the day we were in the woods, the way she sang out when the woodpecker flew past.

"Right, when you were at the park, yes?" He peers at me.

I know what he's getting at. "We sort of took a detour into the woods."

"Yeah, I always knew you were lying about where you took her."

I hide my face behind my hand. "Sorry."

"I trusted you. I knew you wouldn't hurt her."

"No, I wouldn't. And neither would you."

He looks at me, waits, and then looks away. I think he knows what I mean.

"So, how are you?" he asks, changing the subject.

I nod. "I'm okay."

He nods too, like he agrees or like he's glad.

"You on your lunch break?" It's small talk for the two of us, I know, but I feel at a loss as to what to say. Things feel different somehow, now that I know what I have missed, now that I understand what I could have had.

He shakes his head. "I quit work."

"You did what?"

"I got another job."

"Oh." I guess he'll tell me the rest.

"Lilly Carol is the real reason."

I wait, thinking it has to do with her schedule or her summer break.

"The trees."

"What?" And I hadn't thought of this.

He drops his hands in his lap. He looks uncomfortable sitting in the chair, the way he always does when he's inside. Even as a kid he always wanted to be outside, hated being in the house. He would come over to get Nathan, knock on the door, and he'd wait for him on the porch even if it was raining or cold. He just always preferred to be out.

"The trees," he repeats himself. "Once you climbed up your pines, Lilly Carol started asking me questions about my work, about the trees and lumber, where it came from and what my role was, and finally, I just had to quit."

"Wow, okay. I guess I should apologize."

"Nah, it's not your fault; I was tired of it anyway. Billy is a terrible manager."

I nod. I've heard him say this before.

"I'm going to school," he says, surprising me. "Start in two weeks, Emergency Medicine."

"That's great, Ray," I reply. He always talked about being a first responder, always had an interest in that field. After the accident, though, he never mentioned it again. I often wondered if he still had the itch; but I never brought it up.

The nurse comes in, checks the I.V., takes my lunch tray, asks me about my pain. I think Ray might leave; but he stays.

When we're alone again he asks, "Why did you ask me what I was doing here? Why would you think it's odd that I'd come to see you?"

I'm not sure how to answer. There's the night he came to the tree and I was terrible to him, and that was the last time I saw him, and then there's Charlene's news about Lonnie and the beach. I was surprised to see him because I thought he was at the beach with his ex-wife.

"I heard Lonnie came home." I just decide to put it out there. I see no reason to pretend his family isn't getting back together. I'll have to face it all soon enough.

"Yeah, she's better, wants to see Lilly Carol regularly."

"I figured that was it," I say, without telling the rest of what I figure.

"She's moving down to Morehead, got a job at a fish place there."

"Oh. I thought she was moving here; I thought she was coming back here."

He shakes his head. "No, she likes the beach, thought Lilly Carol might like to visit her there on the weekends and in the summer. She asked me to help her find a place; so I went down with her. That's why I wasn't here earlier. I came back as soon as I heard you were in the hospital."

I'm shaking my head. "You're not getting back together with Lonnie?"

"No, why would you think that?"

"I—" There's really no reason to tell what I thought and why I thought it.

"Are you okay, Kate? You seem kind of funny."

And I see it perfectly this time. The red-cockaded, the trees, all of it. It's Nathan's curve ball, and this time I'm not going to flinch. This time, my head is not in the clouds, I'm not thinking about flying away; this time I'm going to stand right where I am and take the swing.

Fifty-Six

People look at me differently. Or maybe it's just what I see now. The view from here. Late in the summer this year, I was invited to be the special guest speaker at the Red-Cockaded Festival, the first annual celebration of the sighting of the bird, held at the Garvers' farm, now a music venue known as The Brownfield. Due to the Safe Harbor Agreement that Hatch and Brownfield made with the state wildlife commission, there are no buildings, no development per se; but they can host community events, bring in tourists, and even charge the birders to go into the woods.

The farm is really just a wide open space, and at the festival they built three stages and hosted rows of booths, selling arts and crafts and barbecue and beer. There was a bird-calling competition with contestants from all across the state, a seed-spitting contest, and even a woodpecker pie bake-off. It was the red ones that won, of course, a tie between a cherry crumble baked by Franklin Massey's new bride from Swansboro and a strawberry cheesecake, created by Millie and baked by Marge, my sister by marriage.

A lot has changed since I left the trees, but nothing is more surprising to me than my relationship with Marge. It turns out that I sort of like her and that she can actually be nice, telling me she's glad that my father and I are now reconciled and happy that I've moved in with Ray, marrying him once I was released from the hospital, wedded in a simple ceremony in the woods, under the loblollies, and consequentially becoming Lilly Carol's stepmother.

I still tease her, can't help myself, but she doesn't bruise so easily and has even come to embrace environmental concerns, attributing her new passion to me and spearheading the effort for the festival, even volunteering the Methodists to help sponsor the event. She organized the bird-calling and even commissioned the women to knit special prayer shawls decorated with tiny little red woodpeckers, designating all the money to be given to the Audubon Society.

Tiffany spent a lot of time with me after she graduated and before she headed to college last fall. She wanted to learn everything I knew about the red-cockaded. She's written articles and already presented a paper to the biology faculty at Duke. She seems to think the pitch wells that the woodpecker drills after it pecks the bark off the tree do more than simply serve as a means to keep snakes and raccoons from robbing the nest, as previously supposed by scientists. She thinks the gray wells attract the insects that the woodpecker eats, and she'd like to study the flow, to better understand the diet of the endangered bird and the substantial increase in the population of the bark beetle.

Jim and Bernard came back for the wedding, of course; Jim officiated. Now they are here again for the bird festival. I watch him with Bernard, the manner with which they work as a couple, the gentle way they are with each other, and I have to say that I've never seen my friend so relaxed and at ease. The Good Lord Bird Bed and Breakfast, named after a moniker given to the lost ivory-billed woodpecker, opens in a month and Ray and Lilly Carol and I plan to be their first guests.

For months after I lived in a tree, I walked with a limp, needed a cane and physical therapy; but for the most part there has been a full recovery. Lilly Carol was quite resourceful and taught me a great deal about how to get along without actually having to walk. When we were first together, first making our life as a family in our shared home, and we needed to move from room to room, Ray picked her up first, took her wherever we were going, and then came back for me. It was another big turn of events and I discovered what it really is to lean on someone else. It's just one more part of this new life I have come to count on, come to enjoy.

I cried a lot when I came home from the hospital. I still do. Everybody around me seems to be used to it now. At first, they thought I was just sad that I came out of the woods or that I was in pain because of the broken bone; Daddy even worried that I was having PTSD after what happened with the owl. But they eventually came to understand it was not sadness or sorrow that fed my tears. Then, later, they thought I was overwhelmed with joy, getting married and all. But now that I still cry, almost a year since the wedding, they know it's just what I see, how I've changed, the way my heart has opened.

I even forgave Hatch and Brownfield and bear no grudge against Tonya Lassiter. I decided that once the forgiving started, once I handed down the first pardon, there was no reason not to share it with everyone. The pain of holding onto the harm done to me seems much harder than just letting it go. And I truly believe that at one time we all had wings, and what keeps us from flying is not the loss of feathers or the progress of evolution. Rather, I think it is the way we remember and record, binding ourselves with ropes of blame, unwilling to put aside the trouble we have known.

That day in the hospital when I told Ray I loved him and what Nathan said about the web, he knelt by my bed and we both wept. He said he had known since I was a girl that I was the one he loved;

but at first he didn't know how to tell my brother, and then when he died, he didn't know how to tell me. Once I went to college and the series of events that became our lives began to unfurl, he accepted our relationship as one more thing he messed up, one more bird that got away.

But now we are together, and all I can say is that I see so much more than I ever could before. I wake up and see my husband, my brother's best friend, lying next to me, and I see what it is to be so lucky because I didn't miss my chance to have love. I walk past Lilly Carol's room and watch her sleep, see a child so peaceful, so innocent, and I know that at any moment she's going to wake up and brighten the day even more with her loveliness. I see my father happy, and I see what it is to be ordinary, just to stop by his house or to walk beside him and share a story or finding, to see him, in peace, grow old. I see colors that I never noticed, kindness and generosity I never knew. I see friendships deepen and stars in the dead of night whose names I still know. I open my eyes and I see life bursting forth from seeds dropped and sprouting in every corner of the earth.

It's funny, I know, that it took climbing a tree to see all of this, that I couldn't find this vision while my feet were planted firmly on the ground. But it is what it is and it took what it took; and if I had it to do it all over again, I'd reach and pull every limb until I got to where I finally am.

Everything in my life is different. It is perfect and clear and right. And I wouldn't take anything for what I see, for what I've learned and know, for what I have been given from the view I have from here.

The End.